Praise for *In This Ground*

"Startlingly incongruous parts—graveyards, guitars, and mushrooms—come together in satisfying and unexpected ways. Sharp writing and an unconventional plot make for a darkly enjoyable read."

—*Kirkus Reviews*

"*In This Ground* brings both music and joy to an otherwise mournful landscape. Castrodale challenges us to come to terms with what is important in our lives by confronting the inevitability of death, and she does so with such frankness and grace that we are compelled to embrace, rather than fear, the unknown."

—Wendy J. Fox, author of *The Pull of It* and *The Seven Stages of Anger*

"Castrodale makes a cemetery not only come to life but also become a central character. Deep in the soil of this unlikely ground, [she] has buried great heart. She channels Richard Russo in her ability to command a large cast of characters about whom we care greatly."

—Jen Michalski, author of *The Summer She Was Under Water*

"That a graveyard can be a stage for so much vigorous, multilayered life is one of the many surprises in Beth Castrodale's warm and wonderful novel. The paths of vividly drawn characters intersect to create a vibrant canvas of uncommon richness and breadth. With the deftness of a magician and uncanny insight, Castrodale weaves together the present moment with its contending dramas and the past with its tragedies, in this moving and deeply satisfying novel that illuminates how hearts break and how they mend."

—Lynn Sloan, author of *This Far Isn't Far Enough* and *Principles of Navigation*

"This novel possesses a mythic sweep. Yet the characters are so sharply drawn, so intimately detailed, they feel like people we all know—people who, while full of regret and self-deception, hidden pain and longing, still manage to find a bittersweet redemption in living. *In This Ground* shows Beth Castrodale to be a writer well attuned to the music of the human heart."

—Jeff Fearnside, author of *Making Love While Levitating Three Feet in the Air*

"If I didn't already love hanging out in cemeteries, Beth Castrodale's *In This Ground* would prompt me to take a sudden field trip to my local graveyard, to stalk plotted rows with a fresh perspective, one that discerns the politics of burial and exhumation, and the complexity of death. But even more compelling is the novel's compassionate treatment of the living. Park your car in the upper lot and prepare yourself for all that unfolds when unexpected alliances form under the luminescence of mushrooms and moonlight."

—Jodi Paloni, author of *They Could Live with Themselves*

Praise for *Marion Hatley*

"Like Marion Hatley's own creations, Beth Castrodale's début novel is sewn, sentence by elegant sentence, with exquisite care and beauty. With clear-eyed assurance it explores the burden of secrets, the virtue of perseverance, and the joys of renewal. As a portrait of a community—and life itself—it is deeply compassionate and utterly wondrous."

—David Rowell, author of *The Train of Small Mercies*

"A reflective, compassionate, and gracefully written tale."

—*Kirkus Reviews*

"A beautiful story, beautifully told. Marion Hatley's skills at creating women's underthings designed to free them from the constrictures of the past are emblematic of the freedom she ultimately achieves."

—Lee Jacobus, author of *Hawaiian Tales, Crown Island,* and *The Romantic Soul of Emma Now*

"An expert and articulate historical novel. The period details, class protest, and feminist protest are particularly engaging, as is the central character, Marion, whose resourcefulness recalls that of Zola's Denise Badu in *The Ladies' Paradise.* In Marion's case, her redesign of conventional corsets speaks to humanizing social constrictions for women as well as easing physical ones."

—DeWitt Henry, founding editor of *Ploughshares,* Emerson Professor Emeritus, and author of *The Marriage of Anna Maye Potts*

Beth Castrodale (signature)

In This Ground

A Novel

Beth Castrodale

GARLAND PRESS
Shrewsbury, Massachusetts

ISBN: 978-1-940782-04-1
e-ISBN: 978-1-940782-05-8

Library of Congress Control Number: 2018941060

Published by:
GARLAND PRESS
P.O. Box 4142
Shrewsbury, MA 01545
www.garlandpress.com

Cover design by William Boardman
Interior design by Diane Vanaskie Mulligan

Printed in the United States of America

For John, my music

I come to this tomb to shed an old skin, to come anew, to rise up like rising water. Do not shut me out from life. Do not let me forget. Do not leave me to stand idle and alone in this hall, surrounded by dreams, for dreams—however beautiful—are vapors and desire, all insubstantial. Give me hands and mind and soul and heart. Give me music, a bright star and some reason to rise and walk.

—From *Awakening Osiris: A New Translation of The Egyptian Book of the Dead,* by Normandi Ellis

Chapter 1

"True is the friend who knows which stories to take to the grave."
Ruth Bedell
Journalist, Editor
April 23, 1925 - October 18, 2003

—Gravestone for Section D, Lot 239

Section D, Lot 454
Late morning, early May

Pete Kovak, a.k.a. New Pete, a.k.a. Noop. He hadn't replaced an Old Pete when Ben hired him the previous week, nor was there a Senior Pete.

While training Pete to take over his job, Haley had just started calling him those names—and passing judgments Ben could have done without.

"Noop must have been bat-shit hyper as a kid," Haley had said to Ben more than once.

He's still hyper, Ben thought. *And he's still a kid. To me, anyway.*

It remained to be seen whether the hyperactivity could be channeled to useful ends. Based on what he'd observed so far, Ben believed Pete was on course to be either a Grade A Fuckup or, possibly, the most productive grounds worker that Bolster Hill Cemetery had ever seen.

This morning, the occasion of Pete's first graveside service, the odds were favoring the former proposition.

Ben had warned him that at these times, their most important job was to stand back and stay silent. But as mourners assembled by the grave, Pete started drumming his fingers on his thigh, and by the start of the committal prayer, he'd moved on to the change in his pockets, churning it slowly at first then working up to a steady three-four jingle so that by the time of the pastor's closing words, Ben had to tug Pete's sleeve and bring him to a full stop.

Now that the casket had been lowered, the last of the friends and family were heading for the East Gate.

Pete glanced in their direction then sprang into action and jumped the vault lid.

"Hey!" Ben called.

Pete swayed on landing then caught himself.

"I forgot. Sorry, man."

The rule was to wait until all the mourners were out of the parking lot, out of view, before any moves were made to fill the grave.

"Why don't you go get the dirt."

"I'm on it," Pete said, before taking off.

With Pete off for the truck, Ben called Haley for the backhoe and began clearing the site of flowers and chairs and turning back the artificial turf. Resting against a neighboring stone was the temporary marker, a laminated poster on two wooden posts that the funeral director had left for them to stake in once the grave was filled: *Anthony James Lekovic, Beloved Son and Brother.*

At the foot of one of the posts lay the ziplocked picture that the funeral director had mentioned in passing. "They meant to scan it for the marker, but obviously that never happened." It was a school picture of a goofy, skinny kid with a toothy smile, a kid at least ten years younger than the one they were about to bury.

Ben went to fold the last chair, pausing at the sight of a newcomer, a thirty-ish woman, tall, dressed in an oversize work shirt and khaki shorts. With that clothing and her purposeful stride, she looked like an adventurer from a nature show, and a *Key Largo*-era Lauren Bacall.

Ben guessed she wouldn't appreciate strangers paying too much attention to her looks, the very thing he was now doing. He turned away and kept himself occupied until she was safely past.

When he looked back in her direction she was well on her way toward the North Gate, presumably to the grave of the Unknown Vagrant, which had been drawing people in greater numbers than at any other time during Ben's twenty-odd years at the cemetery. The previous day a tour bus from Ohio had unloaded a crowd of senior citizens, some of whom, according to Haley, had heard of the mystery man on their local public radio station. At the gravesite they snapped pictures and took or waved away fliers from a rotating crew of demonstrators, who stood behind their usual signs: *Don't Dig Him, Leave Him; R.I.P., U.V.*

A mechanical whine sounded from the hill, and there was Haley in the backhoe, trailing Pete, who was going a little fast in the truck. Ben pledged to hold his tongue and did. Within twenty minutes the three of them got the vault covered, the back fill dumped and spread, the sod replaced, and the marker into the ground, ziplocked picture at its feet.

When they'd finished reloading the truck Haley tossed waters to Ben and Pete, and Ben downed his quickly. When that was done he found himself once again looking northward, though the grave of the Unknown Vagrant was out of sight, and so was the woman.

Pete followed his gaze and said, "Do we have a date for the exhumation yet?"

"Nope. But as soon as I know, you will."

Pete drained his own bottle and tossed it into the truck bed. "I still don't get what all the fuss is about, but whatever. I'll do what I'm told."

Ben had given Pete only the shortest version of the story: that they'd been ordered to move a historical gravesite from just outside the North Gate to inside the cemetery, because it was dangerously close to an ever-busier Route 4. In as many years, three visitors to the grave had been struck by speeding cars, the most recent one fatally.

But a certain segment of the population "had issues" with disturbing the gravesite—thus the chanting sign holders and flier distributors. Their numbers had only grown since the posting of the Don't Dig Him, Leave Him Facebook page, where an especially ardent opponent of the exhumation was sharing a video diary of her efforts to stop the dig. Somehow, the diary had gone viral, drawing even more protesters to the gravesite.

To avoid the risk of additional accidents there, protesters and other visitors were required, sometimes with police enforcement, to stand within a pyloned safety barrier around the grave, and along that stretch of Route 4, the cops had started ticketing speeders more aggressively.

The longstanding interest in the Unknown Vagrant had always puzzled Ben, even though he'd grown up hearing about his oddities, including the self-made, sixty-pound leather suit he was said to wear in all seasons, as he walked his regular state-to-state circuit. The lesson Ben took was, if you're the right kind of weird, in a public way, you might get enough attention to last past your lifetime, enough to earn a chapter or two in books of local history, or a feature in a television newsmagazine.

"Well," Haley said, "I'm sorry I won't be able to join you boys in that worthy endeavor." Thursday was to be his last day on the grounds. After a week's vacation he'd be starting in as the go-to man for Carl Jenks, president of the cemetery's board. As grounds manager and Haley's supervisor, Ben had had first dibs on that job, but he'd never wanted to work in an office.

"Meantime," Haley said, "we've got other fish to fry. Not big fish, but fish."

"What do you mean?"

"You been up to Section D yet, Ben?"

"Not today. Why?"

"There's more crap than ever on the shrine."

"I cleared it off yesterday. Late yesterday." And last night was nothing but a regular Monday night, a school night.

Pete glanced anxiously between them. He started to speak but Haley cut him off.

"I know you did. But I saw what I saw."

4

"Well, we better clear it again."

"What the hell are you talking about?" Pete asked.

Haley looked from Ben to Pete and back again and smiled. "You haven't told Noop about the shrine?"

"Told me what?"

Ben gave Haley the eye but didn't say a word. Haley started this, so he could finish it.

"Pop quiz," Haley said to Pete. "Tell me who's buried in lot 421."

Pete shrugged. "How would I know? Even if it was Jesus Christ, how could I tell from some number?"

Haley laughed. "Well, it isn't Jesus Christ. But on the humble scale of Bolster Hill it's close enough, I'd say. Wouldn't you, Ben?"

"Enough, Haley," Ben said.

Haley turned back to Pete. "Let's cut to the chase, then. Do the Unknown Vagrants mean anything to you?"

"The Unknown Vagrant? The guy we're digging up?"

"I mean the Unknown Vagrants, plural. Or just *the Vagrants*."

"The band?"

"The band. I bet you know at least one of their songs."

"Yeah, I do." Pete closed his eyes and wagged his hand, as if to summon the memory. "Hold on, it's coming to me. It's coming to me. Ah-*hah*!"

He stomped one boot to the ground, turned his face to the sky, and started exuberantly singing "Leave Me in Peace," the Vagrants' breakout hit, which grew more loathsome to Ben every time he heard it.

Ben and Haley let Pete go on until he ran out of lyrics, which thankfully was before the end of the song. All through the performance Haley looked a little dazed, no longer so smug.

In Ben, an old resentment had resurfaced: that a song he'd written as a seriously drunk and depressed nineteen-year-old, a song spared by mere whim from his trash basket, had crawled its way up to the Billboard Top 100 months after he'd left the band. In the reviews and interviews preserved on the internet,

Nick Graves—Ben's stage name, one he'd believed to be far more *rock* than Ben Dirjery—was never praised or blamed for the number. And in recent weeks and months, since WBHL had resurrected it as an anthem for the exhumation protesters, no deejay had mentioned Nick Graves in connection with the Vagrants, not to Ben's knowledge.

While Haley and Pete continued their Q&A, Ben tossed his empty water bottle into the truck bed then occupied himself with pulling weeds in the next lot. He could have walked off— should have—but he couldn't help but stay and listen.

"So," Pete said, "what's this got to do with who's buried in lot 421?"

"You know who the lead singer of the Vagrants was?"

"Uh, yeah. Vince . . . Vince something."

"Vince Resklar."

"Wait. Vince Resklar's buried here?"

"Yep. He grew up just a few miles away."

Since Vince's death, his grave had been a nighttime assembly point for certain local youth, in recent years a steady number of second-generation Vagrants fans, mostly relatively well-behaved music heads. But since WBHL had resurrected "Leave Me in Peace," since an old, post-Ben video of the band performing the song had been posted to the Don't Dig Him, Leave Him Facebook page, things had changed: a new and more substantial crop of kids seemed to have taken to the band, and also to Vince's grave. They'd started leaving beer cans and drunken tributes around it, and they'd worn down the grass and stirred up the dirt. With summer approaching and school drawing to a close, things were bound to get worse.

Haley finished his own water and tossed the bottle. "Now," he said, "a truly curious young man might also be wondering if our fair cemetery has any other special connection to the Vagrants. Do you want to answer that one, Ben?"

Years before, not long after Haley started at the cemetery, Ben had made the mistake of going for drinks with him after work. The third or fourth beer had loosened Ben's reserve; so had a Vagrants song ("Yes, I Can't") that started blasting from the juke box an hour or so into their time at the bar. It was as if some kind stranger had fed those coins right into his ego's hollow coffers, and in repayment for the kindness, Ben told Haley he'd been an early member of the band.

When, the morning after their beers, Ben asked Haley to keep this information to himself, Haley didn't understand why. "If I was you, I'd be proud of being a Vagrant," he'd said. Ben's reply: "Well, you're not me." In the end, Haley agreed to keep the promise, but Ben had little confidence that he hadn't slipped up on occasion.

Now, Haley seemed to be taking pleasure in testing Ben, as if he wished to set off a final show of fireworks before exiting the grounds.

Rising from a patch of dandelions, which he'd been pulling up from the roots, Ben found Haley and Pete staring at him, waiting. Their stares seemed to trigger the buzzing at his right thigh.

Gratefully, Ben pulled the phone from his pocket.

"Sorry, guys. I need to take this." A lie. "Pete, clear off 421. It's right over there, on the other side of Acorn Path, just past the obelisk. Haley, I'll catch you after lunch in Millionaires' Row"— Ben's term for the mansion-like mausoleums that housed the once-wealthy dead. There, some crumbling masonry needed attention.

Ben wandered down the slope, holding the phone to his ear in case Haley and Pete were still watching him. He kept moving ahead, just to get away from them.

There she was again, the woman in the work shirt and shorts, marching back from the North Gate and cramming one of the protester's neon-colored fliers into the pocket of her shorts, not bothering to fold it. No tourist or curiosity seeker, it seemed to Ben. She looked like someone who was here by mistake, and she made quickly for the exit.

At last, in the more obscure reaches of Section B, he checked his phone and found a text from Cole, his daughter: *don't forget, i have drum lesson tonite.*

OK, he typed back. *I'll make grilled cheese before you go.*

As Ben made his way back to the office, and the fridge,

and the peanut butter sandwich that was his lunch, he thought of another possible question from New Pete: *Why did Vince Resklar die so young?*

Perhaps Pete already knew some version of the answer, even though he'd moved into town only recently. Or he'd find an answer, from Haley or the internet or some other source—God willing, without involving Ben.

Chapter 2

Until his death, in 1887, the Unknown Vagrant, also known as the Roamer, spent more than thirty years walking the same 365-mile route through the countryside of three states, completing the same route every thirty-four days, and stopping at certain small towns with the regularity of a passenger train. His travels were predictable enough that, all along his route, pies and bread were baked to coincide with his arrival and handed to him like tributes to a royal.

His celebrity resided chiefly in his mystery—in why he was driven to make his regular circuit; in why he communicated only in hand signals, never speaking or staying anywhere long enough to form bonds or obligations; in why—even in the hottest days of summer—he wore a heavy, hand-stitched leather suit; in what he might have abandoned in favor of life on the road.

—From *The Wandering Enigma: A History of the Unknown Vagrant*, by Wallis Bertrand, 2009

Section D, Lot 232
After dark, mid-May

Don't smoke the whole thing at once, or it'll kick your ass.

Cole's chem-lab partner and "supplier" didn't tell her that barely a quarter of the joint would kick her ass—or whatever you called what she was experiencing now: the sense that tiny invisible people were spying on her from behind the other gravestones, and that one might sneak up to the stone now serving as her headboard.

Oh God, oh God, oh God.

The darkness and relative privacy of this place. Its openness and fresh air, and the hope that these would keep pot smoke from settling into her clothes and giving her away to her dad. All the things that had made the cemetery seem like an ideal spot for trying this joint played against her now, feeding her paranoia.

A tree branch creaked like shrill, wordless teasing. A car door slammed, bringing who? what?

Stay low, Cole thought. *Stay flat to the earth.*

After lying back, she started drumming her thighs: a comfort, compulsion, and means of protection for as long as she could remember. Whenever she was afraid or nervous, she slapped out a beat in response—against any handy surface, including herself. Almost always, the threat eased. This time, she tried out her new funk beat, her fear retreating as the rhythm took hold.

A voice echoed from the other side of the hill.

Over here!

Where?

Here!

Male voices. Soon, they coalesced at one spot. Two voices—no, three: two guys, one girl, talking and laughing. Then, the clatter of bottles.

A moment later the girl started singing a vaguely familiar song, one of the guys joining in on the second verse to add a new and strange harmony.

Four or eight, four or eight by twelve, which one?

A Vagrants song—not "Leave Me in Peace," the one that made her dad, Ben, change stations in the car, or turn off the radio altogether. Cole knew this other song only because her most recent Googling of the Vagrants had turned up a seemingly new site loaded with MP3s, which she transferred somewhat guiltily to her phone. At her own house not a single Vagrants CD, record, or cassette had ever been in evidence. In fact, only scraps of rock and punk remained in her father's music collection, neglected. These days, while he lounged or cooked or toiled over his hobby of growing mushrooms, bluegrass, Dixieland jazz, and crackling old ghosts of a cappella were his background music—all hand-me-down vinyl from Grandpa Ross.

When, in her father's presence, Cole drummed on her hips, a table, or the car dash, he shot her an eye. The sound annoyed him, surely. But it was also as if she'd reeled up something ugly he'd rather have kept submerged.

He seemed to have no love left for guitars either. Before the divorce his hardly-played acoustic, a gift from Cole's mother, Leah, had stood in a corner of her parents' bedroom, collecting dust and the occasional tossed-off sock or T-shirt. After the divorce it vanished from the bedroom, joining an old Rickenbacker in the recesses of a closet, the only electric left of three.

Once, years before, the presence of the guitars prompted Cole to ask her father if he'd ever been in a band.

"Not really," he said. "I just messed around with some musically inclined friends. Until I grew out of it."

I grew out of it. This became his standard explanation for putting music making behind him, and Cole never worked up the courage to follow up with this question: *Then why haven't you sold those last two guitars?* This question, she feared, might trigger him to do just that.

Still, she had one memory of him playing a guitar, the acoustic, when she was a little girl. Long after her bedtime, the unfamiliar sound of it drew her into the hall outside her parents' room. Standing in the dark, she listened to the slide and strum of his fingers on strings, which surrounded her with sounds like colors—in particular blues and greens. Looking back, she wasn't sure this hadn't been a dream.

Four or eight, four or eight by twelve, which one?

As the song wound down in the distance, Cole thought again of how she'd first heard of the Vagrants back in middle

11

school, how she'd also learned that Vince Resklar had been in her father's class at Bolster High. When she asked her dad if he ever hung out with Vince, ever played music with him, he said that they didn't know each other that well, that they'd moved in different circles. As for why he seemed to hate the Vagrants' biggest song, "Leave Me in Peace," Cole figured it had to remind him of the protest over the exhumation, a protest that had been annoying him more and more. But she couldn't help but wonder if the song's resurgence also reminded him of an uncomfortable truth: that an old classmate had done something more with music than just mess around with it.

Over the hill "Four or Eight" faded out, and seconds later the female singer started in with "Leave Me in Peace."

Cole thought of how it would have pleased Meg Tirella, if she were anywhere in earshot. With the help of a teacher, Ms. Gale, and some other honors students at Cole's school, Meg had set up the "Don't Dig Him, Leave Him" petition website, surely another bullet point for her college applications. It was doubtful, though, that she'd be drinking or smoking pot in a cemetery after nine on a school night.

Cole tried to picture Ms. Gale drinking in a cemetery and didn't come close. Though she looked younger than any other teacher in the school it was impossible to imagine her at seventeen—at least not the loud, stupid kind of seventeen. Her type of serious seemed elemental, the type you had from birth.

From time to time, in Honors History, as Ms. Gale passed back term papers or lectured or questioned the class, Cole thought she caught a judging, appraising look. *So you're the gravedigger's daughter. What do you know that we don't about the exhumation?* In reality, it was very possible Ms. Gale had no idea that Cole's father was a gravedigger, much less that he'd be part of the dig when the time came. He'd asked that Cole say nothing on the subject if questioned, and because she knew next to nothing, that would hardly be a problem.

Now, Cole focused on the singing. Unaccompanied, with its strange harmony, the tune was ghostly, almost pretty—a long, sad plea.

Leave Me in Peace.

Those words expressed a part of her father's nature, a part that had intensified recently. Maybe Cole only noticed this side of him more now that it was down to the two of them during the school year. Her mother wasn't there to keep conversations going at meals or on drives, to offer distractions or run interference, and so in the silences over the table or across the living room, Cole found herself furtively studying him in his default state, one of self-contemplative disgust. The disgust was not unjustified. He'd fucked up with her mother. Big time. But his brooding went deeper, or so it seemed to Cole, and ultimately had nothing to do with anyone but himself.

At some point he'd catch her studying him and try to smile, or if they were lounging together on the couch, watching TV, he'd give her foot an apologetic squeeze. There was no fighting the surge of worry she felt then. Summer was coming. Her mother was coming. And soon the two of them would be off to visit colleges—for how long, Cole didn't know—leaving him alone with the graveyard and the empty house, and his new hobby, mushroom farming.

Whenever she watched him plug mushroom spores into logs or check the progress in his "fruiting chambers," he seemed aware that she found his new interest a little odd. As if to calm her anxieties, he'd assured her that he wasn't growing anything hallucinogenic or otherwise illegal. "I'm just keeping myself occupied." Cole tried to tell herself that this was a good thing, not some rare sign of depression, or the first step on a dark, slow journey toward a bad end. She was certain her fears came solely from the fact that mushrooms grew on things that had died, in a cool, damp gloom.

Over the hill the singers hit the final note and held it, and the sadness of the sound brought to Cole's mind her mother's painting of the Unknown Vagrant, which hung in the downstairs hall. The painting showed him striding forward in a cloud of dust, looking over his shoulder at the viewer. In that dust cloud, the only clear thing was his eyes, peering over the collar of his leather suit. To her, those eyes, two polished coals, broadcast a warning like her own protective drumbeats: *Back off.*

The portrait had fascinated Cole for as long as she had memories of anything. It led her, as a child, to ask for bedtime stories of the hermity wanderer, and to request that she be dressed like him for two Halloweens running, a request that her mother fulfilled by piecing together a suit from scraps of leather and suede. Even now, whenever the subject of the Unknown Vagrant came up, Cole saw the dark eyes from the painting and felt certain he'd want to be left alone for all eternity, a belief she thought best to keep from her father.

Cole's phone alarm chimed, startling her. It was 9:40, and she'd told her dad she'd be home by ten. As far as he knew, she was at Maya's, studying. He didn't know that the two of them had broken up the week before; Cole was just getting used to that reality herself.

She silenced the alarm and pocketed the Altoids tin containing the remainder of the joint. Within a few minutes she was over the North Gate and back in her car, no longer paranoid, just starving. She started the engine but kept the lights off as she crossed the lot for the road, passing two shadowy compacts parked nose to nose by the entrance. If the other kids had been there she might have stopped to give them the same advice her dad had once given her. *At night you should park up there, under those pines. Away from the road.* Near the entrance the cars, and consequently their drivers, were low-hanging fruit for the police.

On this night, though, Cole was to cross no one else's path. After the first bend in the road she flipped on the headlights and picked up speed. Almost like she'd smoked nothing at all. Good.

As she neared her house she thought, not for the first time, that the distance between her father and Vince Resklar was possibly something to be thankful for. Vince had died by crashing his car into a tree, and drugs and alcohol had been found in his system. Luckily, no one else had been in the car.

Chapter 3

Some citizens protesting the exhumation of the Unknown Vagrant don't want the body to be disturbed at all, saying the mysterious rambler, as private as he was, would have been horrified by the prospect. They claim that removing his current grave marker, and creating a memorial for him within the cemetery, away from Route 4, would address the safety concerns. Other protesters have no problem with moving the body. But both camps strongly oppose the recently green-lighted plan to subject the Vagrant's remains to DNA tests and a skeletal analysis. According to those who have pushed for it, such testing might shed light on the Vagrant's ethnicity and health history. Most important, they claim, it might indicate whether he suffered from autism, one possible reason for his regular circuits through three states.

—From "Protesters Call Tests of Unknown Vagrant Remains 'Intrusive,'" the *Bolster Register*

Cemetery Office
Mid-morning

The office hadn't changed since Ben's earliest memories of it, back when he'd pushed toy trucks across the gritty concrete floor, back when his father, Ross, was alive and going about the job Ben now held, shuffling from task to task in his cowboy boots, clouding the air with cigarette smoke, stopping occasionally to tousle Ben's hair.

Now as then, shelves holding years of dig registers took

up much of the western wall, the most recent register on top of the shelves for easy access. Along the southern wall was a battered, stained sofa of gold Naugahyde, the resting place for fatigued grounds workers or, more rarely, visitors overtaken by summer's heat, winter's bluster, or grief of all seasons. (Ross had tended to grumble about the former users, forever suspecting hangovers.) Along the eastern wall stood mostly neglected file cabinets and the never neglected refrigerator, containing workers' lunches, cans of soda—compliments of Ben—and in the crisper drawers, occasional bottles or cans of beer—courtesy of Haley—a tradition Ben hoped would disappear with his former co-worker.

Along the northern wall, by the entrance, stood a forties-era office desk and, behind it, a squeaking, off-kilter swivel chair, now occupied by Carl Jenks. As usual, Jenks wore a crisp, fitted cotton shirt, the French cuffs fastened with monogrammed cufflinks, his trousers equally crisp and fitted. Every time he graced this office for the monthly "status of the grounds" meeting, Jenks gave the impression of a man who had gone to bed an investment banker, woken up the president of a not-for-profit cemetery, and decided the venture might be worthy of his talents and his bottomless stores of energy. Though he was seventy-something years old, he showed no signs of wanting to retire, often to Ben's chagrin.

Jenks was peering through his reading glasses at the status report Ben had typed up just that morning.

"How's that mausoleum work coming? The repointing, I mean."

"It'll be done by the end of next week," Ben said. He sat in a folding chair, across from Jenks.

"What about the irrigation problem in the East Garden?"

"It's all taken care of."

"Good. Sounds as if things are under control around here. Mostly."

The *mostly* made Ben's stomach lurch.

Jenks pocketed his reading glasses and sat forward in the creaking chair.

"Ben," he said, "this goes beyond our agenda, but I'm feeling the need to express myself: Those protesters are officially the biggest pain in my ass."

What do you want me to do about it? Ben wanted to say.

He cleaned up whatever the demonstrators left behind and, when the opportunity arose, he asked the noisy ones to quiet down, out of respect for the dead and the mourning. But the truth was, because the Unknown Vagrant's grave was outside the cemetery's gates, there was little he could do to send the protesters on their way. As long as they stayed behind the security pylons and off of Route 4, they had the right to demonstrate, and if they strayed, that was a matter for police to handle.

"Well," Ben said, "the exhumation isn't far off. Won't that kind of take care of the problem?"

Jenks fixed him with his *Are you some kind of idiot?* stare.

"Mark my word," he said. "The dig'll get those people even more riled up."

Maybe, maybe not, Ben thought.

"And that'll keep them going at least until those DNA results come in. Then they'll have a whole new reason for outrage."

Ben finished his coffee and set the mug on the desk. "I'm hoping it won't come to that, Carl. But if there's anything else you think I should be doing in the meantime, let me know."

Buying time for Jenks to settle down, Ben retrieved the coffee pot from the top of the file cabinet and refilled their mugs. He was buying time for himself, too, steeling his nerves for what he needed to say.

"I have an off-agenda item, too," Ben said, sitting back down.

"Oh yeah? What's it about?"

"Take a big guess."

Jenks slumped, as if he'd just lost at cards. "Green burials."

"Yes."

"Can we do this some other time, Ben? Today's pretty busy for me."

Ben picked up the folder he'd left by his chair and handed

it to Jenks. "It's that new report I told you about. It'll take you five or ten minutes to read it, and that's all I'm going to ask of you, for now."

One thing Ben didn't have to bother Jenks with was an explanation of green burials. He'd gone over the basics with him many times.

In green burials, the body went into the earth without a heavy casket or embalming chemicals, and most certainly without concrete grave liners or casket-encompassing vaults, whose manufacture and transport were significant sources of carbon emissions. Shrouds or other containers for the body had to be biodegradable, and made of natural materials.

So far at Bolster Hill all forms of green burials had proved a tough sell, mainly because of their prohibitions against liners and vaults. The cemetery's board, like many other cemetery managers across the country, had long required these structures, contending that they prevented graves from sinking over time, making the grounds easier to maintain, and "more pleasing to the eye."

In arguing for liners and vaults, Jenks liked to say, "Remember the tourists," referring to Bolster Hill's much-touted status as one of the "gems" of the garden cemetery movement: a nineteenth-century trend of developing graveyards that looked as much like Victorian-era parks as places to bury the dead— with winding paths, artificial lakes, statuary biased heavily toward winged figures, and wedding-cake-ish ornamentation on just about every structure that could support it, especially mausoleums.

At the last board meeting Ben had argued—for the second or third time—that better soil filling would keep any graves from sinking and thus detracting from the cemetery's historical charm. He'd also recapped all of his former arguments for green burials—statistics showing a growing demand for them; their potential to attract new customers and reduce expenditures on grounds keeping; the simple fact that they were the right thing to do. He'd made this argument not just at the meetings but in extensive reports he'd prepared in advance.

More and more, Ben was trying to appeal to board members' commercial instincts: a growing number of studies, like the one Ben had just handed Jenks, showed not just rising demand for green burials but also increasing financial benefits. Bolster Hill, he argued, could stand by and let competitors take the lead on capturing that demand, or it could get out ahead of them.

Now, Jenks didn't bother to open the folder. He tucked it under his arm and rose from his chair. "I'll look at this thing as soon as I can."

Ben imagined Jenks stuffing the folder into a drawer or, worse, pitching it into the trash. Those visions inspired anger, and he couldn't hold it back.

"We got five phone calls about green burials last month alone. I'm sure you get even more of them in the central office."

Jenks fixed him with another of his stares. "I couldn't tell you, Ben. I don't answer the phones."

Here, Ben didn't say what was on his mind: that someone in the central office should damn well be keeping a record of such requests, and making sure the information got to the board, and to Ben, who was leading the cemetery's Green Initiative.

Ben took a deep breath to collect himself. When he spoke again, he tried to temper his words. "I'm not letting go of this issue. I hope you know that."

Jenks smiled, as if he truly were pleased. "Of course you aren't. And I admire that, Ben. Really I do."

Flattery will get you nowhere, Ben thought. Not where this issue is concerned.

But once Jenks departed, Ben began to doubt himself. As he sat back down in the folding chair he wondered, not for the first time, if all the energy he'd been devoting to green burials was worth it.

Ben traced his interest in them back to his first sight of a concrete burial vault, when he was eight or nine. He'd been watching a lot of war movies then and, perhaps because of this, the vault reminded him of a soldier's bunker. It had to be hoisted up and into the grave with a truck-mounted crane, after Ross and the crane operator set up the winch and cables.

By that age, Ben already knew that "nothing stays pretty" after death: his father's words, after Ben had pushed him for reassurance that the "magical chemicals" from the funeral home could keep a body unchanged, no matter how much time had passed. In Ross's words, "Nature will have her way with all of us, son, no matter what tricks we try to pull. If you want someone to stay the same forever you better take a picture."

After seeing his first vault, Ben had new questions for his dad: Why the concrete bunker? Isn't the casket enough? Some of the coffins Ben had seen looked like they'd survive a nuclear bomb.

"It's the rules here, son."

"Yeah, but *why*?"

His father explained how the vaults kept the ground from sinking and kept things looking nice, how some families liked the sense of security they offered. But though Ross never said as much, it seemed he felt the pointlessness of them, or that's the look Ben remembered seeing on his face as vaults were lowered or concrete liners placed.

Nature will have her way with all of us.

With time, to Ben, that line of Ross's became less an expression of hopelessness and more a form of comfort. Wandering through the woods behind his house, or into the more obscure, less groomed parts of the cemetery, he noticed how things broke down just as readily as they grew: fallen leaves and tree limbs, last year's grasses and milkweed, the occasional dead bird. No human intervention was required; in fact, the less of it, the better. That, anyway, was what Ben came around to believing.

But that belief was of little help to him now. If he were to convince Jenks and the rest of the cemetery board that green burials deserved their approval, something far more persuasive was required. What that something was, Ben had no idea.

Chapter 4

The Unknown Vagrant, or whoever pieced together his leather suit, certainly had a way with the sewing needle. Extant photographs of him suggest that great care was taken in the construction of this garment.

—From a plaque accompanying a miniature re-creation of the leather suit at the Bolster Hill Historical Society

Grave of the Unknown Vagrant
After dark

"I think this fellow is getting enough attention. He doesn't need any help from us." Peg looked between Martha and the grave, which was lit by yellowish streetlights. For now, it was free of protesters, though a couple of their fliers had blown up against the cemetery's fence.

"It's not about attention," Martha said. "I'm thinking of an understated message. Something about hidden identities. Secrets. I'd go really low-key, with cool colors."

Of course it's about attention, Peg thought. *Why else are we doing this?* But she kept her mouth shut, and after setting a time to meet back up with Martha, she marched away from the tomb of the unknown hobo and into the heart of the cemetery.

Martha was a true artist. Peg was an unapologetically bourgeois maker of sweaters, gloves, and afghans. Their paths had crossed through the weekly stitching sessions of the Bolster Needlers, which Martha took part in to, as she'd put it, "explore new forms." Knitting was no new form to Peg. She'd joined in on the sessions to socialize and knit somewhere other than in front of her TV, and to pass on help or advice when asked. Among the younger Needlers was TT, a twenty-four-year-old knitting prodigy and the first one to mention, in Peg's hearing, yarn bombing.

"Sounds dreadful," Peg had said, though she was intrigued. "No, no, no," TT replied, as she pulled one of the last shanks of yarn through her miniature hedgehog. "It's am*aaaa*zing."

Through TT, and pictures and stories she found for herself online, Peg learned that yarn bombing was the stealthy decoration of light poles, fire hydrants, bike racks—just about anything anyone might pass by—with knitted or crocheted cosies or gewgaws. Some called it vandalism; others, like TT, called it art.

"You just try to get people to take a second look at everyday stuff," she explained. "You get them to stop and think and maybe be, like, *Wow, someone cared enough to make this thing for this place.* Even though it might get ripped down in a day, in an hour."

TT's words left Martha a little misty-eyed, or so it seemed to Peg—as if she were already imagining the artistic potential of yarn. Peg pictured more practical outcomes: specifically, the spiffing up of the tarnished statue of Phineas Bolster, which looked remote and neglected, even though it stood at the center of Bolster Square. In Peg's mind Phineas wore a sporty yet distinguished vest of sky-blue cashmere.

Bolster Square was not to be her destiny, however. When under TT's leadership the Needlers divided the town for "tagging" on June 24th, chosen because it was the birthday of TT's grandmother, apparently a prize-winning knitter, Martha was the first to poke a finger to the map.

"Dibs on the cemetery. Now who's in with me?"

Peg shot up her hand in a spasm of nerves, nothing else could explain it. As the meeting moved on, she allowed herself to be eased into the consequences of her impulsiveness, first by the cemetery's relative obscurity, second by Martha's proposal of an advance planning mission, which the two of them had set off on tonight. Nevertheless, before leaving home with her camera, pen and notepad, and assorted other supplies, Peg granted herself permission to back out of the whole endeavor if this evening's scouting left her the least bit queasy or doubtful.

Now, she swung her scarf-dimmed flashlight along the rows of stones, pictures of others' yarn bombings replaying through her mind—giant pom-pom hats pulled over the roofs of tiny cars, knitted flowers blooming in median strips, crocheted tendrils hanging from tree limbs or lampposts. But what about this particular place? What was fitting? Certainly not pom-pom caps on the gravestones, certainly not yarn hands reaching from the earth—a vision that had interrupted her bedtime reading the night before. In this place almost all yarn doodads, maybe even flowers, were bound to look vulgar.

Peg's flashlight caught a paperboard sign ahead, staked to the right of the path: *Memory Garden.* Having no better ideas about where she might go, Peg followed the sign's arrow forward, to the crest of a small hill, where stone benches surrounded an oval the size of a small pool, dark foliage where the water would have been, and in the middle of it all a type of platform, concrete or stone. Angled along the perimeter of the oval were two concrete structures calling to mind card catalogs. Whether they were sculptures or something more purposeful, Peg had no idea.

All in all, this spot didn't look much like a garden. In the absence of any signs telling her she'd either arrived or had farther to go, she headed for the closest bench and plopped herself down, not out of fatigue, though it was long past her bedtime. *So what exactly am I going to do?* Peg asked herself. Checking her watch, she saw she had about a half hour to figure something out.

Hoping the darkness might aid her concentration, Peg shut off her flashlight and watched her surroundings reappear in the weak moonlight: platform, foliage, benches.

She thought back on the last Bolster Needlers' meeting, a "brainstorming session" for the yarn bombing which featured a special guest, one of Martha's painter friends, Catherine. As the Needlers sat or stood around TT's kitchen table, Catherine laid

23

out color prints like tarot cards—prints of her work and those of other artists, a few of them fellow locals—under labels for each tagging destination: *Bolster Square, Goodale Park, Welton Road, The Cemetery.*

"Some inspiration for your yarn work, perhaps," Catherine said shyly before pushing away from the table so that others could have a look. Peg lagged back to finish her coffee, waiting for the crowd to diminish, watching TT, Martha, and a few others express genuine excitement over the prints, while others seemed more reserved. When Peg herself bellied up to the table she confirmed that the prints were mostly abstract—too abstract, she assumed, to be of any use to her. Many of them were blocks or swirls of color or mere suggestions of recognizable places or things. She was more comfortable with clear plans and patterns, and such rules as she broke in her own knitting were limited—some contrast-color shag on a rolled collar, maybe, or a dolman widening at the arms—and in keeping with the greater scheme.

In The Cemetery section were three paintings, all postcards and none clearly related to graveyards, though there were hints of mortality. In one a vine of blooms, fresh purple or wilted or shriveled to brown, climbed in dimness toward a high window, possibly in a basement. Among the flowers were tiny, random things: a plump, pale hand, a silver cup, a blue-black bird. When she turned over this card and the others Peg saw they were from the same fall exhibit at the little gallery in Baines, which Peg had heard of but never visited. "Losses," the exhibit had been titled.

The most abstract of the three was the one that had stayed with her, though at first it made little impression: a churn of oranges, reds, and grays over a dark field.

The artist was Leah Dirjery, her name ringing a vague bell.

Now, Peg saw that the foliage before her was casting a bluish glow, from tiny footlights scattered among the leaves. For some time, she stared into the glow, until, without thinking, she withdrew the postcard from her shirt pocket. Angled toward the light its central, orange swirl was visible, like a storm pattern on a weather map.

The thing that had drawn her to the painting, she'd come to realize, was how it called to mind summer sunsets in her and Roger's kitchen. Not long into the first summer at their house, the red-gold light caused them to linger in the kitchen, after the dinner dishes had been cleared and leftovers packed away. They took to sitting side by side at the table, glasses of whiskey or wine before them, facing the glow through the western window. They talked or didn't, held hands or didn't, as they watched the red-gold fade to blue.

During Roger's last summer, they kept up the tradition until they couldn't anymore, and the condo Peg moved to after he died lacked a western exposure. In some sense, that was a relief.

Looking between the postcard and the dim, frankly depressing space before her, Peg began to imagine some possibilities. At the very least this spot could use some color, and maybe the faintest suggestion of hope. If that wasn't too much to ask for something created for a cemetery.

While the ideas were fresh in her mind, Peg made some notes and sketches and took a few flash pictures of the space before her. When she remembered to check the time, she was already a few minutes late for meeting up with Martha.

As she walked back to the grave of the Unknown Vagrant, Peg again wondered what Roger would have thought of the painting that had so moved her. Another true artist, he'd worked in wood, and even in her little condo she'd found homes for pieces of furniture he'd finished over the years, and for the projects death had interrupted. Among his creations were small drawered boxes, tilted or curved, for jewelry or other doodads; a chess set with wooden skeleton keys; various attempts at abstract sculpture. Everything Roger had made was a captured conversation, with himself and with the world.

Let me have just one good conversation with that space, Peg thought, as Martha came into view. *If I can do that, I might make something decent.*

25

Chapter 5

If the wind was blowing strong from the west, we could smell him well before we saw him. Imagine a barn in high summer, full of sweat-soaked saddles. That would get the smell about right.

—An observation about the Unknown Vagrant from Emma Meryl, homemaker. Source: *Bolster County Tales and Curiosities*, 1893

Sections A, B, and D
Mid-morning

Monday. Curation day. Ben shuffled through the dew with his garbage bag, scanning the rows for trash, expired flowers, other grounds violations. Collected so far from Section A: the now-withered pansies on the Dobson lots, a collapsed PBR box with empties on the stairs of the Paige Mausoleum, an "I ♥ My Three Wheeler" badge in the no-man's land past Clover Path.

Ben crossed into Section B, moving toward the West Gate. At first glance, the coast looked clear. He started in along the rows.

Whenever a burial was scheduled, the central office sent the family the "gravesite ornamentation regulations," which Ben imagined making a direct trip to the trash can. He imagined this because violations turned up regularly, at the time of the burial or days, months, sometimes years, down the line. Stuffed animals, plastic bouquets, patio candles, and yard pinwheels were the usual offenders. But now and then some real originals turned up, especially—and for reasons unknown—in Section B of the grounds, where deposits over the years included a pair of fuzzy pink bed slippers, dentures in a country club Scotch glass, and the key to room 45 at the Bolster Hill Motor Lodge. Accidental leavings? Common trash? Not these particular things. The slippers had been weighted with marbles and aligned as if at bedside, the denture glass set neatly on a bar mat, the motel key enclosed in a satin-lined watch box.

Something small, not a box, came to mind as Ben crossed Poppy Path into a new block of graves.

This row. No, the next. Ben approached and stared down the line, and there was Bertha Mains's "90" birthday candle, still at the base of her stone. One month and counting, long past commutation time. But Ben's previous defense returned: who could see the candle unless they were looking for it? Jenks for one wouldn't be. Once again, Ben let it go and moved on.

Jenks liked to say he preferred prevention to cures. He'd instructed Ben and, before him, Ross to keep watch at grave-side services for pinwheel planters and their like, and to find some appropriate interval to take them aside and ask that they kindly refrain from leaving the offending objects behind. Any violations remaining on the grave could by all rights be whisked into the trash, according to Jenks.

But the rules Ross followed and passed on to Ben were these: No mourner would be stopped from leaving anything on a grave—above all not during a service. They would be given room to do what they felt driven to do, unharassed. If the leaving was a "Code J," Ross's term for anything that might put off Jenks, its sentence would be commuted to the five days given to cut flowers, unless the object was especially visible or egregious. In Ben's memory, the only things Ross had trashed immediately, before being made to by Jenks, were inflatable boobs the size of truck tires, left on the grave of a strip-club owner and a *Rot in Hell* sign, its letters painstakingly burned into a wooden plank, deposited overnight on the grave of a revered councilwoman with no known enemies. Ross didn't have a personal issue with the boobs, or with a *Rot in Hell* message when justly delivered.

His problem was that these things drew attention away from the graves they were propped against, and from everything else in sight of them.

As for dealing with Jenks, "He wants to come off as the lawman," Ross had told Ben any number of times. But if you disagreed with him judiciously and not too frequently, and whenever possible through actions instead of words, you could usually get some wiggle room on the Code J's. "If he knows you're picking up the trash—the real trash—you shouldn't have too much trouble with the other stuff."

Heading north into Section D Ben made his way to Anthony Lekovic's grave, its temporary marker the only thing visible from a distance. As for flowers and wreaths, there hadn't been many to start with, and the morning after the service some friend of the Lekovics had dropped by to deliver what remained of them to the Bolster Hill Manor nursing home. No sign of the ziplocked picture either, until Ben reached the grave's edge.

It was leaning against the right marker post, partly hidden behind a tuft of grass, the picture blurred by a fog of condensation. Ben dropped to the grass and picked up the bag, finding the lock breached, water pooled in one corner. He unzipped the lock and laid the picture on his knee, then turned the bag inside out, gave it a few good shakes, and dried it as well as he could against his shirt.

Now, he noticed the picture was too thick to be just one. Ben looked along the edge and saw three prints sealed together by the damp.

Just put them back. He started to, then changed his mind and began working a thumbnail between the layers, pulling one picture from the other, and laying each across his knees to air. The first picture was the one Ben remembered: of a goofy, skinny kid so far from starting his criminal record, so far from the heroin overdose that was said to have killed him, that both might have seemed impossible. The next picture showed the same kid a few years later, just as skinny but now much taller and no longer goofy. He sat sprawled on a couch, almost scowling, in real or put-on displeasure with picture takers, with his surroundings, with God knew what else. The only thing excluded from this displeasure was the black dog curled up beside him, long muzzle in his lap. The boy had the dog in a one-arm hold, his fingers laced into the fur.

The last picture showed the dog in profile in a carpeted hall, nose lifted, ears perked toward a door, as if he was waiting for someone to come through it. Ben blew on the pictures and tested the surfaces—still a little tacky, but that would have to do. Carefully, he placed them side by side in the bag and closed the seal, pressing it tight and double-checking. Then he leaned the bag back against the post, behind the tuft of grass.

It was day six, just past commutation time. But for now, the pictures would stay.

Next, Ben headed to Vince's grave, where he moved quickly, as if bussing a table. He tossed beer bottles, cigarette butts, and candle nubs into the trash, and pocketed two guitar picks, more out of habit than desire. With Jenks, there was no wiggle room for ornamentation here or at the grave of the Unknown Vagrant, both of which had turned into "sideshows" in Jenks's words and therefore required especially ruthless patrolling. Ben was relieved to have this excuse.

Giving things a final scan, he spied something pink held down by a rock.

Ben guessed what it was. Unfolding the little scrap of paper, he saw he was right.

Vince,
Love all your songs, esp. Getting Out.
Sending you kisses,
KTR

"'Getting Out' was *my* fucking song," Ben whispered, taken aback by the crazed sound of his voice.

After trashing the note, he wandered down the hill and toward the North Gate, where just beyond the fence four pro-testers, a smaller group than usual, waggled signs at passing cars.

29

Ben's attention was drawn not to them but to something new within the gates, a banner stretched between the tops of two obelisks.

He charged toward the banner, toward the side facing the road. It showed a silk-screened photograph of the Unknown Vagrant, alongside a message in big red letters: *Leave Me in Peace!*

With two leaps, Ben ripped down the banner, prompting a cry from beyond the fence.

"*Hey!* What are you doing?"

Ben turned to see one of the sign holders, a regular, shaking a fist at him.

"My job!" Ben cried, shaking the banner in reply. "You keep this stuff on *your* side of the fence."

"Give it back, then!" another called to him. But Ben was already striding to the East Gate, toward the dumpster in the arbor, trash bag in one hand, banner in the other. A sense of satisfaction and righteousness nearly cheered him.

Into the dumpster went the whole works, with a slam.

Chapter 6

Each of our companion grave markers is constructed from the sturdiest granite or metals, symbolizing the eternal strength of your relationship, and the beauty of our work speaks to the passion and romance of your long-treasured love.

—From the Artful Markers website

Main Parking Lot
Early evening

As she waited for Cole, Leah scrolled through old text messages, deciding which ones to keep or delete. The further back she went the more quickly she hit "delete," until she came across a text Ben had sent her at 2:52 a.m. on a Monday more than a year before, long after they'd split.

She tapped the text, reopening it.

behold #541:
http://www.artfulmarkers.com/companionmarkers

Clicking the link, she discovered that item 541 was still there: a "companion" grave marker consisting of two knee-high twists of steel, joined by smaller rust-colored twists. These wrapped and wrapped about each other, imitating the mindless drive of grape-vine tendrils.

She lowered her phone and looked past the spot where Ben's truck would be, if he hadn't gone home for the day. About one hundred yards beyond that spot, on the other side of the "Spring Garden," was their double plot: a wedding gift from Ross and Liz. It had been excluded from Leah and Ben's divorce settlement as if by neglect and left undiscussed.

Before she met Ben, Leah hadn't thought about what she'd want done with her body after she died. For one thing, she'd been far too young to contemplate the matter and, frankly, would have found it morbid. Had she not met Ben, she very likely would have delayed the decision as long as possible, perhaps until it was beyond her power to make. Her preference would have been cremation, and she would have been fine with having her ashes scattered to the winds. Taking up real estate after she died—real estate marked with an etched stone—seemed senseless to her, and selfish.

As for Ben, he seemed never to have questioned his father's belief that everyone should "leave at least a shadow on the earth." The gift from Ross and Liz had made this belief a near command.

A shadow for whom? Leah sometimes asked herself. The small circle of people who knew you in life, maybe only your children? When they died, who would care?

At the time she and Ben received the gift of the burial plot, she told no one of it, certainly not her own parents, who would have found it macabre at best. It was bad enough, in their eyes, that their daughter was marrying a musician who had gotten her pregnant, a musician employed as a gravedigger.

As a consequence, Leah never had to explain to her parents what she herself had come around to seeing: that to Ross and Ben, buying a plot for oneself or a loved one, far in advance of death, was no more odd or macabre than making room in one's home for an inevitable guest—as nice and welcoming a room as possible. Decisions about where the plot would be located, and how it would be marked, were nothing that should be left to possibly thoughtless or indifferent survivors.

The phone rang, startling her: Cole.

"I was just about to call you."

"Sorry, Mom. My lesson's wrapping up a bit late. I'll be there in a few minutes."

"Want me to just pick you up?"

"No thanks. If we leave my car in the cemetery lot, it'll be easier for Dad to take it to the mechanic."

"All right. And what's the name of the place we're going to?" She wanted to GPS it.

"Max's Drums, in Reading."

"Okay, thanks. See you soon."

Leah flipped back to the picture of the grave marker, studying its curves and twists as if they carried a message, one that given enough time could be figured out. At some point in the middle of this the old song bloomed from a corner of her mind: *Four or eight, four or eight by twelve, which one?* Leah caught herself whispering the words and stopped.

Focus, she thought. Keep or delete?

Surely this was a drunk text, regretted by Ben soon after he'd sent it. Which is why she'd never responded to it. Surely its survival in her message queue would embarrass him.

Then she thought again of that marker, a physical manifestation of a wish of Ben's—that their union, however imperfect, leave a lasting shadow. Though she'd never shared that wish, sweeping it into the trash didn't feel right.

A crunch of gravel turned her attention to the entrance. There was Cole.

Keep.

Chapter 7

[W]e force the [dying] to understand that they must meditate on the formless God; that there are no houses or buildings, no material life, no family; that he came to the world alone and that he will leave alone; that he came out from the Brahman* and that he will also merge there.

*The Absolute; the source of everything

—From an interview with Shuklaji, manager of a home for dying pilgrims and their families in Kashi (Varanasi), India. Source: *Dying the Good Death: The Pilgrimage to Die in India's Holy City*, by Christopher Justice

General Grounds

Mid-morning, Memorial Day

Memorial Day brought its typical blue, cloud-stacked sky and streams of visitors through all the gates—mostly the middle-aged, bearing flats of flowers, children or grandchildren running ahead of them or lagging behind.

Now among the middle aged himself, Ben wheeled about his own flats of flowers, working his way through his usual circuit of relatives' graves: the Meryls, then the Cobbs; maternal grandparents, then paternal; his own parents last. Up until this year Ben's last stop had always been the Unknown Vagrant's grave, but he didn't want people swarming around and bothering him as he did his planting there. He might sneak the flowers in later, once the crowds had dwindled. Or maybe he'd just put the duty off till next year.

As Ben went about his work, he looked out for the bewildered or clearly lost, ready to consult the list of names and lot numbers in his back pocket, ready to hand out copies of the cemetery map. As was his custom, he let pass the Code J's arriving in their usual Memorial Day abundance—pinwheels, stuffed toys, wind chimes, vases or wreaths of plastic flowers.

On his way to the plots of Grandma and Grandpa Dirjery, Ben passed Vince's grave, which was always free of visitors, free of flowers, on Memorial Day. As far as Ben knew, no relatives of Vince's remained in Bolster. His father had never been in the picture, and shortly after Vince's death, his mother had moved to New Hampshire to live with a sister and as far as Ben knew had never returned. As for Vince's shrine keepers, they kept vampires' hours, never appearing before sunset. Ben was certain they would return this evening, leaving their usual junk behind.

By a quarter past ten Ben had reached his final stop, his parents' double plot with its separate stones—

Rossmore B. Dirjery	Elizabeth R. Dirjery
June 28, 1940 –	August 4, 1943 –
September 2, 1992	April 12, 2008

In these stones and the distance between them, his mother perpetually got the last word. The first word had come from Ross, who'd for years expressed his hatred of separate grave markers for the married: "It's like two strangers trapped together on an elevator. For all eternity."

The last word came two weeks after Ross's death, when a stone for him alone was delivered for the double plot. Ben checked the monument order to make sure that a mistake hadn't been made, then he called his mother.

"What a relief," she'd replied wearily.

She explained to Ben that years before, Ross had indeed ordered a companion marker for their plot, without her permission. She'd learned of the marker, and of the fact that both of their names and birthdates had been engraved upon it, a few days after his death, when she'd found the old receipt from the monument company. Immediately, she canceled the original order, requested a marker for him alone, and ate the cost of the stone that had already been engraved.

"I'm not dead yet, honey," she told Ben. "And as long as I'm living, I never want to see my name on a gravestone."

What she didn't say, but what Ben presumed at the time, was that she was keeping her options open, to be buried next to someone else, someone more faithful and devoted than Ross Dirjery. Or to not be buried at all. But when the time came she was laid to rest beside Ross, beneath a marker she never saw, leaving a mix of truth and fiction. The fiction was the shared plot and its suggestion of fidelity. The truth, Elizabeth's doing, was in the separate stones and the space between them.

Ben rose up and retrieved from his wagon a flat of lobelia flowers, one of his mother's favorites. As he overturned the flat and shook free the roots, he felt his phone buzz with a call. Seeing who it was, he answered.

"Hey, Leah."

He heard a rushing sound on her end, wind or the passing of cars. But her voice came through clearly enough: "I got Cole lined up for some college visits, three the last week of June."

"That's great, thanks."

"Would it be okay if I picked her up on the twenty-fifth?"

"Sure."

Briefly, the rushing-wind sound intensified.

"Are you at Greenwood?" he asked. "Or on the way?"

"On the way."

Greenwood Cemetery, one hundred or so miles south of Bolster Hill, was where six generations of Leah's family, most recently her father, had been buried. Before they split up, she and Ben would hit Greenwood first on the Sunday after Memorial Day, then Bolster Hill, making for a full day of graveyard gardening. Cole's compensation, in the years she'd gone along for the ride, was a stop for frozen custard between cemeteries, and permission to drum in the car.

Until the divorce, Memorial Day itself had been out of the question for the outing, because Ben was always on duty then.

"You're not talking and driving, are you?"

He'd asked Leah and Cole this question so many times it had become a family joke. This time, however, safety wasn't his primary concern.

"No."

Most likely, then, the driver was Adam Forsythe, someone Leah had been dating long enough—four months?—to identify him to Ben by name and occupation, enabling extensive Googling. Adam Forsythe, architect, winner of obscure yet impressive-sounding design awards. Marathoner, maker of artisan cheeses. Bald or shaven-headed possessor of take-no-shit good looks.

And future spouse? To Ben's mind, bringing Forsythe to the family plots in Greenwood was in the same category as having him meet the parents.

"I know I'm being neurotic, Leah. Sorry."

"You're not being neurotic."

Ben imagined Forsythe taking in Leah's end of the conversation, adding *neurotic* to his mental catalog of the flaws and oddities of Leah's ex. Then again, in Forsythe's eyes, Ben probably wasn't worth the effort.

"I should let you go, Leah. Thanks for the heads-up about the college visits."

"Sure. Talk to you soon."

Pocketing his phone, Ben turned back to his mother's grave, reminded once more of his and Leah's own double plot. Sometime before long they'd have to make a plan for it—sell off one or both spaces, probably.

But one thing at a time, first things first. Ben knelt back down and reached for a clump of lobelia, tucked it into the newly turned earth.

☙❧

"So my back's to the fountain, and I'm facing uphill. Right in front of me is Poppy Path."

"I thought it was Petunia Path."

37

"No, it's Poppy."

"Well, if you're where I think you are, there should be a big maple to your right, where Whatever Path joins the main way. She's just to the left of that."

Meredith spotted the maple and, as quickly as she could, dragged her wagonful of flowers toward it. In the silence on the other end, she pictured her mother where she'd left her, waiting expectantly in her sunlit kitchen, one plaster-casted leg propped on a chair, the newspaper spread before her on the table.

"Ruby Marie Steinlen," Meredith announced upon finding the stone.

"Well done. Now did you get the geraniums?"

"Yes, Ma."

"The *red* ones? She hated the pink ones. And what's the point of the white ones?"

"I know, Ma. I got what you asked for."

The geraniums were tired-looking remnants from a picked-over lot at the garden store. In an attempt to make up for them, Meredith had also purchased a small rosebush full of red blooms. She unloaded this and the other flowers from the wagon and set them down by her grandma's stone.

"Okay, let me get this stuff planted. I'll be back in an hour or so."

"Hey, Mer, one more thing. Did you happen to spot my friends?"

It took Meredith a moment to figure out what she meant. "Yeah, they're out there with their signs. Same as always."

"Good. They should get a lot of attention today."

"For what it's worth."

A pause of disapproval. "Well, *I* think it's worth something."

As soon as she'd opened her mouth, Meredith knew it had been a mistake. The last thing she wanted was to start this whole argument up again. "I know, Ma, I know. And I respect your opinion, now as always. See you soon." Meredith ended the call and pocketed her phone.

Her mother, Judith, didn't know any of the protesters. They were her *friends* only in that she supported their stance against digging up a mysterious dead person. This solidarity was a continuation of her long and, at one time, bordering-on-obsessive campaign against Meredith's choice of career, which was to dig up mysterious dead people. The campaign reached its peak six years earlier, just as Meredith was accepted into a forensic-anthropology master's program.

Since then, as Meredith progressed through her master's and then doctoral studies, Judith's objections had become less frequent and more subtle: leaden silences when old friends or family politely asked Meredith about her projects *du jour*; dazed looks of revulsion when Meredith offered answers. But the Unknown Vagrant controversy had granted Judith a fresh opportunity to be more direct and vocal. Coming into this visit with her mother, Meredith knew just the roughest details of the controversy. Given that she was on break from her work, until her post-doc fellowship started in the fall, she would have been content to leave it at that. Yet Judith took to speaking out against the exhumation, repeatedly—her complaints like provocative shoves at Meredith, who was equally guilty, in her mother's eyes, of disturbing the peace of the dead.

"Listen, Ma," Meredith had said just yesterday, after an especially unpleasant exchange. "They have a court order. They're going to dig this guy up, no matter how much you or anyone else belly-aches about it. So why don't you devote your energy to something more productive?"

Meredith had lacked the energy to raise her old objections: that no ethical anthropologist disturbed the peace of the dead out of idle curiosity; that in many circumstances it was the living, the surviving family and friends of the dead, who gained some peace from the work, or at least a chance at some answers. *Think of the families of the Disappeared in Guatemala. And in Bosnia and Kosovo.* These words went through Meredith's mind but she did not speak them, knowing her mom would take them for preaching, and she wouldn't be wrong.

Now, for the sake of Grandma Ruby, Meredith resolved to push aside this old dispute. Reaching into the wagon for the first of the tired geraniums, she sensed a motion at the corner of her eye and looked right. A somber-faced girl was approaching with a flat of marigolds—yellow, orange, blood-red—all bright against her cocoa-colored skin. The girl kept her eyes on the flowers, passing Meredith as if she weren't there.

Once the girl had vanished over the hill Meredith set down the pot of geraniums, feeling suddenly adrift, her purpose here as uncertain as the connection between this orderly place and death.

Yellow, orange, blood-red marigolds. They called to mind Varanasi and all of its untamable disorder. Just a month before, Meredith had traveled to the sacred Indian city, for what she'd intended to be a vacation. In retrospect, there was no fitting description of what her experience had been.

✦

Not three hours off the plane, she'd already broken one of her cardinal rules of foreign travel: that unless absolutely necessary, she was to avoid other Americans. Yet here she was trailing, out of fatigue and the narrowness of the streets, a man she guessed to be a fellow Midwesterner. She trailed him past stalls of vegetables, jewelry, bright silks; past roaming humans, cows, and dogs; past weaving bike- and motor-rickshaws; past plump brown monkeys gnawing fruit in the shadows.

She had her reasons for so willingly following his lead:

The 41 hours of travel time—Chicago to Shanghai, Shanghai to New Delhi, New Delhi to Varanasi—with the usual distresses, layovers, and biorhythmic confusions . . .

The fact that it was 5:30 a.m. in Chicago, where she still resided in body if not in soul . . .

The unfamiliarity of everything around her, not only sights but smells: of incense mingled with cooking smoke, of dung and piss, fresh and aged . . .

The increasingly suspect lassi she'd downed at a street stand in front of the guesthouse . . .

The heat . . .

The gravitational pull of the stranger himself . . .

The longer she trailed him, the more dependent Meredith

felt. She kept her eyes on his back as if she were clinging to a raft on high seas.

She'd met him just minutes before in a tea shop. Having dropped in to purchase a bottle of water, she noticed him at a corner table, typing energetically into a laptop. His red Clash T-shirt, just like the one her college boyfriend had worn, signaled *Westerner*. But she hadn't yet heard him speak, and his light brown skin suggested he might be a local. Judging from the steaming mug before him, he'd spent at least enough time in Varanasi to have grown used to the native water.

As Meredith set her bottle and rupees on the cashier's counter he cast her a surly look and went back to his work. That would have been it, had Meredith left the shop immediately. Instead, far from him but foolishly close to a street-side window, she took a seat, uncapped her water, and unfolded her map of the city. As she tracked streets and pathways to Manikarnika Ghat, a shadow slid over the map and stopped.

She turned to see a thin, mustached young man peering at her through the window, hands cupped around his eyes. Taking her notice of him as permission, he smiled, nodded, and made his way into the shop.

"Shit."

This was her sixth encounter with a tout, an aggressive provider of tourist "aid," since stepping off the plane. Now, she resolved to make a quick, efficient escape, without spending a single rupee. By the time he made it to her table, she'd folded up her map and capped her water bottle.

"Hello, miss, hello! Where are you from?"

His words echoed oddly in the confines of the shop.

"No," she said. With luck, on the streets, *no* was enough to end such encounters, or so the guide books claimed. But here she felt trapped.

"I see you can use a guide, miss. Where can I take you? I would be so happy to help."

"No," she repeated, stuffing the map and bottle into her shoulder bag. "I don't need any help."

She rose up, suddenly unsteady on her feet.

"I'll bring you to the best places, with the best views. No one else is a better guide than me."

As Meredith pushed past him he reached for her sleeve.

"For God's sake, no!"

With this, the laptop man bolted forward, shouting something in what Meredith presumed to be Hindi. When the tout was gone she sat back down, a little nearer the door.

"Thank you," she said, immediately embarrassed by her assumption that this man spoke English.

He regarded her with mild irritation, as if she herself had stirred up the trouble. Still, she couldn't help but find him attractive. He reminded her of the fifties-era Harry Belafonte.

"Where are you trying to go?" he said flatly. His accent, or lack thereof, suggested the Midwest.

Manikarnika Ghat had been her intention; now she considered a return to the guesthouse. She was tired, and a little woozy. But something else had come over her as well, something new and strange. The man's voice sounded as if it were being piped through a tube, directly into her ear. The red of his T-shirt was vibratory, edged in blue. She closed her eyes and opened them, trying to pull herself together.

"Are you all right?"

"Yes, sorry. I'm fine." It was a wish more than the truth, coming from the small part of her that wanted to press on. "Manikarnika Ghat is where I'm trying to go."

He looked out to the street and remained quiet for a time. "I'll take you there."

"That's very kind, but I see you're busy."

Still staring out the window, he seemed to be weighing his own priorities—his work, his private life, whatever that was—against her vulnerability and exhaustion.

"I can spare a half hour or so." Here, he attempted a smile. "Anyhow, I could use a break."

And so this man, Wes was his name, led her through the streets and alleys, where turn by turn the jostle and racket of traffic diminished by degrees. Now, shadowed by door arches or shop columns, old men and women squatted or reclined on rugs, middle-aged children at their feet, watching, waiting.

Down one alley, between high stacks of wood for sale, a leathery man lay on a sheet, drawing uneasy breaths.

Farther along, male voices united in a chant both monotonal and commanding. Forward or behind, left or right, Meredith wasn't sure where it was coming from. As she and Wes proceeded, the chanting grew louder, and rounding a bend they found its source: six men bearing a litter on their shoulders, three on either side. Bound to the litter was a body wrapped in orange and gold cloth and garlanded with marigolds.

"Rama nama satya hai! Rama nama satya hai! Rama nama satya hai!"

Without a word, Wes led her in pursuit of them, though even without him she would have known what to do from here. But she could not bring herself to set him free, and together they followed the men and their litter toward the river light and the first sight of the Ganges, brown under the dull sky. At the heights of the ghat, they parted ways with the men, who continued down toward the river, its murky edge strewn with marigold garlands, charred wood, unidentifiable leavings.

More bodies, also shrouded and biered, rested against the stairs to the river, where boats bore loads of firewood. Between the stairs and an assembled crowd of workers, onlookers, and tourists, six pyres burned, the wind carrying the smoke across the water, away from where Meredith stood with Wes, high above the scene. Still, the smell of it reached them and she found it strangely familiar, inoffensive. She was relieved to be out in the open, away from the press and tangle of the streets.

As for Wes, he had the same accustomed manner Meredith had noticed at the tea shop, and staring out at the pyres, he seemed oddly at home.

"So," he said, looking her way, "what brings you to Varanasi?"

"A friend of mine from grad school. She said this place was not to be missed." In truth, Trina's recommendation had been more complicated, and not without reservations. She'd complained of the touts, of the heat, and of the sense—irrational, she acknowledged—that she might vanish into the chaos without a trace. "I'm a tourist, in other words."

"What do—or did—you study?"

When Meredith told him, he laughed. "Bit of a busman's holiday for you, isn't it?"

"I suppose. But give me some credit for leaving my tools at home."

Feeling another wave of dizziness, Meredith lowered herself onto a wall that ran along the outlook. Wes hesitated then took a seat beside her.

"Can I assume you know the story of this place?"

"I think so. The tourist version, anyway."

"That should do."

The guidebooks and web links Meredith had consulted described Varanasi (a.k.a., Benaras, Kashi) as Hindus' holiest city. Those fortunate enough to die and be cremated here, on the banks of the Ganges, were believed to attain the ultimate prize of moksha, freedom from the cycle of death and rebirth.

"What about you?" Meredith asked. "What brings you to Varanasi?"

Another attempt at a smile. "Well, there's a very long explanation, and a very short one. And in the interest of not boring you into a coma, let me give you the short version." He nodded toward the men who were building a seventh pyre, or tending to the ones already burning. "Have you heard anything about those guys? The doms?"

"A bit."

As tenders to the dead the doms were the lowest of the "untouchable" caste. Yet even within their ranks there was a hierarchy, or so Meredith had read. At the top of it, apparently, were wealthy men whose fortunes were made from the prices that could be charged for the passage to moksha, from the wood to burn the bodies to the commissioning of what remained of them to the Ganges. At the bottom were the men now at work on the shore, who from day to day, dawn to dark, lived and breathed in the smoke from the dead.

"I've been interviewing scores of them, for a research project. I'm looking into how their work affects their attitudes toward death. And life."

"Not purely out of curiosity, I presume?"

"Curiosity is part of it, to be sure. But it's also my job."

Wes went on to explain that he was an associate professor of psychology on a research sabbatical from some small Ohio university whose name was vaguely familiar to Meredith.

"With any luck, there's a book brewing in here." He patted the laptop bag at his feet. "Or there'd better be. I've made certain promises to the sabbatical committee."

"It seems as if you've gathered a lot of material."

"Well, let's see what I can make of it."

The wind shifted, bringing up more smoke and the smell of sandalwood, with some sharper undertone.

"Is there any short version of what you've learned so far?"

"Mmmmm, I'm not sure."

Wes turned his attention to the closest pyre, where a tall man in a red turban was jabbing a pole into the embers. His T-shirt and lungi, once white, had been grayed and smudged by smoke.

"That fellow there could give you the gist of things, better than I could."

"The one in the turban?"

"Yes. That's Sanjeet, one of my most eloquent interviewees. If today's like any other day"—Wes stopped to glance at his watch—"he'll be breaking for tea soon. I'll see if I can flag him down then."

A fresh round of the chant sounded from the ghat stairs— "Rama nama satya hai! Rama nama satya hai!"—announcing the procession of another garlanded body down toward the river. At the water's edge three men from an earlier group were immersing a body likewise garlanded and wrapped in bright cloth.

As for the pyres, they burned at every stage—some reduced almost entirely to ash, others still showing human forms. In the pyre next to Sanjeet, two charred lower legs protruded, until one of them collapsed to the ground. Seeing this Sanjeet took his pole and shoved the fallen limb into the embers, the gesture so ordinary he might have been stoking a campfire.

Ghastly. But oddly comforting, just as Trina had claimed.

Now, Meredith thought she was beginning to understand what Trina meant.

Throughout her childhood and early adulthood, death was never allowed to be ordinary, unremarkable, human. It was alternately an abstraction, its particulars hidden and considered unspeakable, and a horror, the horror coming mostly through movies, thankfully not through personal experience. During grad school something changed, and Meredith's work with death's physical aspects allowed neither abstraction nor horror; it required, instead, both precise focus and professional distance. But what continued to be missing, for the most part, was the feeling of engaging with anything human. At work sites she dug, chiseled, and brushed for hours, closely observing and charting what she found, allowing herself at certain times to sing or chat or joke with her co-workers, the bones before her transformed into objects—out of necessity, she believed. Getting too emotionally involved in her work might incapacitate her.

But now and then, this resolve broke down, most memorably during her month in Guatemala, spent on a former military base. Meredith had come in on the end of the exhumation of a mass grave, which had so far yielded twenty-six skeletons, all of them male. She and one of the other interns uncovered the twenty-seventh male and then what was to be the only female: a girl of twelve or thirteen. The last to be found, she'd been among the first to be thrown into the pit, her bones showing multiple breaks. But the most human thing about her, the most deeply human thing, were the hand-embroidered slippers that held her foot bones, pale blue and stitched all over with pink and yellow flowers, the initials GL on each toe. Despite the initials, despite the DNA evidence, the team that remained in Guatemala never matched the girl with a surviving family member.

Now, looking in the direction of the river, she watched Sanjeet pass the stir-pole to another dom, then cover the short distance to a blanket where other men sat, taking tea. There, and all along the shore, even where the bodies were queued for burning, nothing obviously tragic met the eye. Nothing in need of cover or abstraction. This easy intermingling of death and life, she found it essentially and reassuringly human.

Wes was on his feet now, waving both arms and calling to the men at tea. Up came Sanjeet, who walked easily toward Wes, smiling.

"Hello, friend!"

"Hello!"

Across the shortening distance the two men exchanged words, all in English. Good, clear English. But Meredith, feeling more and more removed from reality, struggled to join the words into anything sensible. What she could join were the identical, vibrating reds of Wes's shirt and Sanjeet's turban. In seconds the men stood side by side, and Meredith had no choice but to look away.

Sanjeet would not be ignored. He sat down between her and the river.

"So you want to know what I've been telling my friend here. What I think of my work."

"I think so. I'm not sure."

Meredith couldn't remember what she'd wanted, what she might have asked. She was barely holding on to the sense that she'd fallen under the influence of something, and that her perceptions of herself, of the world, were no longer to be trusted.

Now, she wanted only one thing, which was to lie down. And so she reclined along the wall and watched the smoke drift across the sky. Trail after trail of smoke, until the sun broke through the clouds and she was forced to close her eyes. When the sun dimmed she reopened them, finding Wes's face above hers, and next to his face Sanjeet's. They kept their eyes on her but talked between themselves, as if she couldn't hear.

"This is not what she needs, friend. To hear my thoughts, my story. That is not why she has come here."

"What's her reason, then? In your humble opinion."

"That is not my domain, friend. I'm not the psychologist here."

"Nice work, Sanjeet. Pushing this off on me."

"I am simply deferring to your expertise. Share with her, and me, what insights you might bring to bear on her situation."

"All right, all right, all right. As long as you indulge me with your patience as I stumble along without my notes. Her

47

case history suggests that a significant personal loss can explain her presence here, as well as much of the trajectory of her adult life. She knows nothing of the father who abandoned her before her birth. Her anger and sorrow over his disappearance peaked during her adolescence and were largely resolved through extensive therapy, or so she believes. But we must critically assess the path her life has taken since then: Why the workaholic-level devotion to uncovering the truth about the dead? In utter defiance of her mother? To the exclusion of any but the most necessary or superficial professional or personal relationships?

"As for Varanasi. As for Manikarnika Ghat, she is hoping, perhaps only on a subconscious level, that they will bring about something greater than this comfort she has identified. Some resolution. But what I'd like to communicate to her is that there is no such thing as a resolution in this matter. Even if her father were to rise up from the river, rise up from the dead, and sit down beside her on this wall. And reveal himself as the drunk he was, the drunk who slowly wasted his above-average intelligence, and his modest talents as an actor. And make it clear that he had no redeeming personal characteristics aside from the occasional ability to make people laugh, almost always at others' expense. Even if he were to reveal nearly every charming aspect of himself, he would ultimately return to his dark domain, leaving a sickening aftertaste. And changing little—maybe nothing—for the better."

"Very good, my friend. A thoughtful and thorough assessment, with possibly useful truths. But the comfort she finds here, why do you so easily dismiss it? This problem of her father, it is not insignificant. Yet here he can be seen for what he truly was, what all of us are, in this world: a transitory speck in time. A transitory speck that in his case has come and gone and is well on the way to surpassing the limits of human memory. He is nothing now, and everything. Like that little girl in the blue slippers."

His voice was receding, and the chill that had started in her hands and feet was rolling inward, upward, becoming general. She considered, without any sense of alarm, that she herself might be dying.

At some point a hand grasped her arm, feeling impossibly warm.

"It's going to be all right, miss. We promise you that you have nothing to fear." Sanjeet's voice, the last she would be conscious of until the next day.

Fortunately, she must have been coherent enough to give Wes the name of the guesthouse, for the morning after the visit to the ghat she'd woken in her bed there, fully dressed in the sweaty, smoky clothes from the day before. Headachy but apparently unharmed, her skin and hair still dusted with ash.

Downstairs, the night manager, Gopal, explained how he'd guided her to her room, apparently with Wes's help. He also identified, after some pointed questioning, the probable cause of her temporary break with reality: the lassi she'd purchased from the vendor outside the guesthouse. As Gopal informed Meredith, this stand was known in Varanasi and abroad for its hallucination-inducing bhang lassis. ("I didn't ask for any bang in my lassi, trust me." "Surely that is true, miss. But as you saw it is a very busy stand. The occasional mistake is bound to occur.")

As for Wes, he'd left no information with Meredith or the night manager—not a cell number or address. She didn't even know his last name and struggled, unsuccessfully, to remember the name of his university. Before leaving Varanasi, she returned multiple times to the tea house where she'd met Wes, but she never came across him. She paid several more visits to Manikarnika Ghat but never saw him, or Sanjeet.

Both in India and back in the States, she Googled possible variations of Wes's first name (Wesley, Weston, Westover, etc.) in connection with numerous Ohio universities and their psychology departments, and with research into Varanasi. Every search proved fruitless, and in the end only one thing kept her from entertaining the possibility that she'd hallucinated Wes into existence: the night manager's claim to have seen him. Thank God for Gopal, she thought. Preserver of my sense of sanity.

Now, Meredith tried to focus on planting the geraniums. The dirt in front of her grandmother's stone was so packed that she had to hack it with her trowel. As she struck the dirt, an old anger loosened in her, anger toward her father.

He'd been a drinker all right. Meredith had learned this much, and little more, from her mother. But the wasted acting talents and intelligence, the uncharitable sense of humor, and especially the certainty of his death—what particular cocktail of wishful thinking, long-simmering resentment, and tainted neurochemistry had conjured those specifics? No doubt, she'd jabbered on about them incoherently in Wes's presence.

As she struck the dirt, a picture of her father surfaced in her mind, unwelcomed. He was gripping a glass of whiskey at a bar, his features obscured by the darkness of the place, the void in her he'd risen from. Meredith hacked against this picture, wanting it to dissolve.

Then the trowel's handle split, and she tossed the thing aside.

"Shit-shit-shit!"

She glanced around, embarrassed about who might have heard her, but the only person she saw was in the middle distance: a tall man in work clothes, pushing a wheelbarrow full of flowers. He halted, as if taking in a distress call, then started pushing the flowers her way.

Closer up, she saw that he was forty-ish and weathered in a way that did not suggest dissolution; to the contrary. Though apparently a grounds man, he had a formal, imposing air.

He surveyed the scene around Meredith, and, noticing the broken trowel, dug around in his wheelbarrow. From beneath the flats of flowers, he produced a new-looking trowel and handed it over.

Accepting it Meredith felt herself blushing, uncharacteristically. "Thank you."

"My pleasure. Every Memorial Day, I make it a point to bring a few extras of everything."

"So you work here," she said, noticing Ben D stitched across his pocket.

"Yes."

There was something familiar about him, and now she realized why.

"I saw you clearing up a gravesite here, a couple of weeks ago."

"Yeah, yeah, that would have been me. And I think I remember you, too. You were here to check out the scene by the North Gate, right?"

"The North Gate?"

"Where our local celebrity is buried."

"Yeah, that must have been me. I felt like I had to see what all the fuss was about."

"And what did you think?"

"About the fuss, or the plans to dig this guy up?"

"Both."

She repeated to Ben D the lines she'd grown used to feeding her mom: that the court order for the exhumation made arguing about it all but irrelevant; that, consequently, the protesters were wasting their time.

"What about you? What do you think of all this?"

He went silent for a moment. Then he said, "Well, I see your point, mostly. The decision's been made, so everyone better find a way to live with it."

"I think I hear a *but* in there."

He smiled.

"I guess I keep thinking about something my father used to say, when he was digging the graves here. He said, 'Son, the reasons for digging up a body range from stupid to idiotic to moronic.' The only good reason, in his opinion, was a coroner's inquest, and those are rare. 'Nine times out of ten,' he said, 'the best and most respectful thing is to leave a body the hell alone.'"

A creaking and jouncing interrupted Ben D's thoughts, and Meredith followed his gaze to an old truck that was making its way down the hill. He waved at the driver, then continued on.

"Now don't get me wrong. I see how the grave's a safety concern. It's definitely too close to the road. But if it were up to me, I'd move his monument inside the gates and leave his actual grave alone. Pretty soon, folks would lose track of where his grave is, most of them anyway. And they'd pay their respects and take their pictures within the cemetery. My humble prediction, at least."

"What about the DNA testing?"

"I don't know. I guess I side with the people who question whether that's any of our business."

He lowered his head and laughed. "Enough of that. You didn't come here to listen to me bloviate."

"Well, I asked you a question and you answered it. Very thoughtfully."

"Glad to oblige. And, honestly, the sooner this whole thing is over, the better. I'm pretty damn sick of it, and a lot of other people here are, too."

His attention shifted to a point on the ground, behind Ruby Steinlen's stone. He knelt by the spot and pulled a dandelion up by the roots.

When this was done he said, "Now I have a question for you. Are you new in town? I don't remember seeing you before that last time."

It was true this was only her second visit to the cemetery. When her grandma died the previous fall, Meredith hadn't been able to make it to her graveside service.

"Actually, I'm just visiting my mom for a bit. She moved to Bolster Falls a few years back to take care of this lady here"— Meredith nodded toward the stone—"my grandmother. And when Grandma died, Mom decided to stay. She finds it more relaxing here than in the city, I guess."

"I'm glad. Though I'm sorry about your Grandma."

Chances were, he'd buried her, Meredith thought. But he'd probably consider it rude to bring that up now.

"Well," he said, "I should let you get back to work. See that fountain behind you? I'll be working there for a while, and whenever you're done with the trowel, you can just bring it over."

"All right. Thanks."

Meredith watched him walk toward the triple-bowled fountain, the uprooted dandelion dangling from his right hand. Then, with the help of the trowel, she made quick work of the geraniums and rosebush. When she finished she stood for a moment to admire the blooms in Ruby Steinlen's beloved red, a flare of life that would have to stand in for Ruby's own, at least until summer's end.

Nine times out of ten the best and most respectful thing is to leave a body the hell alone.

Yes, and no. It all depended on the circumstances. In most every gradation between yes and no other possibilities sometimes presented themselves. As Meredith dragged the empty wagon back to her car, she considered what these might be.

Chapter 8

[Mushrooms] are looked upon as vegetable vermin, only made to be destroyed. No eye can see their beauties; their office is unknown; their varieties are not regarded; they are hardly allowed a place among Nature's lawful children, but are considered something abnormal, worthless and inexplicable. . . . No fad or hobby is esteemed so contemptible as that of the "fungus-hunter" or "toadstool-eater."

—From *British Fungi*, by W. D. Hay (1887)

Memory Garden
Early afternoon, late May

As Ben unwrapped his sandwich the sprinkler heads hissed to life before him, quivering the dark green something-such creeper and the silvery vines threaded through it. No one had yet strewn ashes in the garden's inner circle. But later today or sometime tomorrow, during the afternoon interval when the sprinklers were offline, this place was due to receive its first deposit: the remains of Maude Polombo, whose name and dates of birth and death (1938, 2003) were etched onto the first bronze plate to be bolted to the Memorial Tablet. A slanted granite expanse resembling a solar panel, the tablet had been lowered into the greenery just three weeks ago.

Ben could only speculate why, after spending years in some other place of reverence or storage, Maude's ashes would be making their way here. It was hard to believe the aesthetics of this "scattering garden" had been a factor in the decision.

The landscapers had done a decent job with the stonework and plantings given the limited budget and the somewhat restrictive design parameters set down by the cemetery board. Yet even they seemed doubtful about their creation, and the bunker-like columbarium structures, built to accommodate more than four hundred urns, certainly didn't add to the garden's charms.

"Wait till we get those flowers in over there," one of the landscapers told Ben yesterday, while explaining the ins and outs of the automatic sprinkler system. "And when those maples and cherries get a little bigger"—he cast a hopeful glance toward the saplings—"it'll feel like a different world here."

It was all willed optimism. But perhaps that was what landscaping boiled down to, at least in a graveyard. To Ben's mind the grounds expressed themselves most honestly in Oak Corner, where in spells of drear, nodes of mushrooms bloomed within hours, and in profusion, under the old oaks and pines. He found himself venturing there more and more, especially after rains.

As a child, Ben mostly ignored the mushrooms in Oak Corner and everywhere else. Later, as he started working on the grounds, he took more notice of the local fungi, nosing around now and then with a guidebook to see what varieties he might identify. More recently, though, his interest in mushrooms had evolved into something of an obsession, an obsession Ben saw as rooted in decay, just like mushrooms themselves. The decay was in his marriage, which had been in a long, fairly slow decline until he advanced the process considerably, all by himself.

Three springs ago, on the evening of the cemetery board meeting and mixer, he wasn't quite aware that he was looking for trouble. But the few who said, "Leah couldn't join us tonight?" fanned the long-smoldering coals of his resentment. "No," he said. "She's got a show in Heath."

"*Another* show? How wonderful."

Ben could have joined Leah for her show's reception. Should have, really. But when it turned out that the reception was scheduled for the same evening as the cemetery events, he refused to concede that Leah's moment in the spotlight was more worthy of his attention. Instead, he waited to see what

55

Leah would say, just as she was waiting for him. Between them on the kitchen counter, next to Leah's drained wine glass, lay the reception notice.

"I really have to be there for the opening night, Ben."

"Of course."

"And I completely understand if you can't join me."

Of course I'll join you, was what she was waiting for.

"I appreciate that," was all he said.

A darkness flickered through Leah's features, then vanished. Anger? Disappointment? She waited for a moment, as if to make sure he had nothing to add. Then, in what had become her usual after-supper routine, she pushed away from the counter and retreated upstairs to her studio.

The meeting and mixer itself was nothing remarkable at first. After the usual updates on budgets and fundraising, Ben took the stage to outline the modest achievements of the cemetery's Green Initiative (reduced usage of water and pesticides) and to review the initiative's goals (the creation of a storm-water retention pond, the reintroduction of native plants). When that was done, he introduced the keynote speaker, Dolores Fielding, now in a dark purple dress instead of her typical work clothes. Unshadowed by her usual broad-brimmed hat, she revealed herself as a delicate-featured woman in late middle age. Yet as she smiled and nodded out to the crowd, she looked as earnest as the winner of a science fair.

Ben had known Dolores for years. Summers and falls, as far back as he could remember, she wandered regularly to Oak Corner with a basket over her arm. That's where he'd fist spoken to her, at the dawn of his interest in mushrooms. At the time, a spell of summer rain had brought an abundance of milk caps and boletes to that part of the grounds, and it was only because of his encounter with Dolores that Ben learned these mushrooms' names. A week or so afterward, she tracked him down and handed him the now-dog-eared mushroom guidebook, still in the top drawer of the desk in the cemetery office.

In the years since then, Dolores and Ben took to waving to each other across the grounds, rarely speaking. Still, Ben felt they were somehow bonded, through devotion to the grounds and through the simple passage of time. The Green Initiative had deepened their connection, with both of them supporting a total ban on pesticides in Oak Corner, home of certain edible mushrooms.

After Ben introduced Dolores at the cemetery meeting, she took the stage and the remote control for the projector, which she clicked to bring up her first PowerPoint: "The Mushroomerous Glory of Bolster Hill Cemetery."

Ben found nothing surprising in her opening points, about the existence of at least fifteen mushroom varieties in the cemetery; the ideal conditions provided by the trees and grounds of Oak Corner; the desirability of encouraging intelligent but not excessive foraging. What transfixed him, if only because of their hugeness and color, were the labeled pictures that followed—pictures of selected cemetery mushrooms, each projection as large as Dolores.

Agaricus campestris: "Meadow" or "Field" mushroom—edible

Amanita muscaria: "Fly Agaric" or "Fly Amanita"—variably poisonous

Amanita phalloides: "Death Cap"—dangerously poisonous

Calvatia gigantea: "Giant Puffball"—edible before fully mature

Cantharellus cibarius: "Chanterelle"—incredibly edible

Grifola frondosa: "Maitake" or "Hen of the Woods"—stupendously edible

Gymnopilus spectabilis: "Big Laughing Gym Jim" — hallucinogenic

She described the flavors of the edible ones and the

dangers of the poisonous ones, and warned the adventurous, with what seemed to be more than a hobbyist's authority, that *Gymnopilus spectabilis* might leave them waiting and waiting for nothing, or enjoying, for hours, "the depthless hilarity of the mundane: tying one's shoes, watering one's lawn, or examining one's face, feature by feature, in the bathroom mirror."

Finally, she set down the remote control and stepped to the edge of the stage, closer to the board members, and their significant others and children, closer to other Bolsterites who were here out of interest in the cemetery, in mushrooms, or both. "In closing I want to say that to deeply engage with the fungus of this cemetery, and not just the hallucinogenic variety, is to have a deeply transformative experience. I urge every single one of you assembled here not to deprive yourself of such an encounter."

During the applause, Ben made his way to the stage, intending to congratulate Dolores and also ask her where she'd found Big Laughing Gym, a variety that had so far eluded him. He was captivated, but not entirely surprised, by the notion of her sampling such a hallucinogen.

But he never made it to Dolores. Midway to the stage he felt a tug at the arm of his suit coat. Turning, he found Alyssa Weir, whom Ben recognized only by her name tag, which he then connected to the terse, all-business emails about her re-design of the cemetery's website. The terseness did not prepare him for her youth and beauty, or for her intense yet amused study of his face, suggesting an interest extending beyond matters of business.

"I just wanted to personally thank you," she said, "for everything you are doing with the Green Initiative."

Ben expressed gratitude for the compliment and exchanged a few polite words with her, but he found himself relieved to be pulled away into other conversations, away from an attraction that could only lead to trouble. Yet he never lost track of Alyssa, even as the crowd thinned under the tent, even as he drained his third and fourth beers. Two hours or so into the mixer, once they'd drifted back together, Ben was able to follow Alyssa's description of the website redesign, responding now and then with his own impressions and questions, all the while fighting interference from the separate conversation playing through his mind—

She's clearly interested in you.

Don't kid yourself.

Would you fuck her if given the chance?

Who are you kidding that she would want to fuck you?

No harm in thinking about it.

Thinking about it is how the trouble starts, asshole. <u>Married father</u> and asshole.

Another interference was Dolores's final slide, which remained projected till the mixer's end. As Alyssa talked on, smiled, listened, the screen-filling orange cap of *Gymnopilus spectabilis* framed her pretty head, a bright but earthy halo, a warning sign. A warning sign that Ben, in the end, did not heed. By the end of the month he was fucking her. By the end of the year he'd sent a text intended for Alyssa to Leah's phone, exposing the affair and beginning the separation that just a few months later ended in divorce.

During this turmoil Leah was first furious, then morose, then resigned. But heartbroken? As much as he might have wished her to be, Ben couldn't say she was. In spite of everything she seemed to function as well as ever, maybe even better, confirming his suspicion that the affair had only hastened her departure from their marriage. More quickly than he thought possible, she got a good job and apartment in Boston, and through her daily phone calls and weekends with Cole, Leah continued to be the type of parent that Ben could only dream of being, supporting Cole's drumming and interest in music in the ways they deserved. Meanwhile, with a persistence Ben couldn't help but admire, Leah never stopped painting.

By the time of the divorce Leah had long given up on asking Ben about his own music, and on the day of their pos-session-thinning yard sale, before her move to Boston, Ben sold all but one of his electric guitars, sparing the Rickenbacker 360 because it had been his favorite, once. He also spared the acoustic, a Christmas gift from Leah, from several years before. A number of times after that Christmas she'd asked him, in attempted nonchalance, "Why don't you ever play that guitar I gave you?" Each time, Ben felt like she was really asking, "Why are you no longer the man I fell in love with? Or thought I fell in love with?"

Though both of Ben's parents were gone by the time of the affair, his mother returned now and then, in his mind. In the early days after his cheating came to light, she sat at his kitchen table, coffee in one hand, cigarette in the other, giving him that same searing *You shit heel* look she used to turn on his father. For good reason.

"Leah was on her way out, Mom, I *know* it. I just beat her to it."

Because marriage is only a board game, huh? Something you upend in a fit, like a selfish, tantruming child.

At times, Ben wondered if his parents' deaths had cleared the way for him to be who he really was: a later-model Ross Dirjery, equally incapable of marital fidelity. Ross was no longer a living example of how not to be a husband, and Liz was no longer around to pass judgment, other than the imagined variety.

Within a few days of Leah's departure Ben, in need of some distraction from his crisis of the soul, read his way through four books on mycology and mushroom cultivation. Within a few weeks he'd filled her former studio and part of the basement with spawn bags and substrate trays, sterilizers and humidity domes, dehydrated manure and branches from dead trees. Weeknights after Cole went to bed and weekends when she was otherwise occupied, Ben plugged logs with spawn, tried his hand at various spore-culturing methods. To Alyssa, mushrooms were repulsive, whether in food, in nature, or in Ben's temperature- and humidity-controlled cultivation environments. It had to be somewhat perverse, then, the pride he took in labors whose fruits helped push her along, fairly quickly, to better things.

When it came to Cole, though, mushrooming offered little comfort to Ben. From time to time he was struck anew by the fact that she willingly remained under the same roof with him, if only to make it through the school year and then to summer visits with Leah, in Boston. He was grateful for the fact that Cole had only once called him an asshole and never directly expressed her hatred of him, though part of him wished she would. Perhaps her restraint wasn't that at all; perhaps his faults, as great as they'd revealed themselves to be, had simply come as no surprise.

Every so often Cole made her way to the basement or studio, to watch him from the doorway, asking few questions about what he was doing and making no complaints about it. Always, she looked sullen and a little stunned. *Why this obsession, Dad? Why this, of all things?* How to answer her, if she ever actually asked? *I'm filling time, filling space, deeply engaging with fungus.* That would be only partly a joke. Fungus had come to feel like something of his essence—something alternately useful and poisonous, sprouting on rot.

Now, in the Memory Garden, the sprinklers shut down on their one o'clock cue, signaling it was time for Ben to get back to work. As he balled up his sandwich wrapper and bag, he felt his phone buzz. Retrieving it from his pocket he saw it was Jenks.

"What's up?"

"Looks like we finally have a time for that dig."

"The Unknown Vagrant one."

"Yep. It'll be July eighteenth, specific hour to be determined."

"I'll put it in my calendar. Does anyone else on the crew need to know?"

"For now, let's keep this between you and me. That team that's coming in, they just need someone to help plot the dig and maybe work the backhoe. I figure you can manage that alone."

"I'll be ready."

As he rose from the bench, Ben took one last look at the garden, trying to imagine the flowers yet to be planted, the saplings grown to trees, the whole site rescued from institutional ugliness. He didn't succeed.

Hadn't he shown Leah the garden plans, back in the early days? Probably not. If he had, she would have said something he'd remember. She would have suggested some insightful yet practical corrective he'd feel compelled to pass on to the

61

board—a "Why didn't I think of that?" kind of thing. To Leah, nothing was aesthetically incurable. But no one in this world needed more problems to solve, least of all her.

Chapter 9

Della Hoxie Brown
Sister, Singer, Friend
Born: April 24, 1935
Gigged: June 21, 1953 – Aug. 6, 1994
Died: Aug. 7, 1994

—Gravestone for Section D, Lot 232

Section D, Lots 232 and 421
After dark

Cole lit the joint and lay back, Della's headstone her headboard. She was only a few puffs in when the singing resumed down the hill, and she smoked and listened and stared at the stars, until a beat came to her. With her free hand, she slapped it out on her thigh.

The two voices, male and female, circled and circled each other then came together in the same strange harmony Cole remembered from before. The song itself was new to her, only parts of the chorus intelligible:

My memories so clear, of the car that was never here, and [??????] on the passenger side. As I made my way to pass, she scratched at the window glass, and [????] for passing up the ride.

A bird chirping cut in: Cole's ringtone.

Shit-shit-shit!

She bolted upright, silenced the call (from her mom, she saw), and snuffed the joint against her sneaker. Then she just

63

sat there, her heart pounding, noticing that the singing had stopped.

A voice called from down the hill. "Hark! Who goes there?"

Reply or not? Leave or not?

Just go down there, she decided, curiosity defeating fear. She wanted to find out who was behind those voices. The *Hark! Who goes there?* sounded goofy enough to be friendly, like a kind of invitation.

Cole returned the joint to the tin, stuffed both back in her pocket, and started down the hill.

She found the others where she knew they'd be, at the grave of Vince Resklar, a dark huddle of three, no four, kids.

"Here's our night bird," announced a girl at the foot of the grave, as if Cole had been expected.

"Sorry," Cole said. "My phone."

In the dimness she began to make out the faces—no one she recognized from school, though all the kids were about her age. Bolster Academy students, most likely. Though they seemed to have rolled out of bed and into their jeans and T-shirts, they had that look of confidence that bordered on indifference.

"I've been listening to the singing," Cole said. "It's really great."

"Thanks," said the girl at the foot of the grave. Though it might have been a trick of the dimness, she had the whitest skin and blackest hair Cole had ever seen. Never had someone looked so fit to sing in a cemetery.

Across from the girl, a guy peeked around the headstone and waved. "Yeah, thanks," he said.

The two singers, Cole presumed.

In the silence that followed, she sensed it had been a mistake to come down here.

"Well, I just wanted to pass on the compliment."

As Cole turned away the girl called out to her: "You're welcome to stay, if you want."

"Yes," said another guy, who was retrieving a beer from the cooler behind him. Unlike the other three, he wore a short-sleeved button-down, not a T-shirt. His hair looked freshly cut, and wet-combed. "You're not one of the ruffians, clearly."

Cole guessed he was the source of the *Hark!* command and wondered if he used old-style language all the time. She hoped he did. It took a *fuck-you* type of courage to proudly broadcast any weirdness, a courage she admired.

"Yeah, have a seat." This command came from the guy in front of the headstone. He patted the ground to his left.

There wasn't time for this, not enough anyway, but Cole sat down on the indicated spot and introduced herself. She learned in return that the girl at the foot of the grave was Miranda and the guy in front of the headstone, her singing partner, was Grif. Between Miranda and Grif, on opposite sides of the grave, sat Nate and Alex, Alex being the old-style speaker, and the keeper of the cooler.

"Beer?" he asked, nodding toward the stash.

"No thanks." Cole turned down the offer, mainly because she hated the taste of beer. She also wondered if she alone thought it was kind of odd to be drinking on the grave of Vince Resklar, given how things had ended for him.

"Limeade then?"

Limeade. Another weirdness?

"Sure."

Once she'd taken her drink, Cole remembered her question for Alex. "What did you mean by *ruffians?*"

"Well," he said, popping open his own beer, "if you've kept these hours in the cemetery more than once over the last month you may have heard some noise at this location that was, how should we say, unbecoming of a memorial site."

"You mean the drunken yelling."

Alex smiled. "Yes, indeed. You must be a regular."

In fact, this was only her fourth night in the cemetery. The first night she'd heard the eerie but harmonious singing, uninterrupted by any distracting noise. Instead, the singers seemed surrounded by a reverent silence. The other two nights the sounds Cole heard were all about drinking, and the singing— no, the drunken yelling, and laughing—was only a side effect. With time the noise only got louder, chasing her off to a more remote site. Even from that distance the sound of the partying, including the occasional smash of bottles, was detectable. The only bit of relief, for Cole, was that her father could not hear the partiers' rendition of "Leave Me in Peace."

Alex continued, "The makers of that joyful noise were the ruffians."

"Not you guys, then."

"You border on offense to even think it."

"Sorry. So what happened to them? Do you know?"

Alex glanced from Miranda to Grif. They said nothing, nor did Nate. Seeing that no one was raising any objections, Alex turned his attention back to Cole. "A few nights back, we found we could no longer peacefully coexist with them."

"So?"

"So we chose to get rid of them."

With difficulty, Cole swallowed her sip of limeade and set down the can.

Alex went on: "We didn't murder them, of course. We didn't resort to violence of any kind. We just persuaded them, rather diplomatically in my opinion, that a cemetery wasn't the place for their hooliganism."

Cole wasn't sure what to believe, though murder was surely a stretch. "So what about you guys? Why do you come here? I mean, to this particular grave."

Miranda patted a notepad on the ground to her left. "For the inspiration."

When she offered no further explanation, Grif said, "Miranda writes most of our lyrics. For some reason, they come easier to her here. The rest of us, we're just kind of along for the ride."

"And some singing practice," said Miranda.

"So you guys are in a band."

"We're trying to be." Grif took a sip of his drink: also limeade, Cole noticed. "We're what you'd call a work in progress."

"I am, too," Cole said. "I mean, I've been playing drums a lot, trying to get better at it."

Right away, she felt embarrassed by the outburst, which

she blamed on the pot. She hadn't smoked enough of it for paranoia to set in, but she felt way more relaxed than she ever did at school—looser in limb and, apparently, looser in tongue.

"That's awesome," Grif said.

Miranda pulled a stretchy from her pocket, twisted her black hair into a bun. "Are you playing with anyone?"

"No. Not yet." Cole didn't count the run of winter weekends she'd spent practicing with a bassist from the school jazz band. He'd divided his attention between their sets and televised Bruins games, until Cole couldn't take it anymore and went back to playing on her own.

"Well," Grif said, "if Nate didn't have us covered we might be needing your help."

"Thanks. But I'm really not sure I'm good enough yet."

"Who's ever sure?"

Cole looked to Miranda. "So Vince Resklar's your inspiration?"

"Well, I love his music. All the Vagrants' music. And I know it might sound weird or superstitious, but I find it really helpful to sit here and work on the songs. It's not like I hear Vince dictating words from beyond the grave, nothing like that. It's just that being here gets things flowing, for some reason. Especially when I'm feeling blocked or distracted."

Miranda looked to Grif, as if expecting a response. But he just stared moodily into his limeade.

In the silence, Cole heard the sound of approaching voices. Quiet voices, not those of ruffians.

Shit, she thought. They were about to get busted, and her father would have her head. No one else seemed nervous, though, and Cole soon realized why. Seconds later, just behind Vince Resklar's stone, Meg Tirella materialized.

"Cole?"

"Hey, Meg."

"You know these guys?"

"Sort of. We just met."

Meg glanced around the circle. "Cole and I go to Bolster Public together."

67

"Aha."

Cole motioned between Meg and the others. "You guys all met here, too?"

Nods all around.

"I absolutely love their singing," Meg said.

"Awwwww, thanks." Miranda swatted at a bug then whisked it away. "How's camping down there this evening?"

Given that it was Meg, Cole guessed that "down there" was the grave of the Unknown Vagrant or, more likely, someplace close by but inside the gates, where Meg and her comrades would face less scrutiny.

"Pretty quiet. We're just getting a new sign ready for tomorrow. The last one got trashed by some jerk who works here."

Miranda pouted in sympathy. "I'm sorry, that sucks."

"Not as sorry as I am," Meg said. "It was a really cool one, with a picture of the Unknown Vagrant on it. Took me hours to make."

Cole was pretty sure the trasher was her father, and she couldn't bring herself to be embarrassed by what he'd done, or ashamed of the satisfaction she now felt—that not every work of a "star scholar" (the *Bolster Register*'s description of Meg) is met with universal praise.

Alex gestured between Meg and the cooler. "Beer? Limeade?"

"No thanks. I'm actually here on business. Just wondering if you've had time to consider my proposal."

For a long moment, no one said anything. Miranda looked to Grif, who, once again, was staring moodily into his drink. Alex and Nate trained their eyes toward the center of the grave, as if they wanted to disappear into it.

Finally, Miranda spoke up. "Sorry, but we haven't really decided anything yet."

Grif straightened up. "I think we *have* decided on something, Miranda. Or was I somehow mistaken?"

More silence. Then Miranda said, "Listen, Meg. Can you give us a little more time? Maybe a few days?"

"Sure, no problem."

"You know where to find us."

Once Meg was gone Cole saw that Grif was blushing, deeply blushing. He lowered his head and scrubbed a hand through his curly mess of hair, as if to collect himself.

"Sorry," he said, finally. "But I really don't want us to start playing out as some sort of cover band."

"*One* song," said Miranda. "All I'm proposing is one song. We do one of theirs, then the rest would be ours."

He lowered his head again, seemingly thinking things through.

"Grif, it's for a good cause."

"Cause?" Cole asked.

Miranda looked her way, wearily. "What fun for you, huh? To step into the middle of an argument. Anyway, the story is, Meg and some of her friends are trying to put together a protest concert. A protest of those plans to dig up the mystery man. We had no clue, and we made the mistake of singing some old Vagrants tunes here. And she overheard them, which put her on our case."

Grif lifted his head and stared intently at Miranda. But he seemed not to see her; he seemed to be working something out in his mind.

"Okay," he said, finally. "One song. As long as it's not 'Leave Me in Peace.' I'm sick beyond fucking sick of that one."

Thinking of how her dad reacted to this particular tune, Cole couldn't help but smile.

Her phone alarm chimed, as loudly as it had chirped earlier. From time to time, she upped her phone's volume so she could hear it while practicing her drums, but now the sound was ear-splitting. As quickly as she could, she silenced it.

"I gotta get home, sorry." She also needed to call back her mom, who was probably checking in about their next visit.

Cole grabbed her half-empty can of limeade and got up.

"Yeah, I should get going, too," said Miranda, yawning, stretching, then collecting her notepad. Soon, she was on her feet, followed by Alex and Nate. The last one up was Grif, who stood taller than anyone else but had the slouch of someone who didn't want to make a big deal of his height.

"Hey Cole," he said. "Before I forget, a friend of mine from Carlisle is looking for a drummer for his band. A rock drummer. Are you interested?"

"Yeah, sure. I mean, I could at least talk to him."

"Let me get your number and I'll pass it along."

As she headed for the exit, hoping to avoid Meg and the other protesters, Cole found herself thinking of the Unknown Vagrant, of her childhood dreams of him. In the dreams he walked not along the road but through the cemetery, up and down the biggest hills and past the mausoleums, past the ornamental lake and toward the woods that had since been cleared—as if he'd escaped his grave or never entered it, as if he was on a mission to find something and wouldn't stop until he did.

Chapter 10

Hamlet: Hath this fellow no feeling of his business, that he
sings at grave-making?
Horatio: Custom hath made it in him a property of easiness.

—William Shakespeare

Section C, Lot 537
Some June afternoon, 1986

Lunatic ranting.

Once again, Ross followed the sound to its source—this
time the shoulder-high hole that would soon be occupied by the
late Dr. Lance Carew—and found Ben crouched in its depths,
singing into the mallet he should have been swinging.

"Son?"

Still blind to Ross, Ben went on with the singing—really
more like shouting.

"*Son*?!"

Ross grabbed a clod of dirt and pelted Ben, who finally
dropped the mallet and pulled down his earphones, which
broadcast a tinny version of the rant. Ben stared up at Ross
with stony irritation, as if he'd been interrupted from important
business—business having nothing to do with shoring up a
grave dug into a treacherously unstable seam of sand and clay.

"Do you have a death wish, son?"

Ben didn't answer right away, as if he had to think about
it. "No."

"Then get out of there. Now."

Ben climbed the ladder as told, taking the mallet with him. Once he'd surfaced he switched off the little tape deck at his belt, finally silencing it.

"I know what I did wrong, Dad, so you don't have to tell me."

"You tell *me* then. Just to put my mind at rest."

"You brace the walls from top to bottom, not bottom to top. And you don't step into the grave until those first braces are in there."

"And *how* are they in there?"

"Tight and level."

"Good. Now let me take over for a bit. You go on your break."

"You don't trust me."

"I'll trust you more when you've had a break. But I'll need you back here by three, all right? And no later."

Within ten yards of the grave Ben had slid the earphones back on and returned to his lunatic singing, leaving Ross to once again reflect on the deep spell of absent-mindedness the boy had fallen into. Whether his music was a symptom of the problem or part of the cause Ross, couldn't say. Ben listened to it nearly nonstop, if not on the portable tape deck then on the record player in his room—the songs by bands whose names Ross had glimpsed on the Magic-Markered labels of the handmade cassettes: the Damned, Fear, the Misfits, Mission of Burma, the Germs. As a courtesy to his parents Ben usually used his headphones, though Ross had heard enough of the tunes to get their essence of threats and loathing.

Whenever he saw Ben nod along with them, as if in a trance, Ross wanted to believe the shout-singing was a release valve for normal teenage anger and frustration. He did not want to believe it was more insidious in nature, sowing the seeds of dissolution or something worse. Usually, optimism won.

But not for Liz. She worried that by way of his obsession with music, Ben was subtracting himself from the world. Ross didn't disagree. But if this cemetery counted for a world, any sane young man would want to subtract himself from it, the sooner the better. So more and more, Ross found himself in a confusing position: One part of him wanted Ben to listen to him and follow his orders; another part of him wanted Ben to ignore him and go his own way, despite the hazards.

Whatever alternative worlds his son was or wasn't envisioning, Ross couldn't say. The music, the guitar lessons, the hours Ben spent with that record-store clerk, Vince—these might be nothing more than passing whims. But if whims played any part in imagining a future beyond this cemetery, they deserved as much space as Ross could safely and sensibly give them.

By 2:57, all the top braces were in place against the uprights, making it safe to step into the grave. At 2:59, Ben reappeared to do just that, still nodding to his music. By 3:15, or so Ross imagined, Addie would be standing by her door in that slinky red thing she'd warned him about, watching out for his arrival. Thanks to his son's punctuality, he wouldn't have to speed.

Ross tapped his ear, his now-customary signal for Ben to pull aside an earphone. "Can you hold down the fort till four thirty, son? I've got a little errand to take care of."

Ben nodded and threw a stack of bottom braces into the hole, then carried the mallet down the ladder to get started.

Turning his thoughts to Addie and her little red number, Ross started humming the catchy ditty he'd heard on the radio that morning, until he waved his farewell into the hole.

Ben stopped to glare up at him, chasing the song from Ross's mind.

⁂

As the tape rewound, Ben peered over the grave's edge, watching his father recede toward the East Gate, then vanish. The second he was gone Ben hit *play* and let the pummeling of drums, the thrash of guitars, lift him up and out of the hole and toward the center of the cemetery, the farthest he could get from the living.

New Day Rising!

The savage joy of the song made this place bearable, even

73

spectacular. As Ben moved through the grounds, music in his head, patches of sun felt like promises of deliverance, stretches of shade were assurances of privacy. The monuments and graves? All background. Whenever music filled him, nothing could be dead.

He rewound the song to give it another listen (the sixth? the seventh?), telling himself that this time, he'd follow his guitar teacher's urging.

"Any amateur can listen for pleasure," Mr. Dubovic had said, multiple times. "Musicians listen and *study*. They listen and ask themselves what it is this other musician is *doing* and *how*."

Ben had tried this strategy several times, and so far, it had been a recipe for discouragement. Whenever he came down from the clouds, from the music in his head, and back to the earth—especially, back to his room, the shitty knockoff strat in his hands—every song he loved, every song he attempted, felt weighted by his own incompetence, and by his growing doubts that he'd ever overcome it.

Hüsker Dü chords, deceptively simple, were a special problem. Even if Ben got them down right, which was greatly uncertain, there was no way he'd ever play them as blisteringly fast and joyfully as Bob Mould.

Why not give up then?

No. Not yet.

Every now and then, maybe entirely by accident, something good came out of his messing with the guitar.

This time while listening to "New Day Rising," Ben tried to visualize the strumming and fingering, tried to make sense of the chord progressions, but everything went gray in his mind.

He rewound the tape and tried again, but now the music slowed and warped as if mocking him. Then it stopped entirely.

Opening the player Ben found the tape partly unspooled, and backed up behind the cassette. He withdrew the cassette and hand-wound the tape, but when he tried to play it again the sound was warped even worse than before: ruined.

Ben had other tapes back at the gravesite, including two

new ones from Vince, but that was the last place he wanted to go right now. So he charged ahead, directionless, gripping the tape deck like a gun.

Trapped here, music-less, Ben thought of a more enduring source of his anger: his father.

Ben wasn't an idiot. He knew what Ross's errands were— *who* they were. At the cemetery office, he'd answered calls from two of them; most likely, there were more.

The one woman never left her name or a message.

"Ross?" she'd ask. The silence that followed her question seemed one of sadness more than hope, or desire.

"This isn't Ross. This is his son. Can I take a message?"

"No thank you, I'll try back later," she always said, in a single breath, before quickly hanging up.

The other one, Addie, wasn't afraid to leave her name or a coded message, spoken in the voice of a sexy spy.

"Tell your father he can pick up the cake tomorrow, at two."

This was her message just last week.

"What cake?" Ben asked her.

"He'll know."

Later, Ben asked the same question of his father, once he'd returned to the office and the pink message slip.

"What cake?"

"A token of thanks from the funeral home, for all the business over the years."

Hearing this, something finally broke in Ben. He grabbed the mug of pens from the desk, shattered it against the opposite wall.

"Bullshit, Dad!"

Ben waited to see if, finally, his father would open the door into his private world, even just a crack. It was a possibility Ben had dreaded, almost as much as he hated the closed door: his father's evident insistence on secrecy, his belief that he had an absolute right to it.

What happened, though, was this: Ross glanced toward the shards of the mug, the scattered pens, then shrugged and barely smiled.

Isn't that the damnedest thing, objects taking flight like that? That was what he seemed to be thinking. Then he left the office.

Now, as Ben trudged ahead, toward the partially forested western edge of the cemetery, he tried to calm himself with the sense that justice would be delivered, eventually. His father wouldn't look like the Marlboro Man forever, and his back was already giving out. Ben's mother was spending more and more time at her sister's house. Within the year, she'd ask for a divorce. That was Ben's prediction, anyway.

Closing in on the stand of oaks, Ben saw a crouched figure: a woman in jeans and a work shirt, shaded by a wide-brimmed hat: Dolores Fielding.

With his father's behavior fresh on his mind, Ben remembered the one time he'd seen Ross and Dolores together, back before Ben had said anything more than "hi" to her, long before she'd given him the mushroom guidebook.

In Ben's memory, his father and Dolores seemed to be in the middle of a polite conversation, one Ben was too far from to hear. At some point, Ross stepped closer and casually laid a hand on her arm, looking at her in a way Ben had come to understand only since then. It was the look of a man who knows the power of his charms, who is just waiting for them to take their usual effect.

But Dolores stepped back from Ross, even as she went on smiling, still politely talking and listening. That was Ben's memory of what had happened and, now, it heightened his sense of justice. It also reinforced his determination to never be like his father, not with women anyway. Not if he ever decided to get married.

"Dolores?" He called her name as softly as he could, not wanting to startle her.

Still crouched, she turned toward him and lifted the brim of her hat.

"Ben! To what do I owe the pleasure?"

"I'm just taking a little break from my work."

"Listening to your music, I presume."

"Yep." Ben didn't want to bore her with the details of his tape failure. "You looking for something in particular?"

"I think I just found it. Want to see?"

"Sure."

Ben crouched down next to her, in front of a semi-rotted oak log, dark and damp from recent rains. All along its length, parallel to the ground, were gooey-looking pinkish-brown ruffles, like distorted ears.

"Wow—*cool!*"

Ben loved that there was a place in the world for life forms that took no pains to please the eye or smell good. The gelatinous extrusions before him were almost boastfully ugly.

"*Auricularia auricula,*" Dolores said. "Also known as jelly ear. One of my friends from the mushroom club said he spotted them here, but I had to see it to believe it. They're not exactly common in these parts."

Ben sat back, set the tape deck and earphones on the ground next to him. "So are you going to take a picture of them?"

Dolores looked puzzled. "Why would I?"

Ben shrugged, embarrassed by his question.

"What I mean, Ben, is that I don't think I'd have much to add to the pictures of jelly ears that have already been taken. Matter of fact, there's a few right in here."

Dolores patted her knapsack, which presumably included her guidebook, the same one she'd given Ben a couple of years before. She kept her eyes on him, as if waiting to see that he got her point. He kind of did, but something else was on his mind.

"Dolores? Can I ask you something kind of personal?"

She hesitated a moment, then nodded.

Ben shifted a little, trying to get as comfortable as he could on the twiggy, bark-strewn ground. At Dolores's request and for the sake of the mushrooms, Ben, Ross, and the other grounds workers let dead branches and other debris remain in this part of the cemetery, unless the branches were unusually large or hazardous.

"Whenever I see you here, you seem like you're completely absorbed in something you love. You've spent days, months, years on it. But . . ."

He worried that what he was about to say would offend her.

"But what, Ben?"

"Well, a lot of people would see what you're doing as pointless. I mean, not entirely pointless, because it's a hobby. Something you enjoy doing."

Ben knew he was blushing. He could feel the heat rising up from his neck, into his cheeks.

"So, I guess my question is . . ."

Dolores smiled as if to encourage him.

"Aw, forget it, it's stupid."

She sat back, too, as if settling in, and brushed some dirt from her knees. "Let's not forget it, Ben. It's important to you. Maybe let me ask some questions? In case they're in line with yours?"

"Okay."

"So why all the time with the mushrooms if there's no money in it? And no possibility of the immortality granted by fame—perhaps the fame enjoyed by great photographers? Or maybe just the occasional possibility that what I do or find will give pleasure to someone other than me? Does any of that sound about right?"

He nodded.

Dolores studied him closely, as if some other question might be discerned.

"Is there any chance we're talking about your guitar playing, Ben?"

"Yeah."

For at least two summers now, he was never here without his tape deck and headphones, something Dolores surely noticed. More and more, he simply waved to her as he passed, not wanting to interrupt the near constant soundtrack to his days. At some point, though, during a job that required his full, headphone-less attention as dictated by his father, he'd told Dolores about his guitar lessons, about the time he spent practicing.

Dolores continued: "Is it safe to say you enjoy making music?"

"I think so. I mean, I wouldn't really call what I'm doing *making music*. I'm still just learning things, mostly, and sometimes it's really frustrating. But I have some good times with it, yeah."

"Okay, good. Now is it safe to say that playing the guitar, or learning the guitar, is something you'd like to keep enjoying?"

"Yeah, you could say that."

"Then be careful how much you ask of it, how much you expect from it. That's not to say you can't have dreams or ambitions. But chances are good you'll have to find other ways to pay the bills. And chances are good you'll be remembered for other things—possibly a lot more meaningful things. But the enjoyment you get from playing the guitar, even the frustration of learning it, is not insignificant. It's the kind of experience that adds up to a well-lived life."

Ben sensed a story behind Dolores's advice—her history as a once-promising pianist, maybe, or as a standout dancer who'd suffered a career-ending injury. Whatever the story was, he didn't feel up to asking about it.

He didn't know how to react to her advice either. As hopeful as she'd tried to make it sound, it boiled down to something sad. Like she was trying to convince herself that some old disappointments were truly something good.

"Listen, Ben. I don't mean to discourage you. That's the last thing I'd ever want to do." Again, she smiled. "And should you become a famous musician, I will gladly eat every single one of my words. Deal?"

"Deal."

Ben got up, and so did Dolores. Together, they took another good look at the jelly ears, now glistening in the sunlight that had filtered through the oaks.

"Hey Dolores?"

"Yes?"

"Is there any other mushroom you'd really like to find? One that's especially rare or something?"

"Hmmm. There are quite a few varieties on that list, actually. But if I really had to choose, I guess I'd pick one of the glowing kinds. And if they were going to be anywhere in this cemetery, they'd almost certainly be in this spot. But, of course, I'm rarely here at night."

Ben looked toward the Crane Mausoleum, about a hundred yards to the east. He and Vince had been hanging out there lately, after sundown.

"Well, *I* am," he said. "Not like every night or anything. But when I am, I'll check things out over here."

"That would be lovely, Ben. The most likely candidate is bitter oyster, and it is said to give off a very faint green light. When it's luminescing, that is, which is nothing that can be depended upon."

"I'll keep an eye out," Ben said. "And if I find anything glowing I'll let you know whenever I see you."

"Better yet, call me so I can have a look myself. I'm in the phonebook."

Ben meant what he'd said. He looked out for the green glow that night and nights during the following week, and occasional nights in later weeks and months, until fall brought the cold, sending him and Vince indoors. Eventually, he gave up on the quest entirely, never asking Dolores if she'd succeeded without him.

Chapter 11

SM: I understand the band is named after some anonymous guy who was buried in your hometown cemetery. Why did you choose that name?

VR: Well, it was actually kind of a group decision. But for me, the pure anonymity of the name just stays with you. I mean, I've walked past a lot of graves in that cemetery, and the "Unknown Vagrant" one is the only one I clearly remember. That guy has some weird kind of legend around him, but it's the "unknown" aspect of him that draws me in. To me, that mystery is more interesting than a specific name or any other particular fact. That mystery is a kind of star power.

—From "A Chat with Vince Resklar of the Unknown Vagrants," *Scene* magazine, May 1992

Section D, Lot 357
Midmorning, early June (present day)

Ben spotted her on the way to her grandma's grave, a full watering can in her left hand, backpack slung over her right shoulder. Not wanting to startle her, he waited for her to settle in at the grave. After putting down the watering can, she knelt and started rooting around in her backpack. With her baggy T-shirt, pink running tights, and ponytail, she could have passed for a high schooler.

Once Ben caught her eye, he waved and approached.

"You don't have to trouble yourself with the watering," he said, once he'd reached Ruby Steinlen's grave. "Or the weeding. I'll make sure we take care of your flowers."

She leaned forward and dug a finger into the soil under the geraniums. "Yeah, it's nice and damp there, but . . ."

With one quick move she reached into her backpack and pulled out a blue glass bottle, like something from a nineteenth-century pharmacy.

"Do you regularly apply Giles and Proctor rose food?" The way she held the bottle up close to her face, the way she'd switched to a sing-song voice, she seemed to be performing for a commercial. "Do you regularly inspect the stems and leaves for mites and aphids?"

Ben considered the possibility that he was dealing with a "compulsive," Haley's term for visitors who were certain that they—and only they—had the skills and tools essential to protecting a loved one's flowers from blight. They were a rare breed.

"Listen," she said, back to her usual voice. "I'm kidding. Or kind of kidding. My mom is insisting on the Giles and Proctor and the regular leaf inspection, and I'm just doing her bidding. If she weren't home with a broken leg, she'd be doing it herself."

Ben remembered digging Ruby Steinlen's grave with Haley, but he didn't recall any visitors who might have been this woman's mother. Then again, Ruby had been buried just last fall, making this her first flower season.

"Well," he said, "I'd be happy to use the Giles and Proctor as often as required. And I'll keep on the lookout for mites and aphids, too. Tell your mom that. And if she wants to call me with any special requests, she can. Anytime."

Ben found his wallet, pulled out a business card, and handed it over.

"Ben *DIR*-zhur-ee," she said, reading the card.

"Nice job," he said. "Not everyone gets it right on the first shot."

"Well, Ben. Thank you for helping me with the flowers."

She slipped the card into a pocket of her backpack and extended her hand. "I'm Meredith, by the way. Meredith Kurtz."

"Pleased to meet you, Meredith."

Her handshake was strong enough, her skin rough enough, that she might have been a grounds worker herself.

"Likewise."

"Now," she said, picking up the rose food again. "Let me give you this."

Ben waved the bottle away. "I actually have some of that stuff in the supply shed."

"*Really?* High-class shit like this?"

"Really."

She returned the bottle to her pack, but she seemed distracted, as if something still troubled her.

"Is there anything else I can do for you?"

"Actually, I'm wondering if there's something I might be able to do for *you*. Concerning the Unknown Vagrant exhumation."

The offer, as well-intentioned as it was, left Ben a bit anxious. Part of him wanted to leave the whole matter alone; it had already stirred up enough trouble. Still, he was curious. "What do you have in mind?"

As if for encouragement, Meredith glanced toward Ruby Steinlen's rosebushes, full of orange-red blooms.

"I should begin by telling you that I'm a forensic anthropologist. Do you know what that means?"

Certain TV shows came to Ben's mind, as did an old textbook in the cemetery office. He had no idea where it had come from.

"I think I have a passing acquaintance with the details of your work. You do exhumations yourself, right? And when a body's unidentified, you try to figure out who it is."

"That's a big part of the job, yes. But a smaller part is figuring out when a dig might be pointless."

"What do you mean?"

"Certain conditions, such as highly acidic soil, break down bone and tissue more quickly. If that happens to be the case here, and this guy's been in the ground for over a hundred years, the dig crew might come up empty-handed, or close to it."

Now and then, Ben had done his own soil tests in the

gardened areas of the cemetery, making sure the conditions were right for whatever flowers and shrubs were being planted. In some places the soil was fairly acidic; in other places not so much. As far as he knew, none of the plots had been tested for the reasons Meredith was describing.

"I have some kits for testing soil acidity," he said. "Could I use something like that on the gravesite?"

"Well, that might give you *some* information. But to do the job right you should go deeper into the soil and get something known as core samples. It's a pretty straightforward procedure, and it's minimally invasive."

"Hmmm."

"Ben, I don't mean to butt in where I don't belong. But you told me how you feel about this exhumation, and if there's even a small chance the testing could save some grief, I think it would be worth it."

Ben thought of Jenks, whose approval of just about anything hardly ever came easily. Still, if there was any chance of bypassing the exhumation, he'd probably be thrilled.

Then Jenks's first likely question came to mind. "What about the cost?"

"The testing is fairly inexpensive, I believe. Certainly, a lot less expensive than an exhumation. But I can get some numbers for you on parts and labor."

"Really? I don't want to take up your time with this."

"I'd be happy to. And, actually, I'd be glad to do the testing myself, as long as I'm still in town when the time comes."

Ben felt a subtle sinking within himself, a disappointment unrelated to the business under discussion and all out of proportion to his brief acquaintance with Meredith Kurtz.

"When are you planning on leaving?"

She shrugged. "A month, maybe a month and a half. It kind of depends on how long it takes my mom to get back on her feet."

"Well, it's very kind of you to offer your help. And if you end up doing the test, we'll pay you whatever you think is fair."

"There's no need to pay me. If you guys can cover the cost

of some testing supplies, I'll be happy to do the work *gratis*. Let me just track down some costs, and I'll give you a call."

"Great, thanks."

Meredith turned her attention to the roses and geraniums, and Ben followed her gaze.

"You know," she said, "these flowers are looking pretty good."

"You sound surprised."

"You should have seen the sorry-ass geraniums I got—I guess you did. They've really come back to life."

"Seems so."

Once again, Meredith reached into her pack, pulling out a phone this time. She stepped back and snapped a few pictures of the flowers.

"Proof," she explained. "For my mom."

"Aha."

Once they'd parted ways, Ben watched Meredith walk toward the East Gate, the now-empty watering can swinging with her steps. He wondered whom she might be attached to and how strongly, thankful that she wasn't wearing a ring.

Then he cursed himself for such foolishness. *This is business*, he thought. *Strictly business.*

And he hoped that however the business worked out, it would all be for the best.

Chapter 12

It can't be stressed enough how important it is for the yarn tagger to carefully measure the target object or landscape, especially when creating something large or complicated. Those who skip or flub this step may find themselves short on yarn and shorter on patience.

—From *The Yarn Tagger's Handbook*

Memory Garden
After dark, early June

Peg ran the tape measure from the middle of the foliage, where she planned to place the central pole, toward one of the stone benches along the perimeter. That's about where one of the outer poles would go. Ten feet. She wrote down the measurement and moved on to the next bench, feeling more and more confident about this whole enterprise.

Now that she was back in this space, the sketches she'd made at home seemed just about right: eight outer poles should do it. With crocheted chains strung from them to the center pole, there should be enough color, enough variation in tone and texture, to suggest rays of a setting sun. But not so much color that she'd have to devote twelve-hour days to getting the crocheting done on time.

Once she'd finished her measurements Peg checked her watch. It was 9:19, eleven minutes before she was due to meet back up with Martha. So she sat down on one of the benches and shut off her flashlight, hearing nothing but the chatter of katydids.

It seemed the singers had called it a night.

Peg had heard the singers, a young man and a young woman, not long after arriving. Their voices had been distant enough that she hadn't been able to make out any words, but the sound had stopped her in her tracks—the woman's voice, especially. It seemed to have come from a lost and longing spirit, and no other sound could be more suited to this place.

Still tuned in to the night, Peg heard talking in the distance, then silence. With her flashlight off, she was nearly certain she'd be invisible to anyone who came her way.

Now, it wasn't sound Peg sensed but light—a faint greenish glow emanating from the ground by the largest tree she could see, several yards ahead. As Peg drew closer to the tree, the glow seemed to intensify, almost pulse, as if to reassure her that her eyes were not deceiving her. Then again, maybe they were.

Crouching at the base of the tree, an old birch, she discovered that the light was coming from a clump of mushrooms in their umbrella-ish prime. They'd sprouted from one of the birch's fallen branches.

"My heavens," she whispered, thinking of illustrated fairy stories, the ones in the books that her mother had read to her years before, books she couldn't bring herself to get rid of. *What a strange place this is,* Peg thought. *What a strange and wonderful place.*

Once again, she heard the talking, close by this time. Seconds later, a young woman appeared, her face partially lit by her phone as she carried on a conversation. "Yeah," she said. "If we could meet after my drum lesson, that would be really great. . . . Okay, Mom. Bye."

She lowered her phone and looked Peg's way. Startled, it seemed.

"Good evening," Peg said, hoping to assure the young woman that she was no one who'd make trouble for her, no figure of authority in the cemetery. "I don't mean to pry, but are you a singer perhaps? I've been hearing some lovely singing this evening, and I'm wondering if I might have you to thank."

The young woman studied Peg, straight-faced. Then she said, "It wasn't me. And, actually, I haven't heard any singing. Sorry."

Though her phone conversation indicated that she was a musician—a drummer—it was possible that this stranger wasn't one of the singers. But if she'd been anywhere in the cemetery within the last half hour, there was no way she hadn't heard those beautiful voices. Still, Peg wasn't about to press the point. If a cemetery couldn't be a place of privacy, especially at night, it would be a sorry state of affairs.

The young woman turned her attention toward the glowing mushrooms, as if she'd just now noticed them. Before, the light of her phone must have blinded her to the sight.

"Pretty amazing, huh?" said Peg.

Still staring at the mushrooms, the young woman looked slightly repulsed. Then she turned to Peg and said, "I should get going."

After a quick exchange of *goodnights* with Peg, she was on her way.

Peg considered the unspoken agreement underlying her interaction with the young woman: *I won't ask you why you're here, and you won't ask me either.* She was certain that in countless locales over the world, especially at night, such agreements were keeping peace and contentment.

Chapter 13

I have been paying close attention to the activities of the Infinity Burial Project, and I urge my mushroom-loving friends to do the same. The Project's Infinity Burial Suit, which is threaded with corpse-consuming mushroom spores, breaks down human remains gently and naturally, remediating environmental toxins and producing nutrients to support new life. The suit will provide an environmentally friendly alternative to traditional funeral industry practices, which involve toxic embalming chemicals and other environmental hazards. It will also help counter some prevailing beliefs in our culture: that decomposition can and should be averted, that it is not a natural, even restorative, part of the cycle of life.

—Jade Fiorelli, *The Mushroom Times*

Section D

Late morning

Weed whacking alongside Acanthus Lane, Cole spotted a brown, bubble-ish cluster in the grass ahead: mushrooms, her fourth such sighting in as many days, the most spectacular being the ones from the night before. Their green glow loomed like horror-movie fog, returning when she closed her eyes.

The previous days' spells of rain were the most logical explanation for the fungal abundance on the grounds, yet Cole couldn't help but wonder if her father was spreading spores simply by showing up for work. Literally and figuratively, he'd become immersed in them.

Two nights before, as Cole entered the basement with a basket of laundry, she found him hunched over his workbench, eye-dropping solution into a trio of petri dishes. He looked up at her guiltily but said nothing and continued with his work.

"Dad? What are you doing?"

He finished with the eyedropper and set it aside. "Are you sure you want to know?"

"I asked, didn't I?"

Another look of guilt.

"Okay. Consider yourself warned."

One by one, he spoke for the petri dishes like a priest gearing up for the Eucharist: "This is my skin, this is my hair, and these are clippings of my nails. I'm trying to train mushrooms to grow on them, devour them. And if that works—well, I'll take things from there."

"Take things where? What *things*?"

"This is where it gets kind of weird."

"We're already pretty far into weird, Dad."

Anger and embarrassment seemed to have united in him. He said, "Let's leave it then, all right? Go back to your laundry."

Cole was grasping hold of the clothes basket as if for life. Still, she made herself put it down and step closer to the bench, glancing over the petri dishes in spite of herself. One gummed surface was sprinkled with something like black pepper; another was topped with evenly distributed nail shavings.

"I didn't mean to insult you, Dad. I guess I just don't understand what you're doing."

In the silence between them, he seemed to be figuring things out himself.

"Well, if this little experiment works, I'll get mushrooms that acquire a taste for me, instead of their usual diet—rotted wood and such. Then I'll infiltrate a bodysuit with the spores, a bodysuit I could eventually be buried in. The idea is that the mushrooms would break down my body naturally, without chemicals, and turn me into some really nice compost."

He smiled as if to reassure her, until he saw this wasn't working.

"Cole, you look upset."

"I'm not." A lie.

"If it's any comfort, this wasn't my idea. I read about an artist who's doing the very same thing, bodysuit and all. I figured I'd do a parallel experiment and see what I can learn."

Cole was not comforted. Seeing this, Ben stepped around the bench and laid his hands on her shoulders.

"Honey, what's wrong?"

She didn't want to cry in front of him, but it was too late.

"How soon are you planning on using that suit, Daddy?"

He closed her in his arms quickly, as if pulling her back from a ledge. Then slowly he began to rock her back and forth.

When she'd calmed down some he said, "Honey, I won't be using that suit for a very, very long time. Or never, if I can't get the damn thing to work."

He stepped back to look her in the eye. "Do you want me to stop it with this stuff?"

"No."

"Are you sure?"

"I'm sure. I know it makes you happy."

Happy probably wasn't the best word, yet her father didn't correct her.

"The only way I can explain all this, Cole, is that the thing I'm involved in at work—"

"The *green* thing?"

"Yeah, the *green* thing."

Her father's mission to make the cemetery a little less of a blot on the environment, a mission low on self-congratulation. Just last week, after he'd added some more native plants to the cemetery's gardens, he'd answered Cole's praise this way: "One small step in turning a felony into a misdemeanor."

"Well, Cole," he said now, "the green thing's really gotten under my skin, so to speak. Take that and the mushroom thing, and maybe it's a case of one obsession feeding another."

Cole supposed that was possible.

91

"Whether anything positive will come out of all this, who knows? All I can ask is that you promise to tell me if this stuff becomes unbearable to you. If *I* become unbearable to you."

"That's not going to happen, Daddy."

"Still, can you promise?"

"I *said*—"

"Please, please, just promise."

"Okay. I promise."

Now, Cole thought over various things she might have said instead.

She wished, too, that she'd remembered her father's fairly new routine of jogging before dawn, before work. How many among the terminally ill or suicidal decided that now was the time to start getting into shape?

Though Cole hadn't asked him the reason for this new habit, she assumed it had something to do with the fact that he was closing in on his fiftieth birthday. Not long after passing that milestone, both his father and paternal grandfather dropped dead from heart attacks.

As Cole closed in on the corner of Acanthus Lane and Ivy Path, her phone started chirping in her butt pocket. After doing a quick three-sixty to satisfy herself that Mr. Jenks wasn't in sight, or her father, she shut off the weed trimmer and took the call.

"Hello?"

"Cole? It's Grif."

She stood silent for a moment, trying to match the name with a memory.

"The guy from Vince Resklar's grave." A pause. "God, does that sound weird."

"One of the singers, right?" She pictured the tall guy with the mop of curly hair.

"Right. Am I catching you at an okay time?"

"Yeah, sure. I mean, I'm working, but I was just about to take a break."

"You got a job? Where?"

"Take a big guess."

Another pause. "I have no idea."

"Hint: I'm whacking weeds in the land of the dead."

"The *cemetery*?"

"The cemetery. I'm helping with landscaping, for the summer."

"No shit! How'd you get in there?"

"It's kind of a long story." It wasn't, really. Cole just didn't feel like getting into it now. "I'll fill you in next time I see you."

"Speaking of jobs, remember Nate?"

"Your drummer, right?"

"Right. Well, he got a summer gig on an organic farm. In another state."

Cole felt a clutch of nerves, sensing where this was heading.

"So I'm wondering if you might want to play with us sometime, test the waters. And then if that works out, maybe you could sit in with us for that concert? If that ever happens?"

"The protest thing?"

"Yeah."

"Do you need an answer now?"

"Not really. Take a day or two to think about it."

Cole knew that a day or two, or even a week, even a month, wouldn't make any difference.

"I guess I'm just worried that I'll really suck."

A smaller source of anxiety: how her father would take the news of her playing a gig—if things got that far. Although Cole was sure he wouldn't be thrilled, his worst response would probably be a near-silent acceptance; his best, a grudging "Congratulations."

"I doubt that," Grif said.

Cole rapped nervously at her thigh. How to put this? How to make her point without sounding beyond-all-hope insane?

Finally, she said, "I'll try out with you guys on one condition."

He answered warily. "*Okay.*"

"You have to promise that you will tell me if my playing is not just having-an-off-day bad but hopeless bad. And you have to be absolutely honest."

A long silence on Grif's end.

"I sound neurotic, don't I?"

"No, you don't sound neurotic, and I promise I'll be honest."

As they made plans for her tryout, the new guy, Pete, wandered into the middle distance, a trash bag trailing from one hand like an afterthought. Her dad was right about Pete being a perpetual-motion machine, but to Cole he looked perpetually stoned, too. Whatever the truth was, she had a feeling she didn't have to worry if he caught her on the phone.

"Before I forget, guess where that girl from your school wants to hold the concert?"

That girl, Cole realized, was Meg Tirella. "Tell me."

"Where you're standing right now."

Cole felt another clutch of nerves. "You're shitting me."

"I'm not. She thinks it's the perfect venue, for pretty obvious reasons."

"Well, she'd better have a plan B."

"That's pretty much what I told her. I can't see how it would be in the cemetery's interests to go along with this thing. Unless I'm missing something."

"You're not. They like to talk about how much time and money they put into maintaining the grounds. So I doubt they'd let a bunch of people trample through like it's Six Flags." Cole was oddly pleased by how well she'd channeled Mr. Jenks.

"That's what I thought. The only way it might work is if we flash mobbed and just played till we got kicked out. But that would mean going acoustic, at best."

And probably drumless, Cole thought. Which might be for the best. If Mr. Jenks or, worse, her own father caught her playing an unauthorized show on the grounds, her ass would be in a sling for the foreseeable future.

"I don't suppose you have any pull there, Cole."

"Sorry, man. I'm a totally dispensable peon."

"All right, just thought I should ask. And I don't really give a shit where we play. Someone's back yard would be fine by me."

Me too, Cole thought. Then she hoped she hadn't cursed her chances by imagining herself in the band.

After pocketing her phone, Cole paused before turning the weed trimmer back on. Somewhere, a man—not her father—was singing something like a church hymn. A man with a pretty good voice. As she listened, the sound grew fainter, more distant. When it faded entirely, she switched on the trimmer and went back to work.

⋆⥥⋆

Ben paused with the hedge clippers and, from several yards' distance, watched an older woman advance on Anthony Lekovic's grave. He remembered her from the graveside service, when he'd assumed she was the mother. He'd missed her on Memorial Day, though she, or someone, must have appeared. At the start of that day there was nothing at Lekovic's gravesite but his newly installed granite marker. By sunset impatiens had been planted, bouquets of daisies laid over the fresh sod. Gone were the ziplocked pictures.

She approached the grave warily, trailed by a black mongrel who looked no more certain of their mission. When she reached the marker, she stared at its face for some time, as if it carried some coded message. Then, suddenly, she covered her eyes and fell into tears, prompting the usual mild panic in Ben.

Make yourself useful or leave, he told himself.

When it was time for such choices, his father never hesitated. He understood when to approach someone and play the sympathetic bartender, the therapist. And when, instead, the best thing was to leave a person alone. As Ross told Ben more than once, "The ones who really need you, you'll know them when you see them."

After all these years, Ben never did.

This time the dog tried to answer the call, poking his grayed muzzle at the woman's knees. When this earned him no attention, he circled a spot by the grave then eased himself down with a sigh.

Give her some privacy, Ben concluded; the hedges could be finished some other time. As he headed toward Ivy Path

95

something froze him once again in his tracks: the sound of joyous singing.

There's a dark and a troubled side of life
There's a bright and a sunny side too

Then came joyous Pete, cresting the hill.

Though we meet with the darkness and strife
The sunny side we also may view

The woman at Lekovic's grave looked Pete's way, so did the dog. Pete raised his hand to greet them and sang even louder as he continued on his way.

Keep on the sunny side, always on the sunny side
Keep on the sunny side of life

Stunned out of crying, she waved back absently and followed Pete's progress past the grave and then toward the hedgerow, where he saluted Ben before moving on down the hill.

It will help us ev'ry day, it will brighten all the way
If we keep on the sunny side of life

Chapter 14

Recommended Annual Advertising Campaign, in Advance of Bridal Season
When: March 15 – June 15, yearly
Where: the *Bolster Register*, the *Carlisle Monitor*
What: Daily B&W and Sunday full-color ads promoting 8 x 12 (double) plots.
Suggested promo lines: "A unique and thoughtful gift for the special couple in your life"
"A moving demonstration of eternal love"
"A loving, lasting symbol of commitment"
"A ring is just one way to say 'My heart is yours—forever.'"

—From section 2, "Pre-Need Promotions," of the *Bolster Hill Cemetery Sales Handbook*

General Grounds and Mausoleums
Some June evening, 1990

They crept, headlights off, across the parking lot, Ben leading the way to the tractor and backhoe lot, which was hidden from the road by a stand of hemlocks. He parked the truck and grabbed his guitar from the back, while Tuke retrieved the extra-large bag of cheese curls from somewhere beneath the seats.

By the time they got to Dave's Tercel, Vince was standing by with his own guitar, watching Dave root through the equipment bag on the back seat.

"I know it's in here somewhere," Dave said.

"What's the *it*?" Tuke asked.

97

"The thing Vince asked about. The station list."

"While you're at it, look for the Seagram's."

"Can't you wait a fucking minute, Tuke?"

"No."

"Here," Ben said, tossing Tuke the key ring. "It's in the office, bottom drawer of the filing cabinet that's way back on the left wall. Look behind the last file."

"What's it doing in the office?"

"Never mind. Just get it, and make it quick. And don't forget to lock the door when you're done."

"Cool, thanks," Tuke said, handing the cheese curls off to Ben. "I'll catch up with you guys in a few."

The truth about the whiskey was that the junior grounds man had brought it to work for Ben that morning. In exchange, Ben had mowed all of Sections C and D while the grounds man took time off for God knows what. Through similar arrangements since the start of his summer gig at the cemetery, Ben had obtained cheap vodka and, more important, three cases of beer, now stashed under a tarp in the Sherman family mausoleum.

"Ah-*ha*!" Dave waved a folded sheet like a flag before handing it to Vince, who stuffed it into his back pocket.

Catching the look on Ben's face, Vince said, "You'll see the list in a minute. As soon as we get settled."

From the back lot the three of them, rejoined soon by Tuke, followed their usual course: over the East Gate then across Section C, then finally to the space between the Crane and Bates family mausoleums, which offered both seclusion and a soft, cushiony groundcover like tiny ferns. In high school, it had been just Ben and Vince who met up here on clear, warm nights, after Ben was done with his grounds work and Vince with his shift at Record Scene. They talked about music, listened to music, and eventually played music—first other people's songs, then initial stabs at their own.

Now, the whiskey circulated one way, the cheese curls the other, while Dave stuffed his pipe full of weed then fired it up. Ben didn't turn down anything, though he took it easy on the whiskey and easier still on the pot, which could trigger ugly spells of paranoia. Tonight, especially, he needed to keep himself under control.

"So," Vince said, pulling the station list from his pocket. "You sent our kit to all these places?"

Dave took another swig of the Seagram's before passing the bottle to Vince. "Yep."

"Nice work."

The kit consisted of their four-song demo tape, a press release that Ben had photocopied in the office, a band photograph, and stickers and pins that Vince got made through a connection at the record store.

"The ones with *c*'s next to them, are those the college stations?"

"Yep."

Vince passed the list to Tuke, who gave it a quick once-over before handing it to Ben.

Dave went on: "I'm close to nailing us an interview at the Ithaca station, for the same weekend as our gigs around there. And I'm working on the station at Saint something-or-other, since that'd be just down the road."

"Saint Bonaventure."

"Yeah."

"Great."

Now, Ben and Dave, with occasional interjections from Tuke, added a few more tasks to their to-do list: contacting the new clubs in Burlington and Southridge about possible gigs, figuring out new places to plaster or distribute fliers for the upcoming shows in Carlisle. At some point Vince took his acoustic out of the case and began strumming it in the background, until there was a break in the conversation.

"Hey," he said, "before I forget. That friend of Joe's I told you about? That promoter/manager guy? Tim Waller?" Joe was Vince's boss at the store. "Well, Joe gave him our tape, and apparently he liked it. He liked it a lot."

"So?" Tuke asked.

"So Tim Waller's a big fucking deal," Dave said. "He got Jeezmit signed, to give you just one example."

Once again the holder of the whiskey bottle, Dave raised it in Vince's direction. "That's awesome, man."

Tuke was still taking it all in. "What's next with this guy?"

"He wants to meet with us, I guess. He's going to call me at the store tomorrow, and I'll let you guys know what happens."

They were classic Vince, these bomb-drop understatements, these holy-fuck afterthoughts tagged onto tales of others' best efforts. This was the first Ben had heard the news about Tim Waller, though he'd talked to Vince at least two times since his last shift at the store. Though he thought of Vince as his closest friend.

Ben considered, not for the first time, that Vince might not share his view of their friendship. Furthermore, holding his cards close to his vest was part of Vince's nature, and one possible means of keeping things under his control.

Vince went on strumming, transitioning into the opening notes of their latest effort, moving verse to chorus, verse to chorus, and casting Ben questioning glances as he tested out a bridge. An attempt, it seemed, to draw Ben out of his sulking and back into the circle.

Taking the cue, Ben said, "I wouldn't start it that way, with the major chord. Here. Let me show you what I mean." He retrieved his own guitar and replayed the verse-chorus progression, then started a bridge in F minor, giving it a lot of major from there.

"Yeah, yeah, that's good, that's good. But how about coming back to the minor here, like this—"

"Okay, okay, yeah."

This time they played the whole song together, following each other's moves as they went into the bridge, then repeating the song till everything flowed. As they rolled ahead, Dave started rapping out the beat on his thighs, Tuke mouthing an imitation of the bass.

At some point Ben noticed that the rapping had stopped, and following Dave's gaze down the hill he saw Leah making her way toward them like a reluctant ghost, her pale pretty face turned downward as she checked her footing. Ben put aside his guitar and jogged down to meet her, and as he pulled her toward him he breathed in the smell of her hair. It always reminded him of apples.

Releasing Leah, studying her in what light there was, he thought of the statue in front of the Tate Mausoleum: the beautiful mourner embracing an urn, her veiled head lowered. That statue had been his first crush, his first womanly mystery, filling his young mind with questions: *Who made you so sad? What else would you tell me, if I could bring you to life?*

"Sorry I'm so early," she said. The plan had been to meet in the main lot at twelve thirty, and it wasn't even midnight. "It didn't take me that long to varnish the painting. So I thought I'd just come by."

"How did you find us?"

"It wasn't hard." She smiled. "I just followed the sound."

Taking her hand Ben led her back to the others, whom she'd never met. Dave, ever the gentleman, was the first to rise up in greeting.

"College Leah!" he announced.

"So that's my handle," she said, laughing as she shook Dave's hand.

In truth, Dave and the others knew little more than the fact that she and Ben had met the first week of their freshman year and that, since then, he hadn't been interested in dating anyone else. Though Leah had made it to one of the Vagrants' shows, she'd had to duck out early, before she could catch up with any of Ben's bandmates, and there'd been few other opportunities for her to cross paths with the guys. Dave and Tuke went to a different college, and Vince stuck to Bolster, mostly. He'd expressed no desire to go to college, and as far as Ben could tell, the hours Vince didn't devote to sleeping, eating, or covering his shift at Record Scene were spent playing his guitar and trying to get down songs.

Tuke then Vince followed Dave's lead, standing to shake Leah's hand. Once all the introductions had been made she said, "I didn't mean to interrupt you. I just wanted to say hello."

"It's no interruption, really," Dave said. "We're pretty much just messing around."

"Well it didn't sound like messing around. Whatever you were playing, it was really nice."

"Thanks."

Ben was grateful that no one was embarrassingly fucked up. Not yet, anyway.

Settling back onto the grass, Tuke looked Leah's way and patted the ground beside him, which Ben then covered with his jacket. Once Leah settled into her spot she was offered first the whiskey bottle and then the pipe, both of which she politely declined.

"So are you here for the whole weekend?" Tuke asked her.

"Yeah." Leah smiled at Ben uncertainly. "I think so."

"Yes, she's here for the whole weekend. Unless the Dirjery clan drives her nuts."

Knowing his parents, and knowing Leah, Ben doubted that anything would go horribly wrong. Yet he'd been anxious about her visit, and ever since they'd made a plan for it, he'd been trying to figure out why. One thing he understood was that bringing Leah to Bolster Hill was another way of making his feelings for her plain to others—this time, to those closest to him—and therefore undeniable. And the deeper and more undeniable his connection to Leah became, the more Ben worried that he might thoughtlessly destroy it.

They'd reached this "meeting the parents" phase somewhat unintentionally. When Ben mentioned in passing to Leah that this weekend was Ross and Liz's twenty-third anniversary, she proposed giving them one of her paintings as a gift. Long propped on a milk crate in her bedroom it showed a white hound looking over its shoulder in the middle distance of a dark field. Though the sky threatened a storm, the dog glowed as if caught in headlights.

Ben liked to study the painting in his morning drowse, while he and Leah lay together on the mattress on her floor. The hound was a dead ringer for Luke, Ben's favorite dog—his parents' favorite dog—until he disappeared the summer Ben turned fourteen.

The fact that Leah was willing to give his parents the painting, let alone the fact that she'd created it in the first place, was just another of the many reasons Ben had fallen in love with her. Seriously in love. But they had two more years of college, two more years for her to grow apart from him.

Then there was the problem of Ben himself. With any luck he'd be on the road with the band, possibly for weeks on end. School would suffer. So, most likely, would his relationship with Leah. If it happened that she could tolerate that, what kind of reward would she get in the end? Most likely, he'd continue on as a nearly broke musician. Or, with any luck, as a nearly broke musician with an environmental-science degree and a vaguely imagined future.

"So," Leah said now, from her place between Ben and Tuke, "Ben tells me you guys like the privacy of this place."

"Yeah, that's part of it," Dave said. "But it's more than that. I mean, the cemetery I grew up next to, it was kind of like an army barracks, just rows and rows of the same old kinds of stones. There was nothing interesting about it, and no place to hide. But this place, it's like entering some kind of weird, twisty dream." He paused to laugh. "I swear I'm not as high as I sound."

Leah reached for a handful of cheese curls. "You make perfect sense."

Dave looked between Vince and Tuke. "What about you guys?"

Once again, Vince had started strumming his guitar. Even at times like these he was nearly all business, all music—never one for small talk.

Tuke said, "I like the captive audience."

"*Hah!*"

Tuke nodded toward Vince, then Ben. "And if I may speak for these young men, they enjoy the creature comforts here."

Creature comforts was code for getting laid, something Ben had attempted twice in the cemetery, back in high school, and succeeded at only once—the "success" included rolling himself and his girlfriend onto a patch of stinging nettles.

Not long ago, after having a few too many beers, Ben shared this story with Vince, Tuke, and Dave, and while Tuke and Dave laughed, Vince lowered his guitar and locked eyes with Ben. Then he said, dead serious, "Why didn't you just stay in the back lot? That's always worked for me."

Suggesting multiple girls. Suggesting encounters so satisfying that neither Vince nor his dates had any inclination to depart his car and the hemlock-surrounded tractor lot.

Now, no one translated *creature comforts* in Leah's presence, for which Ben was grateful. Vince didn't even look up from his strumming.

"So," Leah said, "this cemetery is where the original Vagrant is buried?"

"Actually, he's just beyond the gates—thataway." Dave nodded northward.

"A classic outsider," she said.

"Yeah, that's about right."

"Is that why you named the band after him?"

Dave looked from Ben to Tuke then spoke up. "I just like the word *Vagrants*. It's a great band name."

"Me too," Tuke said. Then he nodded toward Vince, who was already back to playing his guitar. "If I may once again speak for our friend here, he likes the mystery of the name. Right?"

Still strumming, Vince glanced blankly at Tuke. "Sure."

"Then," Dave said, "there's the intriguing mystery of the Vagrant himself."

"So I've heard," Leah said. "Ben told me about his wanderings, how no one was ever sure why he made them, or why they were so regular. Do you think you'd ever write a song about him? Maybe try to tell his story?"

These questions got Vince's attention. He stopped strumming and looked to Ben, and it seemed to Ben that, silently, they were repeating the conversation they'd had about this very subject, more than once. Now, Ben tried to summarize it for Leah.

"The problem is, we don't have any idea what that story would be. And it just doesn't feel right to try to imagine it. Especially considering how much the guy wanted privacy. How much he really just wanted to be left alone."

Leah's gaze drifted away from Ben and Vince, toward the

ferny ground at the center of their circle. Ben hoped she hadn't regretted her questions, and in an attempt to cheer her, he put his arm across her shoulders and kissed her cheek.

She smiled, and so did Dave. "Lucky in love," he said.

It felt that way to Ben.

"Hey," Leah said. "I'd love to hear more of that song you were playing."

"It's a work-in-progress."

"Good," she said. "That's the story of my life."

With this, Ben took up his guitar, then he and Vince exchanged their *ready-set-go* nods and started in, Dave and Tuke soon finding their own places in the song. Together they made their way through the latest version, uncertainly during the first round, smoothly during the second.

On the third round, the Vince that Ben most admired and dreaded surfaced—the Vince anyone inclined to jealousy, Ben included, might be tempted to see as a showoff. But, unlike most musical showoffs, Vince was focused on nothing but the song. In fact, he became inseparable from it, adding weird but beautiful twists to the verse and then to the bridge, each change feeling retrospectively essential.

During the fourth round Ben made the mistake of glancing toward Leah and found her attention locked on Vince, a common reaction from any mindful listener. Yet the intensity of her fascination, as if everything but Vince had dropped from her awareness, unsettled Ben, then made him angry. Leah had never looked at him that way.

Ben strummed harder, adding a few new flourishes of his own, until the strumming nudged his anger into words. Usually the backup singer, he now took the lead:

Numbers, here's my numbers, four and twelve, and twelve and eight

He got Leah's attention.

There's a question in them—Answer me, it's getting late.

105

He cast her glances as the song progressed, checking that she was still with him.

I just need to know
Will you let me know?
Four or eight by twelve, which one?
Four or eight by twelve, which one?
You know I know you know what I mean.

Did she, though? At that moment all Ben knew was that she was listening to him, and that she seemed to understand the emotion if not the sense of his words.

As for the sense of them, all Leah would have had to go on was the exchange she and Ben had had just before dawn last Valentine's Day. At the time, he was deep into that strange land between drunkenness and sobriety, a land lit by the glaring fluorescents of his and Leah's favorite diner. She was leaning against him in their cushy corner booth, possibly asleep, the remains of their pancake breakfasts arrayed before them.

"Hey," he whispered into her hair.

After a moment, she came to life. "What?"

"Wanna see something weird?"

She answered by sitting up and watching as he took a pen from his backpack, then fished a clean napkin from the metal dispenser.

On the left side of the napkin he drew a single vertical rectangle. "This," he said, "in cemetery parlance, is a single burial plot. A four-by-twelve. And this"—he drew a second rectangle next to the first one, and tapped it with his pen—"makes it a double plot, an eight-by-twelve. And in my father's eyes, this is true love."

Leah glanced from Ben to the napkin and back, without smiling. She seemed partly fascinated, partly disturbed, as if Ben had drawn her some perverse kind of Valentine.

"I'm sorry," he said. "The idea just came to me, and I thought you'd find it kind of funny."

She sat up straighter and turned to him, looked him in the eye.

"Do *you* believe this is true love?"

"Fuck no. I said it was weird, didn't I?"

Leah seemed not to believe Ben. She kept her eyes on him, as if waiting to hear the true intentions behind the drawing, its deeper meaning. To end the conversation, he called for the check.

The memory of that morning at the diner broke Ben's concentration now. He flubbed the words on the song's next pass then stopped singing entirely. Eventually they moved from this song to another, and another. When they'd wrapped up their impromptu performance, Leah praised the music in general but said nothing about the words to the first song. She said nothing about them during her and Ben's parting with Tuke, Dave, and Vince; nothing while the two of them locked her painting in the office for temporary storage; nothing while she got her first impressions of the house Ben had grown up in, where his parents, now asleep, had left the porch light on, leftover pizza in the fridge, and a "Welcome, Leah" note with daisies on the kitchen table.

Soon after they entered Ben's room, Leah fell into a deep sleep beside him. But Ben lay awake till nearly dawn, wondering what dark corner of his soul those lyrics had come from, and why. Possibly, he'd reeled up old anger against his father, turned it against Leah's attention to Vince—an attention that Ben perceived, rightly or wrongly, as attraction.

Another, far more disturbing possibility presented itself: Ben was becoming more like his father than he cared to acknowledge, even in matters of love.

Chapter 15

"Whether we find it appealing or not is another question, but personally I like being fourth cousin to a mushroom. . . . It makes me feel a part of the world."

—From *Dry Store Room No. 1: The Secret Life of The Natural History Museum,* by Richard Fortey (2008)

General Grounds and Section D

Late morning (present day)

When her phone chirped, Cole was on her knees in a flower bed, yanking out an exceptionally stubborn patch of weeds. Retrieving her phone, she saw that she had an incoming call from Grif Scortino, and with this her stomach turned.

If it was good news, he'd be texting. Bad news—heart-shredding, personal bad news, like *I want to break up with you*—came through calls. At least when people had manners, and courage, which Grif seemed to.

"Grif?"

"Hey, Cole."

"What's up?"

The pause that followed seemed an eternity.

"You're in with us, if you want to be. We all thought you were great."

"Really?"

Cole wanted to scream, jump up and down, but she managed to control herself, expressing her joy with a fist pump.

"Really."

"Oh, man, that's awesome. I'm *absolutely* in."

Cole thought back on the slightly risky fills she'd tried in the last song of her tryout. Almost as soon as the song ended, she was certain they'd been a mistake. Thankfully, she'd been wrong.

"So what's next?" she asked.

"Next practice is Tuesday at seven, the usual place. And you can use Nate's kit again."

"Awesome. I'll be there. And Grif? Thanks a lot."

"Don't thank me. You did a great job."

As soon as she hung up, Cole texted her mother with the news. Seconds later, her mom texted back: "So thrilled for you. Can't wait to hear you perform."

Pocketing her phone, Cole looked toward Section D, where she'd last seen her father, who'd been busy distributing compost. She'd tell him about the band at some point, but not now. Now, she had no desire to dilute her happiness.

As for the concert, she wasn't going to bring it up with him, unless or until that became absolutely necessary.

※

It wasn't the first time this kind of thing had happened— someone Ben should have remembered but didn't, waving to him from a distance; it was a hazard of being a fixture at the cemetery.

As this woman drew closer, certain things about her started to ring a bell: her height and the resolute set of her shoulders, the shirt so crisp it looked pressed, the broad-brimmed straw hat. It was the basket across her right arm that fit all the pieces together.

Dolores Fielding.

Yet it couldn't be. This woman was too frail and withered, her gait unusually labored.

"Ben?"

When she got to the edge of Ivy Path, he set down his compost pail, seeing he hadn't been mistaken.

"Dolores. Good to see you."

She was smiling but clearly tired, and with slow determination she made her way toward the angel statue between them. There, she laid her hand on the angel's shoulder and let it take her weight.

"On a mushroom hunt, I presume," Ben said.

"Indeed I am. Have you seen the shaggy manes in Oak Corner?"

"Nope. Not yet."

"Well, they come on quickly. The only reason I know about them is that Ellie emailed me this morning."

Ellie Whitlin was another aficionado of the cemetery's mushrooms. Ben hadn't seen her recently, but she tended to show up at dawn, or earlier.

"She sent me a picture, but I decided a picture wasn't good enough."

Ben smiled and tried to look at ease, hoping his first shock at seeing Dolores hadn't been too apparent.

"You're welcome to walk over with me, if you have time."

He didn't. But it seemed wrong to turn down the offer. "Sure. Let's go."

Ben let her set the pace of their walk, resisting the temptation to take her arm, not for fear that this might seem too forward. It was more that such a move would acknowledge that something was seriously wrong, an acknowledgment he felt should be Dolores's to make.

Nearing the end of Willow Path, they spotted cluster after cluster of mushrooms beneath the oaks. It was Dolores who took Ben's arm now, bringing them both to a stop.

"My goodness," she said. "My, my goodness."

They made their way forward with even greater care, as if any sudden moves might spook the vision away. As they drew nearer, the clusters resolved into little white rockets poking up in abundance, like taste buds. Still closer up they could make out the shaggy, lifted scales that gave these mushrooms their name.

"Never have I seen so many of these, so early," Dolores said.

As for Ben, he had no recollection of shaggy manes in the

cemetery, certainly not in Oak Corner. Up till now he'd seen this type of mushroom only in pictures, and he knew next to nothing about them, which he now told Dolores.

"Well," she said, "the short story is they're a variety of inky cap, and edible. But you have to pick them at their prime—that means now for most of them here. And you have to use them quickly. Because one day they're delicious and fresh, and the next they're black goo."

Ben noticed that certain ones had already lifted their caps, transforming from white rockets into browning umbrellas. Some umbrella edges had curled up into black scrolls.

"The good news, Ben, is that the shaggies tend to come in waves. We're likely to get a few more rounds of these ones here before things die down entirely."

"I'll have to keep an eye on them."

In the silence that fell between them Ben's thoughts turned back to the composting he'd interrupted, to the broken pump in the Section B fountain. Perhaps sensing this, Dolores said, "I'm glad I ran into you, Ben. I've been meaning to call you about something."

The tone of her voice told him the "something" wasn't some new wrinkle in green landscaping or a reminder about the next mushroom walk.

"And I'm going to be direct about it, because right now that's easiest for me."

Finding himself suddenly unable to speak, Ben made no objection.

"I'm dying, Ben. Exactly how quickly, I don't know. But I'm not making any plans beyond three months. And if I'm here a year from now, that would exceed the current expectations. By a long shot."

Still at a loss for words Ben took Dolores's hand, and after a *May I?* glance for permission, led her into the stand of oaks, where he eased her onto a bench and sat down beside her. Dolores turned so they were knee to knee, so close she had to tip back her hat. She gave him the apologetic look of a parent breaking bad news to a child.

"I know you're sorry, Ben, so you don't have to say it. I know you'll be thinking of me, so you don't have to say that either. But if you're wondering if there's anything you can do for me, I'm afraid the answer is *yes.*"

"Sure, Dolores. Just tell me what you need."

She smiled in the old way, as if she were about to deliver another strange or surprising fact about a mushroom.

"I'm wondering if there's any chance of me getting a green burial in that new wing, if it's open in time."

As Ben's collaborator on the Green Initiative, Dolores had had a front-row seat for at least one of Ben's arguments for green burials—that the cemetery should offer them in the soon-to-be-opened Section E. Though she hadn't been present for the last board meeting, the outcome had been the same: a decision on the issue got tabled for the same reasons as before—the green-burial certification process was a pain in the ass (not true); the cemetery had more important priorities, logistically and financially (maybe). The bottom line was, the can got kicked down the road once again.

Dolores went on: "The website didn't say when that wing would be ready."

Ben was somewhat to blame for this omission. The web page for Section E, the one that would announce the planned opening dates, hadn't been posted yet because of advertising claims that Ben, and a few others, hadn't felt comfortable with—among the claims, that this new wing of the cemetery would be "especially attuned to the needs of the eco-concerned." As the plans stood now, Section E would be no more eco-attuned than any other part of the grounds.

"Anyway," Dolores said, "if I can't get a green burial here, I understand. There are other places I can go."

Yet Ben knew Dolores's parents had been buried at Bolster Hill; quite possibly, other relatives as well. It only stood to reason that she'd want to end up here, too.

To buy some time for himself, Ben took a napkin from his shirt pocket and wiped the sweat from his brow and the back of his neck. With unnecessary, time-consuming care he folded up the napkin and put it back.

"First," he said, "the relatively easy answer. The estimate now is that Section E will be open by mid-September. October first at the latest."

"That might work for me."

"Now the hard part."

Dolores didn't flinch, as if ready to hear anything.

"We're no closer to green burials than we were at the last meeting you went to. The only good news is that I've pulled together some new numbers that make a stronger case for them, at least to me. And I'm going to be running them by Carl Jenks later this week. But even if Carl jumps for joy over the numbers, even if he personally okays green burials, I'd still need full approval from the board. And that's going to take time."

The faintest shadow of disappointment passed over Dolores's face. "It's a long shot, in other words."

"Yes. But let me see what I can do. And I'll let you know what happens with Carl."

"Thank you, Ben"

Staring out over the assemblage of shaggy manes, most in their rocket-like prime, he couldn't help but think, once again, of how all mushrooms at this stage were little structures of hope—as if no browning or wilting was possible.

"Don't thank me unless I can make something happen. I'll give you some news as soon as I can."

"You know how to reach me."

Ben straightened up on the bench. "I probably should be getting back to work."

"Of course."

"I could drive over here with the golf cart in a bit, take you back to the parking lot."

"Thanks, but I'd like to try to run under my own steam. For as long as I can."

Yet Dolores didn't wave away his arm when he offered it to help her up from the bench. Once she was on her feet she gave the shaggy manes one last admiring look.

"Do you think it's strange that I still want to come here, Ben? Given my circumstances?"

"Not at all."

The strange thing, for Ben, would turn out to be the growing number of days, from mid-summer on, when he didn't see Dolores in Oak Corner or anyplace else on the grounds.

Chapter 16

Bolster's Got Talent!

Join us every Wednesday night for open mike nite at the Wallflower Lounge.
Catch acts by local singers, musicians, stand-up comics, and the occasional poet. Or wow the crowd with your own performance!
Doors open at 8 p.m.

—From a flier and online posting

Cemetery Office

Mid-afternoon, mid-June

All morning Pete had been even edgier than usual. Returning from lunch Ben found him pacing in front of the office, making it clear that his issue—whatever it was—couldn't be set aside any longer.

In the seconds it took Ben to reach Pete, various shitty possibilities surfaced in his mind: a clogged irrigation line, a backhoe collision with expensive masonry work, a dig initiated—or completed—on the wrong plot.

"What's up?" Ben hoped his tone conveyed his impatience. Jenks was due to arrive any minute, and he was rarely late.

Pete didn't answer right away. He slapped nervously at his pocket change, suggesting the worst.

"A little bird told me you used to play guitar, Ben."

Guitar. The word conjured something like the Grande Burrito in Ben's stomach. Unseen but weighty, webbed with regret.

"Who's the little bird?" Ben asked, though he was pretty sure he knew.

"Haley."

What else did he tell you?

Ben held back this question, dreading the answer. Most likely, Haley had told Pete about Ben being in the Vagrants, especially if the conversation had involved alcohol. But Ben didn't want to bring that subject to the surface, especially not now.

"Well, I used to play the guitar, Pete. But not anymore."

Pete let this reply sit for a moment, as if waiting for a more detailed explanation. "Do you still *have* a guitar?"

"Somewhere, I think. Why?"

"Well, in case you haven't noticed I like to sing."

"I've noticed." Hearing the irritation in his voice, Ben backpedaled. "And you're quite good at it."

"Thanks."

From the parking lot, the slam of a car door. Jenks.

"Have you heard of open-mike night? At the Wallflower Lounge?"

Ben knew nothing other than the fact that the Wallflower Lounge existed. He'd never been there, for open-mike night or anything else, and he told Pete as much.

"Well," Pete said, "I'd like to try my hand there. Even if it's just one song, just one night. So I'm wondering if you'd be willing to back me on guitar."

The burrito rolled uneasily in Ben's stomach. "I'm not so sure my fingers would be up for it, after all this time. Or my brain."

"No disrespect, Ben. But isn't it one of those things like riding a bike?"

"I don't know. I don't ride bikes. I've never tried to do anything after giving it up for twenty-some years."

"Would you be willing to give it a shot?"

While he was waiting for Ben's reply, something in the

distance caught Pete's attention and broke his concentration. Following Pete's gaze Ben spotted Jenks and waved. Then he turned back to Pete.

"Let me think about this, all right?"

✵

Ben took a ginger ale from the fridge, and when Jenks waved it away he opened the can for himself, hoping it might settle his stomach.

Jenks looked as cool and settled as ever. Despite the day's above-average heat and humidity, his shirt, a pale lavender set off by a charcoal tie, seemed fresh off the press—same as always.

After taking his usual seat behind the desk, Jenks folded his hands and sat forward: commander-in-chief stance.

"Sounds like you have some good stuff for me today, Ben. I'm eager to hear it."

Ben had made a strategic decision to begin with a Jenks-pleaser, hoping that might sweeten the pot. He took a long swig of the ginger ale, then sat down across from Jenks.

"I know you're sick of the protesters, Carl. Maybe sicker of them than I am. And I know you're worried that the exhumation might only make things worse."

Jenks raised an eyebrow, as if to say, *And?*

"What if there was a chance of getting around the exhumation altogether?"

Jenks worked his hands together absently, mulling Ben's words. "I don't much care for chances, Ben. I'm a businessman, not a gambler."

As the president of a nonprofit cemetery, Jenks wasn't exactly a businessman, not in the traditional sense. But Ben respected his caution.

"I'm talking about a chance without a downside, without a risk."

Jenks's skeptical expression didn't ease. Still, he said, "All right. Tell me what's on your mind."

Ben described his encounter with Meredith, and her suggestion about the soil sampling at the grave of the Unknown Vagrant. He reiterated her central point: the higher the acid content of the soil, the lower the chances of discovering any viable remains.

"It's a minimally invasive process, Carl, and pretty cheap, too. The tools required, and the testing, will cost about two hundred and fifty dollars. Meredith said she'd do the sampling work for free."

Jenks stayed quiet, still thinking. Then, he said, "This doesn't sound very promising. Didn't you have to add peat moss to some of those flower beds in Section C, to make them more acidic?"

Ben took another sip of his ginger ale, but his stomach continued to churn. "That was for the azaleas, and they like pretty acidic soil. Anyhow, it's unlikely that conditions are exactly the same across the grounds."

Again, Jenks raised an eyebrow.

"I think the testing is worth it, Carl. Really, I do. What do we have to lose?"

"Then go ahead and do it, Ben, with my blessing. Just don't get your hopes up too high."

Jenks paused in thought, then slowly smiled. "I'll tell you what, though. If this test gets us around the exhumation, I'll owe you something. Exactly what, I'm not sure just yet. But I'll owe you."

Ben wished he could deliver some good news right now, to call in Jenks's favor. He needed all the help he could get. As soon as he reached for the folder on the corner of the desk, he saw Jenks's smile fade.

Jenks knew what the folder contained, the gist of the contents, anyway. Ben had warned him in advance of this meeting that, once again, he wanted to talk about green burials but that now he had better numbers to make his case.

He opened the folder and took out the charts he'd spent recent nights and the past weekend putting together.

"Well, the numbers in this row aren't any news to you." Ben was pointing to the five-year sales projections for Section

E, assuming business as usual. "Now look here. These are the numbers we could get if we went green for just half of the plots, if we address that growing demand."

Already, Jenks was pulling a face. "You know how I feel about vaultless graves."

"I know. But look at the numbers. This is a twenty-percent sales increase. That's pushing half a million dollars."

As a nonprofit, the cemetery's main financial goal was keeping its day-to-day numbers out of the red, and maintaining its perpetual-care account, funded by ten percent of plot sales. If Ben's projections were accurate, the cemetery would be enough in the black to make a modest profit, at least while Section E—and the even-newer Section F—still had available plots. By investing that profit wisely, they'd be able to add to the perpetual-care fund, which Ben and Jenks had always seen as inadequate, and keep the cemetery in good shape long after the last plot was sold.

"How do you know?" Jenks asked.

"I don't *know* anything; these are projections. But pretty good ones, I think." Ben pointed out the list of cemeteries he'd contacted in other states. "All these places started offering green burials within the last few years, with about the same number of available plots. And they were more than happy to share their stats with me, for my own calculations. I got input from a couple of consultants, too. On my dime."

Jenks's face was frozen in an expression of distaste, but he was clearly listening.

"May I?" he asked.

Ben handed over the charts so Jenks could study the numbers more closely, which he did, mumbling to himself as he ran a finger along the rows.

At one point his finger stopped.

"You show a drop in columbarium inurnments and scatterings."

"Only a small one."

"But why?"

"More and more people are finding cremation isn't green

enough. They want to enter the earth simply, without the help of fire or chemicals, or two hundred pounds of casket. And, frankly, we'll make more money selling them a green plot than taking their ashes."

Jenks kept his eyes on the numbers, not looking convinced. "But we'd lose vault sales," he said. For each vault, they charged two hundred dollars.

"Yes. But we'd still make up the difference."

"If these numbers hold any water."

"I think they do."

Jenks looked no more convinced.

"Listen, Carl. I can't force these numbers on you. But I can tell you this. We can either step up and be ready to give people what they want or watch someone else take the business."

"Like who?"

"For starters, Queen of Heaven, Carlisle Heights, Lebanon Grove"—their top competitors.

Jenks yanked his tie from side to side to loosen it. But he wasn't sweating yet, not visibly.

"None of them are offering green burials," Jenks replied.

"How do you know they don't have something in the works? And I mean something *beyond* green landscaping." A not-so-subtle jab at the planned advertising for Section E.

Feeling he was finally getting through to Jenks, Ben added, "The certification process for green burials isn't that involved. I'll take charge of the whole thing myself."

"You promise?"

"We can put it in writing if you want."

Jenks stood and handed back the charts. "Congratulations. You've gotten green burials on next year's agenda."

That meant nothing would happen between now and the first of next year's board meetings: March. It also meant that the first green burial, if the plans could get through the board without the typical delays, would take place early the following year, at best.

"You don't look too pleased, Ben."

"Well, if I were you, I wouldn't be either. We're basically giving the competition a year to get ahead of us. At least a year."

"That's all speculation."

"Let's hope it is."

"Listen, Ben. I don't need to tell you that we never let haste get in the way of careful deliberation here—and sensible, financially sound decisions."

That was true. It also seemed true that nothing, in Jenks's eyes, should get in the way of tradition, the tradition of chemicals, caskets, and vaults that, to him, were not threats to the environment but necessities for a respectful departure from this world.

Ben knew it was time to lay down the only card left to him, the one he'd hoped not to play.

"What if someone asks us for a green burial now?"

"We'd tell them the truth: that we'll be carefully considering that option."

"Next year."

"Yes."

"What if they'll be dead by then?"

Until this instant Jenks's attention had already started drifting away from Ben and his charts. Now, he sat back down, fully present, a perverse look of satisfaction settling over him.

"Who are we talking about here?"

"Dolores Fielding. The mushroom—"

"I know who Dolores Fielding is."

"Both of her parents are buried here."

"Are they?"

"Yes."

"Dolores is welcome here too, of course."

"As long as she's contained in a casket and vault."

Jenks let out a breath of exhaustion. "Jesus, Ben."

"I guess I'm just wondering if there's any way we can accelerate the process, call a special board meeting or something. As a special favor to Dolores."

Jenks cast Ben a level look, as if seriously considering his proposition. Then he shook his head.

"We can't offer *special favors* to anyone, even our best friends, even our family. If we're going to go about this green burial thing thoughtfully—and fairly—we can't take any shortcuts. You need to put all those numbers you showed me into another one of your nice reports. Then get the report out to the board members, and we'll give them plenty of time to make an informed decision."

Informed, my ass, Ben thought. When he'd sent the board his last report, on the status of the Green Initiative, two of them claimed to have looked it over. But when he'd asked the others about the report, most of them said they didn't remember receiving it.

"The bottom line, Ben, is that we can't skirt the process, even for Dolores Fielding. Do you understand?"

Ben understood processes all right. They had their place, and he'd spent much of his working life honoring them, for the most part respectfully. But these gymnastics of dealing with Jenks and the board, they'd pushed Ben to his limits.

Now, Jenks sat forward and gave his knees a slap of satisfaction. "I think you scored some points today, Ben."

Not where it mattered, Ben thought. Not where Dolores Fielding was concerned. But this time he kept his mouth shut.

"Time for me to check out the Memory Garden," Jenks said. "See how things are progressing."

Ben could have told Jenks all he needed to know—that thanks to the newly planted flowers and ever-expanding foliage, the garden was well on its way to being slightly less ugly than it had been the week before.

"Let me know what you think," Ben said.

"Will do."

When Jenks was gone Ben slumped down on the couch and studied the picture on the opposite wall: a lithograph of a yellow-eyed owl. It had been part of the scenery, part of Ben's life, long enough to have been rendered nearly invisible, though certain foggy associations remained between the yellow eyes and those times in Ben's childhood when fatigue or illness, then his father's gentle urging, sent him to the couch. *Why don't you lay down, son?*

Those times, he'd stared into the owl's eyes before drifting off, usually in silence but occasionally while his father talked, hush-voiced, into the office phone.

Consider it done.

A favorite phrase of Ross's, it came back to Ben now, as clearly as if just spoken. The words were in keeping with the resolve in the eyes of the owl, which now seemed to accuse Ben of failure. He'd not won the day with Jenks, as Ross most certainly would have.

Consider it done.

"Fuck you," he said. To the owl, to Jenks, and to himself.

Ben was still staring into the yellow eyes when the idea came to him, as suddenly as if dropped from the creature's talons. He bolted up from the couch and for a moment paced the floor, more out of excitement than uncertainty about what needed to be done.

Finally, he got on his cell and dialed Pete, who picked up on the second ring. Within five minutes Pete was standing before Ben in the office.

"I'll do open-mike night with you," Ben said. "I'll play a whole damned set with you if you can help me with a little side project of mine."

"Okay," Pete said uncertainly. "What is it?"

Ben told him. And by the end of their conversation Pete seemed as grateful as Ben that the next board meeting had been delayed till the end of July.

Chapter 17

Q: Many of the works in the exhibit deal pretty directly with death. But your painting, with all those violent oranges, it calls to mind a wildfire. It makes me think of a natural disaster more than death. Was that at all intentional?
Leah Dirjery: I can't say that was intentional. But in this case, those two things are virtually the same.
Q: Can you be more specific?
LD: I think I'd like to leave it at that.

—From "An Interview with the Artists Behind 'Losses,' Now at the Baines Gallery," the Sunday *Bolster Register*

Dirjery Residence
Mid-morning

Leah pulled into the drive and parked where Ben's truck would have been, if he wasn't at work. After cutting the engine she sat for a moment, taking in what the house had come to.

Built in the mid 1800s and last renovated at the time of her and Ben's marriage, it was teetering perilously between old and charming and old and depressing. On overcast days like this one it might be judged to have taken a definitive plunge. Now more gray than white, the paint showed blisters and scales. Beneath it, dry rot had set in here and there, in the floor and posts of the porch, along window jambs and sills. Down in the cellar and up in the attic, moisture crept steadily through walls and beams, which had begun to bloom with stains and smells of mold.

On occasion—once right before the divorce and a few

times afterward—Leah and Ben talked of selling the house, which would require making it presentable. The proposal was couched in *Maybe we shoulds*, then left to drift. Last time the subject came up, they decided to wait until Cole graduated from high school—but to do what? To once again discuss putting the house on the market, or to actually make that happen? Leah couldn't remember, or maybe they'd left it vague. For now, the sale of the place—and therefore the sorrowful state of it—was nothing she and Ben were eager to talk about.

Perhaps he'd grown attached to the dampness, and the ideal climate it afforded his mushrooms. But there was another attachment that went back further, for both of them.

Leah got out of the car and headed for the back yard, the one part of the property that had been painstakingly maintained. Bordering it was a fence and the garden that bloomed steadily from April through fall. Though at the moment the peonies were drooping, fading, a good two months remained for the blue salvia, lavender, and daylilies, and those toughest of beauties, the roses, would flower in waves past the first frost, maybe through November.

Of all the rosebushes the white one bloomed the most energetically, budding without interruption throughout the season, its fist-sized blossoms bending the branches, their perfume weighting the air. Summer dawns and twilights, its flowers and shed petals floated ghostlike in the dimness, canceling everything around them.

Today marked twenty years, for the white rosebush and for their little boy. As Leah stared into the white blooms, her mind drifted back to that time.

⁂

She and Ben returned to the scene of their interrupted breakfast—eggs congealed in the frying pan, bread poised in the toaster, orange juice warm in their glasses—and left things as they were. They turned on no lights wherever it was dark. They made no phone calls, not even to their parents, all of whom they'd urged toward vacation, one last break before their first grandchild's arrival. Before long, their own phone would be ringing, for all the old reasons and soon enough for this new one.

Dreading these intrusions, Leah grabbed the line to their only phone, yanked it from the wall. She felt herself drawn to the darkest room, the front room, its curtains still closed from the night before. It was the land of unpacked moving boxes and unopened wedding gifts, baby gifts. Too tired and numb to climb up the stairs and into bed, Leah dropped into the rocking chair at the center of this shadowy mess.

All the while she held him. Within the hospital blanket he was still warm, or borrowing her warmth. To the tick of the hall clock, she rocked and rocked and rocked him, approaching the rhythm of something lasting.

The room grew darker as the clock ticked ahead, chiming through quarter hours. At the turn of the hour she counted eight chimes. Eight o'clock, and no sign of Ben.

She called his name.

No reply.

"Ben?"

She pulled herself up from the chair and carried the baby into the hall. There, behind the ticking of the clock she heard a second rhythmic striking, more weighted and distant. She followed the sound toward the back of the house, toward the kitchen filled with the last daylight. Approaching the kitchen window, squinting through the sunset's glare, she found him at the far edge of the yard, in the border garden they'd hoped to return from neglect. He was up to his waist in a hole and still shoveling, as if his life depended on how quickly, how completely, he could escape into the earth.

The hole seemed far bigger than required for the rosebush Ben had bought the day before. It lay on its side a few feet from him, its roots bound in burlap.

Leah walked out the back door and into the garden. When she stood before Ben he didn't glance her way. Yet she stayed where she was, absently stroking the baby's back, steeling herself to say what had been on her mind from the time they'd started back home.

"I'm afraid to look at him," she said. "I mean, really look at him." It seemed she'd only glimpsed him at the hospital, through the fog of denial and disbelief. "That doesn't make sense, does it?"

Ben paused to meet her gaze, holding a shovelful of dirt. "If you're trying to make sense of any of this, you're wasting your time." Then he turned back to his work.

For the sake of peace, she knew it would be best to give him what he most wanted right now, which was to be left alone. But the fact was, she was standing before him, with their child. Peace, for her, was now beside the point.

"What about you, Ben? You don't seem too interested in him at the moment."

"I'm busy, Leah."

"With *this*?" She kicked at the dirt and a clod of it flew, just missing him. "Because *this* is the most important thing right now?"

He chucked the shovel into the earth, leaned his weight into the handle.

"This isn't gardening. This isn't some leisurely fucking distraction."

"No, I don't suppose it is. What I *do* suppose is that you can't wait till he's out of sight, in the ground. As if he never happened. Then you can have your life back."

She turned from Ben and retreated, aware that he was following her.

"Leah," he called. "*Leah!*"

When he caught up to her, when he laid a hand on her arm, she didn't shrug it off. She turned to face him.

"I'm sorry," he said. "It's just that I'm feeling a bit, I don't know—I just need to feel like I'm doing something, *anything*. Do you understand?"

"I think so."

His eyes were locked on hers. For the first time since morning, he saw her.

"And, Leah? You don't have to look at him. Not if you don't want to."

She took a deep breath and with it the scent of the garden, of mingled failure and promise. Though a mold was wilting the peonies, they still perfumed the air.

"I *think* I want to," she said. "It's just that I'm afraid to. And I don't know why."

Yet she had a sense of the *why*. She held the whole of their son, a bundled beginning and end, and for now that felt like enough. Anything more seemed hazardous.

"Then give it a night's sleep. Maybe things'll be a little clearer in the morning. For both of us."

"Maybe," she said, though she doubted it. "What about you. Are you afraid to look at him?"

Ben went silent, thinking. He reached for the crook of her left shoulder, where the baby was nestled, only slightly bigger than his hand. Then he pulled away, as if fearing he'd smudge the blanket.

"I already had pictures of him, ideas of him, in my mind. And in all those pictures he was alive. So I guess I'm afraid of replacing them, canceling them out."

Leah understood. She'd made pictures, too, though she was now struggling to keep them from surfacing.

Ben gestured to where he'd been digging, where just the week before they'd uprooted two blighted rosebushes, the ones the white roses would replace.

"All the way home I imagined putting him here, in view of the house. But I should have asked you before I started in. So think of this as me asking you now. If you don't want him here, if you can't bear him here, I'll put the rosebush in this spot, and leave it at that. We'll figure out something else, for him, in the morning."

Leah wondered what difference it could make once he was in the ground, all but removed from the world. Not much, it seemed.

With Ben's help she lowered herself to the ground. Permission for him to continue his work, which he did. Making a pillow of his cast-aside shirt, she reclined onto her left side, still cradling the baby against her tired shoulder, feeling a throbbing in her breasts.

She listened as Ben found a faster rhythm, striking and shoveling the earth. This resolve of his seemed to exclude her, but most certainly not their son.

Now, twenty years on, Leah brushed aside the fallen white rose petals, revealing parts of things she'd lodged into the soil.

Year one: a tiny toy-block letter M

Year two: a sea-tumbled stone from Acadia, Maine . . .

Year six: a thumb-sized ceramic turtle . . .

Year ten: an eyeball-keychain carnival prize . . .

Year sixteen: a rusted key from her beloved old Plymouth, now in a junkyard . . .

Years. Things. Nineteen in all. All of them her best guesses about what might have pleased him.

She withdrew from her pocket two orange-swirled marbles, one for each decade.

As a child she'd seen worlds in them, whole worlds with their own churning atmospheres. Now, their swirling colors called to mind that evening all those years before, when she lay by the garden as the sky embered slowly from orange to red, when she'd listened to the strike of Ben's shovel, rhythmic and strangely comforting.

In the first light of the next day, they finally saw their son, perfectly formed at twenty-nine weeks, though the size of a slipper.

Michael Ross Dirjery.

Now, Leah pressed the marbles into the soil that was him.

Chapter 18

It's many a young band's dream: (1) Write some great songs and build a strong regional following, (2) pick the best tunes for a four-track demo, (3) get the demo into the right hands at the right time, (4) score a record deal and support for a U.S./European tour. Most bands never make it through step one. But for one local act, the Vagrants, the dream has quickly become a reality. The band has signed with Drunk Tank Records and is preparing to release its début album, "Never Here," on August 1st. Having received a pre-release copy of the album, I can assure you it is well worth a listen, and at least three of the tracks—"Yes, I Can't," "Leave Me in Peace," and "Four or Eight By Twelve"—are single-worthy. Though the Vagrants faced a setback in the middle of the recording process (the unexpected departure of singer/guitarist Nick Graves), that hasn't gotten in the way of a strong début.

— "Vagrants Prepare for Record Release, Tour," *New England Musical Express*, July 21, 1992

Section D, Lot 418

Some August predawn, 1992

Ben froze at the sound of his name.

"Pssst. Over here."

It was Vince, staring down on him from the left edge of the grave.

"You scared the shit out of me." Ben pitched aside his slop scoop, wiped his hands down his jeans.

"Sorry. There's just no good way to come up on a man in a grave."

"I thought you were in London."

"That's next week, I think."

"What do you mean, you *think*?"

"We'll get to that. First, answer me this: what the hell are you doing in that soupy hole at—I don't know—two in the morning?"

"Insomnia."

"Do you always come here when you have insomnia?"

"Not always. But someone's getting lowered into this hole later this morning, and it better not be soupy then."

Vince leaned in to get a better look, as if he were missing something. "Have the dead been known to complain about such things?"

Until quite recently, Ben had questioned this kind of detail work himself. But more and more, he was seeing this place through his father's eyes, not necessarily because he wanted to.

"The dead haven't. But the living sometimes do, the relatives. Or you can just see it on their faces when they're standing by a sorry-looking grave. And I kind of get their point."

"Ben Dirjery. Ever the perfectionist."

Ben gestured to the dirt walls surrounding him. "If these are the limits of my perfectionism, that's pretty sad."

Vince didn't agree or disagree. He sat down on the edge of the grave and fished a cigarette from his breast pocket, struck a light to it. His skin seemed paler, his eyes hollower than Ben remembered, or maybe this was a trick of the ditch lantern, the way it cast up light and shadows.

"What about you?" Ben asked. "Why are you up and around at this hour?"

Vince took a pull from his cigarette and blew a plume of smoke. "My circadian rhythms are permanently fucked."

A consequence—a necessity—of touring, Ben guessed.

"So tonight I decided to go for a drive. And when I passed this place I noticed your truck and thought I'd stop, have a look around. Then I saw your light. And I felt my soul being drawn inexplicably toward it."

Ben didn't respond to the joke. He had no idea how to respond to any aspect of Vince's unexpected appearance here. Yet he understood that in settling himself down by the grave, Vince was extending a kind of invitation, one that would be rude to refuse.

So Ben hoisted himself up and took a seat by Vince, considering how for all the hours the two of them had spent together in this cemetery, they'd never met up at an open grave. Sitting side by side, dangling their feet like two kids on a dock, might once have felt companionable if not exactly cozy given their surroundings. But now something was different. Vince seemed smaller and tenser than Ben remembered, as if his physical and emotional energy had become both more concentrated and more withdrawn. Or perhaps it was Ben who'd changed. Perhaps he'd grown thicker and more sluggish than he'd care to admit.

"Hey Vince?"

"Yeah."

"Leah and I, we plugged the phone back in."

"Okay," Vince said slowly, uncertainly.

"What I mean is, you don't have to drive all the way to the cemetery to reach me."

"Good to know."

When Ben and Leah lost the baby, the Vagrants were touring out West. And the first week in July, he received a letter from Vince, bearing a Tempe, Arizona, postmark, and taking up three pages torn from a Wagon Wheel Inn notepad. At the time Ben received the letter, he and Vince had been out of touch for months, during which their lives had barreled down sharply diverging paths. When Ben learned he was to be a father, he resolved to do all he could to be worthy of the title. That began with quitting the Vagrants, understanding he couldn't do both the band and fatherhood justice. It continued with working longer hours to save money, preparing—with Leah—for marriage and their baby's arrival, and with devoting any remaining time to the increasingly remote prospect of finishing college. Vince, for his part, had been occupied with rehearsing, recording, and preparing for months on the road. That, anyway, was what Ben had imagined for his old friend in the absence of specific details. In the letter from Tempe, Vince told Ben he'd heard what happened with the baby. He said how sorry he was. He said he'd tried calling Ben's phone number at different times but no one ever picked up. He'd gotten worried enough to call Ross, who said it would be best to write to Ben, not explaining, at least so far as Vince had indicated, about Ben and Leah's phone being out of commission, about Leah's case for keeping it that way.

In his letter, Vince never mentioned how the recording wound down. Nor did he make the mistake of bitching about touring. His narrative of life on the road, illustrated by occasional instant-camera photographs, was both specific and evasive.

Some of the specifics that stayed with Ben:

Spent two days in Las Cruces: one gig, one bad case of the flu (me). A hawk stood guard outside our motel window and I watched him for hours, whenever I wasn't sleeping. (This with a picture of a hawk on a rusted railing, his checkered brownish back to the camera.) *Little worried that from now on hawks will remind me of the flu, but it might be kind of nice if the flu reminds me of hawks. . . .*

What the fuck might explain the fact that since we left Texas I've had at least three dreams about waiting in long lines in institutional settings? (No picture for this one.)

The evasive part was that Vince never spoke directly about the music, or about how the shows were going, or about the inevitable comings and goings of women—though one photograph, intended to capture a framed sign on a wall opposite Vince's bed ("Bedtime prayers count double at the Seventh Day Motel") also captured his legs and the left leg, bare and white and shapely, of an unidentified female companion. Her leg, not the sign, persisted in Ben's thoughts.

Dave and Tuke were mentioned, but only in passing and never in reference to their music. A single picture offered Ben's only sight of them: Dave on top of Tuke, pinning him to the grass of some roadside or park, Tuke laughing.

Rick Boskin was absent from both the letter and the photographs, his presence suggested only by his guitar case, propped in the background of a picture of something else.

Ben understood that in all these evasions Vince had been trying to protect him, to spare him, so far as this was in Vince's powers, from envy and regret. Yet Ben also knew that if their friendship was to be sustained it could not exclude music—including the Vagrants', maybe especially the Vagrants'. This meant it was up to him to make the first move.

"I listened to the album," he said, "and it's really good. *All* of it." Meaning not just the tracks Ben had contributed to.

Vince never accepted compliments easily, as if he didn't trust them. When it was clear he wasn't going to respond to this one, Ben said, "So what about this *maybe* with London? You want to tell me about that?"

Vince held his silence a moment longer, his cigarette hand faintly trembling. A case of nerves? That wasn't like him, Ben thought.

"I want Boskin out of the band," Vince said. "Before we do any more recording. If that means he doesn't want to stick around for the first part of the European tour, I'll have to figure something out."

"It's that bad?"

"For me it is. Dave and Tuke, they're coming around to seeing my side of things. Or maybe my misery is just rubbing off on them."

"What do you mean, your side of things?"

Vince took another pull from his cigarette then leaned back so he could look Ben in the eye.

"The guy's the best guitar player I've ever worked with."

Including me, Ben thought.

"But it was a mistake for me to think we could figure out songs together. Maybe I just wanted to believe we could."

"You disagree about things?"

"Yeah, we disagree about things. But it's something more basic than that. It gets down to the level of chemistry, of which we have none."

Vince leaned forward, ready to flick his cigarette ash into the grave, until he saw the look on Ben's face.

"Here," Ben said, handing Vince an empty soda can.

"Sorry. Wasn't thinking." Vince tapped the ash into the can.

"So you were saying there's no chemistry."

"That's right. And I'll take some of the blame for that. I mean, the guy tries. Or tried. In the beginning he came to me with ideas, bits of songs. And maybe I should have given them more of a chance before shit-canning them. But I just have this strongly negative, almost visceral, reaction to what he thinks a song is. Like I'm almost allergic to it."

Vince stabbed out his cigarette and dropped it into the can. "I don't mean to sound dramatic, Ben. But that's the way things are for me."

"What about for Boskin?"

"Well, how would you like it if the guy you're supposed to be writing songs with shut down everything you suggested?"

Ben had been shut down by Vince on a few occasions himself. But he'd also pushed back when he thought a possibly good song—or the start of a possibly good song—was being too easily dismissed. Somehow, the two of them worked through such disagreements and came out the other end with something decent, or with a mutual agreement to cut their losses and move on.

"It's at the point, Ben, where the problem between Boskin and me, it's really gotten in the way. For the whole band. The last leg of our tour in the States, the two of us were barely speaking to each other. The only times I'd see him would be during gigs. I don't think it's any coincidence that our last few shows sounded like shit."

Glass smashed in the distance, almost certainly the work of a bottle tosser.

Vince raised an eyebrow. "Is that something you need to deal with?"

"Not now. I'll clean it up later."

"It must be weird being on the receiving end of this night-time shit."

135

"It's more annoying than weird. You and me, we never left trash behind, much less broken glass."

"Kids today."

"Yeah, kids today."

A wave of drowsiness rolled through Ben. If he headed home now and crawled right into bed, he might actually be able to fall asleep. But there was work to be finished, and for the sake of the caffeine, he cracked open a fresh soda, took a cold, fizzy gulp of it.

"About Boskin," Ben said. "Mind if I play devil's advocate?"

"Go for it."

"Those two songs on the album that were new to me. 'Never Here,' and the other one." Ben couldn't remember the name.

"'Yes, I Can't.'"

"Yeah, that one. Those songs are proof to me that the two of you can put out good stuff. It might be a rough process, and not much fun for either of you, but *something's* working. And I think it might be worth taking some time to figure out what that is. Then maybe you can focus on that instead of whatever it is that's making you break out in hives."

Ben downed more of the soda. As he set the can back on the grass he saw Vince glaring at him. In the eerie underlighting of the ditch lantern, he looked almost psychopathic.

"Okay," Ben said. "What did I step in now?"

"Was there anything in particular you noticed about those two songs? Anything at all familiar?"

Ben never did well under the pressures of inquisition. At the moment the songs were a blur in his brain.

"How about the chorus in 'Yes, I Can't'?" Vince hummed a few bars to jog Ben's memory. "How about this little bit in 'Never Here'?" Vince let some of this one fly, too.

Isolated in this way, captured in hums familiar to Ben from hours and hours of practices with Vince, hours and hours of *What about this?* sessions, the snippets finally fell into place: they were bits of things that he and Vince had come up with together, bits of things that, however promising they seemed at the time of their creation, never became whole songs. Not, at least, when the two of them had been working together.

"I get it, Vince. You can stop."

Vince did, his glare softening into something nearly sympathetic.

"Listen, Ben. I just want you to understand that when you say you like the album, you're complimenting yourself. And I want you to know that it's the last of the decent music I'm ever going to put out with Boskin, because it's the last of the stuff I worked on with you."

A second bottle smashed in the distance, followed by laughter—a girl's answered by a boy's. The sounds of lives still light on complications.

"You see what I'm getting at?"

The soda Ben had gulped seemed to have turned to churning acid. He swallowed hard to keep it in its place. "You want me to come back in. In place of Boskin."

"Just think about it. Right now, that's all I'm asking."

The smart move would be to give Vince an immediate *No,* with all the resolve that might make it convincing. Instead, Ben said, "If you want an answer before the London dates, that gives me a week. Maybe not even that."

Vince shrugged. "Take a couple of weeks. Take a month even. I'm pretty sure Boskin will stick with me through the first part of the tour. And if he doesn't want to, I'll work around that."

"What makes you think he'll go quietly? And what about the recording contract? Doesn't it bind you to him, in some way?"

Vince reached toward his breast pocket for another cigarette, but his hands were now shaking hard enough to make this impossible. Contract jitters? Low blood sugar? Ben tried to push aside the stories he'd heard about Vince and drugs, harder drugs than pot.

Vince changed course and brushed a palm down his jacket, as if smoothing it had been his intention all along. "I bet he'll be as relieved as I'll be to end things."

"What makes you think that?"

"He's already talking to another band."

"How do you know?"

Vince smiled. "A scoop from a reliable source. As for the contract, I'm sure we can strike a deal that'll satisfy everyone. It's nothing you have to think about. Not right now, anyway."

The things that Ben *did* have to think about were of no consequence to Vince. Finishing college. Trying for another child. Those could wait. But Leah couldn't be—didn't deserve to be—put on hold, or worse.

The image of that bare and shapely leg, the one from Vince's photograph, had lingered for some time in the back of Ben's mind. Now, it resurfaced, conjuring more fear than desire. It would be hard to find a better temptation to becoming just like his father, in none of the good ways, than hitting the road with the Vagrants.

More than once, Ben had complained to Leah about Ross's infidelities. At the time this felt like simply letting off steam, but it was also possible that he was trying to reassure her, as much as himself, that he'd been inoculated from the willingness—no, the eagerness—to yield to temptation.

Ben wasn't reassured. Whether Leah had been, he had no idea.

He also had no idea how Leah might react if and when he asked her about possibly returning to the Vagrants. On the one hand, she'd always encouraged him in his music, just as he'd tried to encourage her in her own art. As much as he understood that drawing and painting were essential to Leah, she understood how important it was for him to make time for his music, even if on some days that amounted to idly strumming the guitar in front of the television, between supper and bedtime.

On the other hand, Ben couldn't forget Leah's reaction when he'd told her of his decision to quit the Vagrants, after learning of her pregnancy. Though she'd asked, "Are you sure?" he could tell from the way she took his hand, from the shine in her eyes, that he was doing the right thing by her.

Ben couldn't forget, either, what she'd said after they lost the baby: *You can have your life back.* If *his life* meant no Leah, and no second chance at having a child with her, he wasn't interested.

"Listen, Vince," Ben said now. "I'm honored that you're asking me to work with you again. I truly am. But at this point in my life, I'm—"

I'm someone's husband now. I'm on the path to a more settled life. Ben thought this but said nothing.

"Don't answer me now. Just *think* about it. Can we agree to that? For even just a few days?"

"But I really don't—"

"Hold it right there."

With a now-steady hand, Vince reached into his jacket and withdrew a cassette tape, handed it to Ben.

"Some stuff I've been working on. Why don't you listen to it, see if it sparks any ideas."

Ben took the tape, understanding what accepting it meant. As he tucked the tape into his shirt pocket it occurred to him that Vince's presence here, not to mention the convenient availability of his songs-in-progress, was unlikely a mere coincidence. Vince's unfailing shrewdness irked Ben now, as it had many times before. Still, he couldn't help but admire it.

"I should let you get back to work." Vince pushed himself up and onto his feet.

Ben followed his lead, but not before glancing back into the lamp-lit grave, soon to be home to a retired bank administrator. According to his obituary, he'd rediscovered in his later years "a passion for playing the violin." Had Ben been less of a skeptic he might have been tempted to see personal significance in this detail, on this night.

"How about I call you in a couple of days?" Vince said. "Just to check in."

"Sure."

Vince started for the exit, then turned around.

"The resurrection of Nick Graves," he said. "Sounds almost like a song, doesn't it?"

"Sounds more like a horror movie."

Vince smiled. "All right, Ben. Good night."

As Vince made his way back to the East Gate, Ben stayed where he was, out of the grave. He looked toward the parking lot, waiting for Vince's headlights to switch on; then he watched them glide down the lane to the Old Post Road. Once Vince had disappeared, Ben headed for the parking lot himself and started up his truck. He pushed the tape into the cassette deck and pressed play.

It was just Vince on his guitar—no other instruments, no singing, though here and there Vince hummed hints of vocals or counter-melodies, parts for another guitar. There were no neat breaks suggesting individual songs; tune and style and rhythm changed smoothly, with grace and intention, as if Vince were telling a single, chaptered story.

Ben listened his way through both sides of the tape then hit replay, now and then humming counter-melodies of his own. He hit replay again, and again and again. At some point the first sun hit his windshield, bringing him back to the world and the press of time.

He had to go home and get his parts down before they dissolved into the day.

Chapter 19

On occasion, he was spotted traveling by night, always lanternless. It seemed he was glad for the cover of darkness.

—An observation about the Unknown Vagrant, a.k.a., the Roamer, from *Bolster County Tales and Curiosities*, 1893

Grave of the Unknown Vagrant
After sunset (present day)

Ben checked his phone and saw that it was 8:41, eleven minutes after the appointed meeting time. He continued pacing the roadside, just behind the orange pylons, hoping he'd come around to seeing the comical aspects of being stood up at a gravesite, should that be necessary.

It wasn't. A minute or so later a car pulled into the turnaround just east of him, the spot where he'd told her to park. Once she cut her lights, he walked over to meet her.

"Sorry-sorry-sorry!" She called from her open window.

In the dimness he saw that she was dressed like a cat burglar, in a long-sleeved T-shirt and tights, both black, her hair swept up under a black baseball cap.

"My mom can't figure out the new TV I got her, and one of her shows was coming on."

"No problem," Ben said. He looked to the back seat, spied a long cardboard shipping box and a duffel bag. "May I?" he asked, nodding toward them.

"Help yourself. The door's unlocked."

Ben got the box under one arm and the duffel over the

other. Then he followed Meredith, who was once again toting her backpack, to the gravesite. There, she pulled a tarp from her pack and spread it on the ground next to the grave.

Ben grabbed his keys and broke through the tape on the shipping box. From the return address, Ben supposed it contained the soil-sampling tools Meredith said her university colleagues would send her. Thanks to them, and Meredith, the cemetery would have to cover only the costs of shipping, some miscellaneous supplies, and the lab work.

"Seems pretty quiet here tonight," she said, unzipping the duffel. "Or did I miss something?"

"There were a couple of sign carriers when I got here, but I asked them if they could kindly leave, and they did. Told them I needed to administer a lawn treatment and that no one should tread on the grass here for at least two hours. No one but us, that is."

Meredith paused in unpacking the duffel. "I'm impressed. You're really good with the bullshit."

Ben didn't know whether to take this as a compliment. "That's our line if anyone else comes along. Let's hope they keep buying it."

Their main goal, aside from getting the soil samples, was to work as quickly as possible. As Ben had told Meredith during their planning phone call the night before, his greatest fear was that someone would spot them and suspect that the exhumation was underway. Then, through some magic phone or texting tree, word would spread like wildfire, and a crowd would descend before he and Meredith could bag their last sample. Or so he imagined.

Meredith took a box from the duffel and handed it to Ben: rubber gloves. He snapped on a pair, and she did the same. Part of the protocol Meredith described the night before, the gloves would help prevent contamination of the soil samples. As Ben and Meredith unpacked the shipping box, the rest of the protocol ran through his head: After Meredith marked the sampling sites—eight altogether—they'd remove, at each site, grass plugs the width of the augers. Then they'd use the augers to pull the samples from the ground.

Because Meredith's colleagues had sent her two sets of augers and extension poles, necessary for going deep into the ground, she and Ben would be able to divide and conquer, tackling four sites apiece and having a prayer of getting the job done within a half hour. Already, Ben was beginning to doubt that estimate. He struggled so long to assemble the extension-pole-and-handle contraption that Meredith had to step in to help.

Getting the samples was no easier for Ben, not at first. "Push and twist right," Meredith repeated, until he got the hang of it, feeling like the laggard in gym class. When the auger was full, he followed Meredith's lead, depositing the contents into one of eight plastic containers lined up on the tarp. Then he returned for another sample, *Push and twist right,* until he reached the required depth.

Eventually, Ben fell into enough of a groove that his mind began to drift, the prevailing current leading it to Meredith, about whom he knew so little. In the course of their phone conversations, he managed to learn that she'd recently gotten her Ph.D. in forensic anthropology, and that she'd soon be heading to Arizona for postdoctoral work—something to do with identifying the remains of people who'd died, undocumented, while crossing from Mexico to the United States. He wanted to know more about her, hoped he might have the chance to. But for now, he appreciated the companionable silence that fell between them as they worked ahead on their mission. She might have been Pete or Haley, except for the fact that Ben had never been so aware of Pete or Haley's presence in relation to his own, had never tracked their motions so keenly, almost viscerally.

In the middle of his work on the third site, something weighted dropped from the auger as Ben emptied it, not a stone. Using his phone as a flashlight, he knelt and found a rusted spike the length of a finger. Before he could call her over, Meredith was at his side.

"Is this what I think it is?" he asked.

Meredith stooped for a closer look. "If you think it's a coffin nail, you're probably right. But that's not necessarily a bad sign. Nails can outlast remains."

Still, Ben detected disappointment in her voice, and he himself felt suddenly uneasy, reminded of just where they were standing, remembering that *noninvasive* was only a relative term. This was someone's grave, someone who almost certainly wouldn't appreciate being the subject of a soil probe.

"Come on," she said. "We're almost done."

By the time they got to their final sites, full darkness had fallen, and fewer and fewer cars were passing by. All the while, only a couple of them had slowed, seemingly out of curiosity. Once Ben and Meredith had re-plugged the holes in the turf, packed up the tools and samples, and gotten everything into Meredith's car, Ben checked his phone.

"Nine thirty-six," he announced.

"Not too shabby."

"Pretty damn good, I'd say."

Meredith slung her backpack over her shoulder and reached for the driver's-side door, a gesture that made Ben's heart sink.

"I'll ship the samples to the processing lab tomorrow," she said. "We should have results a few days after that."

"That's great, Meredith, thanks. Thanks for everything you did."

In the pause between those words and her opening the car door, Ben found his courage.

"As a token of my appreciation, would you let me take you out for a drink?"

She smiled a little warily, as if once again appreciating his talent for bullshit. "Sure," she said, after a beat. "I can't stay out for long, but a drink would be nice."

"Great. I just need to make a call. To my daughter. Tell her I'm going to be home a little later than I'd expected."

Daughter. There it was, out in the open. Ben felt relieved, then foolish for feeling relieved. Just where did he think things with Meredith were going to go?

At that moment he decided to look just one drink into his future. Then he got on the phone to Cole.

Chapter 20

Robert Morris Godwin
March 21, 1878 – October 5, 1933
Devoted Husband and Father, Master Locksmith
"Few things are more sacred than privacy." –R.M.G.

—Gravestone for Lot 132, Section B

Parking Lot and Office

Mid-evening, two days later

Every day since last Friday, her father's truck and Pete's old Honda had sat side by side in the parking lot, till nearly sunset. Like shells of the men themselves.

Tonight, by the time Cole pulled into the lot, the truck stood alone. She drove up beside it, cut her engine, and listened. Through her open window came the pulse of night bugs, and over this something more insistent: the sound of her father's guitar, the acoustic.

The previous week, she'd caught him loading it into his truck.

She must have looked as surprised as she'd felt; he paused and gave her a *What?* look.

"I'm doing a favor for Pete," he said. "And it's *quid pro quo.*"

He explained that Pete was planning to sing a few tunes— all or most of them covers—at some hole-in-the-wall bar in Carlisle. Ben agreed to back him on guitar in return for Pete doing some OT prep work for the board meeting, something related to the Green Initiative. Something involving a lot of phone calls. When Cole asked for specifics, Ben seemed reluctant to share them. ("Let's call it telemarketing," he'd said. "For a good cause.") The main thing he wanted Cole to know was that between the OT work and the set rehearsals with Pete, he'd be spending some long days at the cemetery office.

Now, Cole climbed from her car and, wanting to keep things quiet, nudged the door closed. As she neared the office the sound of the guitar intensified. He was cycling through a riff with increasing force, a riff from no song she recognized. She crept toward the sound, toward the light pooled before the office's screen door, and sat down just at the edge of the darkness. She listened as he continued with the riff, now with new, less intense variations. Behind the guitar she heard his voice, a strained cross between growling and humming. He wasn't singing so much as arguing with the music. And behind the strumming and the complaint of his voice, a fainter tune layered the air—a recorded second guitar.

Pete's?

But Pete didn't play the guitar, not as far as Cole knew. And whatever Ben was working on at this moment, whatever he was listening to, it didn't sound like a cover, at least not like any cover she'd heard. Her best guess was that he'd recorded a lead guitar part and was now working out a rhythmic base for it. Or was it the other way around?

"*Shit!*" he cried.

He stopped playing, apparently having screwed up, and the recorded guitar ceased with a mechanical *thunk*.

In the lengthening silence that followed, Cole froze, fearing he sensed her presence. But nothing shadowed the light from the door, and soon she heard the whir of a tape rewinding and stopping, then once again the sound of the recorded guitar, followed by his acoustic.

As he played on, the growl-humming took shape, and he began to sing:

Rocks and dirt and rusted nails
Random as starlight, random as tea leaves

Rocks and dirt and rusted nails
No business of mine, I see what I shouldn't see

Rocks and dirt and rusted nails
Random as starlight, random as tea leaves
Rocks and dirt and rusted nails
No business of mine, I see what I want to see

Cole found her attention drifting away from the words, toward the bass-baritone roll of his voice, rich and strangely familiar. Another nearly lost memory from her childhood, perhaps. Just like the one of him playing guitar behind a closed door, long after her bedtime, when she should have been deep asleep.

Rocks and dirt and rusted nails
Random as starlight, random as—

The office phone rang, stopping him once again.

He answered on the fifth ring. "Yeah? . . . Isn't it on a timer now? . . . Okay. I'll go out and check it. . . . No problem, have a good night."

Cole bolted to her feet, considering her options: stand there and face him or make a run for it. By the time the screen door slammed, she was halfway to her car. She whirled around and headed toward him, as if she'd just arrived.

"Hey, Dad," she called, stopping him on his way to the gate.

"Cole. What brings you here?"

"It was getting so late, I thought you might be hungry. Do you want me to bring you a pizza or something?" That had been the original intention of her visit.

"No, thanks. I'll be ready to get out of here in a few minutes. Maybe we could grab a bite together, unless you already ate."

"Sure," she said. "That sounds good."

"I just need to check a pump in Section A. Then we can hit the road."

Cole followed him through the gate and toward Section A.

As they made their way to the pump station she couldn't help but glance around for other members of the after-hours crowd, excluding Grif, Miranda, and Alex. They—and now Cole, when she was with them—never climbed the gates until the main lot was empty, until the last light had drained from the sky.

Once her dad had checked the settings on the pump, he eased himself onto a bench, patted the spot next to him.

"Sit down a sec, Cole. I need to tell you something." When he saw the look on her face, he said. "Don't worry, you're not in trouble. Though *I* might be."

"What do you mean?"

"One of your teachers called me today. Ms. Gale."

"Shit."

"You know what this is about?"

"I think so. She asked you about having a concert in the cemetery. To protest the dig."

"That's right. She also said it was her idea to call me, not yours. She didn't want you to be in the middle of this."

"What did you tell her?"

"What do you think?"

Cole tried to imagine a G-rated version of *No fucking way.*

"I wish she would have checked with me first, Dad. I would have told her not to bother. I mean, there's a total conflict of interest on the issue, where the cemetery's concerned. Especially where you're concerned."

In the nearly expired light, Cole tried to read his expression. It was as neutral as if he were waiting for a bus.

"I don't blame her for trying," Ben said. "I mean, she had to figure it was worth a shot, considering my daughter is one of her students. And considering you'll be in the headlining band."

He kept the same neutral expression.

"She told you about that?"

"Yes, Cole, she told me about that. But did you think I'd never find out? And did you really think I'd care when I did?"

Yes, she really did. But to spare him the awkward ins and outs of her logic, she didn't bother explaining herself.

"Honestly, Cole? I don't care if you headline a protest of

tombstones, as long as it's something you really want to do. And as long as the kids you're working with keep it clean. Do you know what I'm talking about?"

Cole nodded. "All of them go to Bolster Academy."

Ben shrugged as if to say *Big deal.* "When I was in high school, some of the biggest druggies went to Bolster Academy. And they could afford to maintain a pretty serious habit."

Cole lowered her gaze, worried that a truth was written all over her face: that she herself might be defined as a *druggie*, if that definition still included smoking pot.

Well, you aren't a druggie anymore, she told herself.

A week or so before, she'd finished the joint from her lab partner and decided she didn't want another. She didn't like the way pot made her feel—a little outside of herself and therefore at risk of saying, or doing, something stupid.

She worked up the nerve to look her dad in the eye. "Well, the ones I'm playing with aren't druggies. They don't like drinking either." That wasn't entirely true. Miranda and Alex had downed more than a couple of beers in Cole's presence.

"Good," Ben said, though he didn't seem comforted by her words. Cole wondered if he was thinking about what had happened with Vince Resklar.

"All right," he said at last. "Let's get something to eat."

He got up from the bench, and Cole followed.

"Hey, Dad?"

"Yeah."

"Are you glad to be playing the guitar again?"

Again, the neutral look and shrug. "It's all right, I guess. Better than getting a colonoscopy."

"C'mon, Dad. *Really?*"

"Really. How much fun do *you* think it would be, playing covers? And I don't mean off-the-beaten-path quirky ones. I mean the ones that *everyone's* sick of."

What she'd heard him playing in the office didn't sound like a cover, but for now she wouldn't mention this. Nor would she mention the Vagrants cover her own band was working on.

"It sounds way more fun than a colonoscopy." In fact, it

149

sounded like he was really into the song he was working on, like it was about more than just helping out Pete.

"Next time I'm playing, I'll try to remember that."

Chapter 21

We throw our art out there into the world, and then sometimes it disappears. Nothing lasts in life. There's something about that ephemeral quality that appeals to me.

—Threep Parlour, founder of Yarn Bomb Ojai, quoted in "The Yarn Bombing Movement Hits the Streets," *Highbrow Magazine*

Parking Lot and Memory Garden

Just after 11 p.m., June 24

"Let me carry something," Martha said.

All of Martha's supplies fit in a single diminutive satchel. Peg's, on the other hand, required two hefty-size duffels and a hiker's backpack, to which she'd bungeed the support poles for her crochet work.

Peg hoisted on her backpack, then pulled the stepladder from her trunk. "Think you can manage this?"

"Sure."

They made their way from the parking lot to the Memory Garden in silence, Martha having given up on questioning Peg about her plans for the garden, as had other Bolster Needlers. Peg's repeated response to their questioning ("You'll find out soon enough") had been enough to tamp it down.

Lately at the Needlers' meetings, Peg crocheted coil upon coil, chain upon chain, corkscrew upon corkscrew of reds, yellows, and oranges, so intent upon her work that she paid only partial attention to the chatter about others' yarn-bombing works-in-progress: the knitted woodland creatures for Goodale Park, the elaborate light-post swags for Welton Road, the colorful bike-rack and bench cozies for Bolster Square.

Now and then Martha cast Peg worried looks over her knitting, as if wondering why her usually talkative friend had withdrawn so deeply into herself. Always, Peg smiled to reassure her friend. In truth, she'd rediscovered a nearly pure contentment in crocheting and knitting, which had evaded her since Roger's death. The needlework was newly purposeful for her, not a mere distraction from sadness.

As for why Peg had deferred questions about the ultimate purpose of her crocheted coils and chains, she would have put it down to fear, a fear of setting up expectations and, consequently, risking disappointment, both her own and others'. Even now, as she and Martha set down the makings of the work for the Memory Garden, Peg wasn't certain her execution of the thing would equal her plans.

"When should we reconnect?" Martha asked now, checking her watch. "Eleven thirty? Quarter to twelve?"

"How about twelve?" Peg said. "I think I'm going to need a little more time."

"That sounds fine," Martha said. "I'll come get you then."

Peg watched Martha depart for the grave of the Unknown Vagrant, knowing what lay in store there; Martha had spoken openly of her plans as she'd gone about her knitting. She'd created a sweater-like shroud for the Vagrant's gravestone: comfort and protection for the legendary recluse—in Martha's words, "a shield from banal curiosity." She'd also crocheted tendrils to stake in front of the stone, in the same dark blues, greens, and purples as the shroud. Martha intended them to suggest truths that might bubble up from the grave.

"Beautiful," Peg had said, when Martha showed off her finished work, and that was the truth.

Now, as Peg unbungeed the poles from her backpack, as she started unpacking the coils and chains, she feared the adjectives that might be used in connection with her work when the next day dawned. To steel herself, she tried to picture Roger at her side.

"Keep going, stay focused," he would have said. "And remember: the most important thing is to please yourself." He'd said that so often about his own art, and about Peg's knitting.

As Peg worked ahead, she looked toward the birch tree and its fallen branch, which glowed green even at this distance, seemingly brighter than before. Was it possible the mushrooms had multiplied?

She took their glow as encouragement, a sign that there was reason for hope.

Chapter 22

Today is the last day of the world. The sun will not set, the light never wane. We've reached the knot of eternity. . . . The word of light has been spoken and has lived by our hands, in our bodies and in the things we made. . . . As I turn to dust, I turn to light.

—From *Awakening Osiris: A New Translation of The Egyptian Book of the Dead,* by Normandi Ellis

General Grounds and Memory Garden

Early morning, June 25

"Leah, it's Ben. If you get this message before you pick up Cole, could you stop by the cemetery for a minute? It's nothing to worry about. I just want to show you something. Only if you have time. Okay, thanks."

On the chance she'd show up, Ben took his breakfast out to the parking lot and watched the road. Sure enough, as he downed the last of his egg sandwich, her car emerged from the fog and pulled into the lot.

As Leah got out of her car and made her way toward him, he was struck by how different she seemed. A new haircut? He didn't think so. A bit more color in her cheeks? Maybe, maybe not. The bottom line was, she looked more at ease, more content than she had in some time, and Ben wanted to feel happy for her. It was the least he could do.

"Sorry to take you out of your way," he said.

"That's all right. Cole and I have plenty of time."

She glanced over his shoulder, toward the front gate. "I hope you don't have some kind of disaster on your hands."

"I don't think so. But you might have to be the judge of that."

"*Me?*"

"You'll see what I mean. Just follow me."

On this morning, the cemetery was spooky in a Victorian sort of way—the grass a bright English green from the rain, the low fog obscuring all but the nearest stones and statuary. The two of them tramped forward with care, Ben looking out for the first signs of the new addition to the Memory Garden. Soon enough, its colors emerged from the mists.

From a central pole, rays of yellow, gold, orange, red, and rust extended out to thinner poles of various heights, which encircled the garden. Each ray was made up of chains, corkscrews, or coils of yarn. The result was an imitation sunset, its beams forming a canopy over the scattering ground and the surrounding benches.

"Holy shit," Leah said.

Ben couldn't tell whether she was impressed or appalled, or both.

"Someone did all this overnight," he said. "If you can believe it."

"Yeah, I can believe it. It seems you've been yarn bombed, my friend."

"There's a name for this?"

"Yep. One of my art-school buddies blogged about it a month or so ago. But if you go looking, you'll find pictures of this kind of stuff all over the internet."

As Leah explained this phenomenon, this "temporary form of public art," Ben again took note of the ever-widening canyon between himself and popular culture.

"Let me ask you something," he said when she'd finished. "What do you think of this?"

"Of yarn bombing?"

"Of *this* yarn bombing."

"Well, what do *you* think, Ben?"

Feeling cornered, he tried to dodge the question. *"You're the artist. Not me."*

Absently she shook a pole, watched water droplets scatter onto the foliage. She seemed to be taking in the structure of the thing.

"But you know this space better than anyone, and that means something. It gives you a kind of authority I don't have here."

"I doubt it."

"Come on. Just tell me what you think."

He described to Leah his first impression of the thing, how it seemed to have been woven from above rather than raised up from below, like the web of some alien spider. He told her how he'd come to appreciate that despite the brightness and strangeness of the work—or maybe because of them—it seemed to suit the space. It took the parts of the Memory Garden and made some kind of whole.

"So you like it," Leah said.

"Yes, I guess I do. Actually, I like it very much."

Ben waited for Leah to express her own views, but whatever they were, she kept them to herself.

"There's another reason I wanted to bring you here," he said. "Hold on a sec."

He crossed the garden to the farthest pole and reached up to one of the yarn chains extending from it. Clipped to the chain was a ziplock bag, and inside the bag was a postcard. Ben took down the bag and handed the postcard to Leah.

On the back of the card, some unidentified person, presumably the yarn bomber, had written "Perpetual Sunset" in large block letters. Beneath this, in smaller letters: "Inspired by the work of Leah Dirjery." The painting on the front of the card was Leah's, and Ben remembered the art exhibit it advertised, another exhibit he hadn't made it to. At the time, he'd been afraid to ask her how this particular painting connected to the show's theme ("Losses"), sensing there was a whole sad story behind the work, a story he most likely played a part in.

Now, he regretted showing her the card. She seemed close to tears.

"I'm sorry, Leah. I didn't mean to upset you."

"It's okay," she said, handing back the card, collecting herself. "*I'm* okay."

She stepped back to get a wider view of the yarn bombing, looking from pole to pole, from the lowest point to the highest.

"You know, I'm actually honored that I had the smallest thing to do with this. It feels genuine."

That was, perhaps, the highest praise the work would receive from her.

"Well," he said. "Enjoy it while you can. It won't be here long."

"Ah," she said, as Ben's meaning came to her. "The ire of Carl." Carl Jenks. "Has he seen this yet?"

"No, he's off for a few days. But when he's back, he'll blow a gasket about it. Or sooner than that, if someone gets word to him."

Another scene sure to repulse Jenks was the Unknown Vagrant's grave, variously sheathed in or sprouting knitted gloom. Thankfully, the yarn bomber—or bombers—had left the rest of the cemetery, including Vince's plot, alone.

"Let me ask you something, Ben. If there were a way to keep this thing, would you like that?"

"It's not up to me, Leah. There's a whole approval process it would have to go through."

"I'm not talking about approval processes. For now, let's just start with you. Would you like this thing to become a permanent installation, if such a thing were possible?"

"Hell yes. It's a huge fucking improvement over things as they stand now."

"I agree. So do me a favor. Before you have to rip this thing down, take a bunch of pictures of it, from all sides and angles. Then send them to me. And when Cole and I are back from the college visits, I'll ask my sculptor friends for some suggestions."

"About what?"

"Well, they might know of all-weather materials that could be substituted for the yarn. And if they think something more permanent is possible, I'd be happy to work up some drawings for the cemetery board. Or whoever needs to approve this stuff."

From the parking lot, a door slam: most likely Pete reporting for duty.

"It sounds like a lot of work," Ben said. "Are you sure you have time?"

"I'm guessing it would take a few hours, tops. And I'm happy to do it."

As they neared the gate to the parking lot, Leah paused and turned to Ben.

"Do you have any idea who the yarn bomber might be?"

"Not a clue. Why?"

"I'd like to get in touch with this person, if possible. Maybe pick their brain."

"If I learn anything, I'll let you know."

With that, Ben watched her continue on to the gate, a spring in her step. Then she vanished into the fog.

Chapter 23

Without music, life would be a mistake.

—Friedrich Nietzsche

Office and General Grounds

After sunset

Haley parked next to Ben's truck, happy to see it was still there despite the hour. So was New Pete's car, which would have been indistinguishable from other late-nineties Civics if not for its bumper sticker: "Warning: Driver Singing."

Why the late shift—for both of them? Possible reasons played through Haley's mind: a last-minute request to open a grave, a DEFCON 3 issue with the ever-troubled irrigation system, another crisis with the pumps in Sections A or B.

Approaching the office, Haley saw that the lights were on, but when he tried the door it was locked. He rapped at the door, waited, then took the old key from his wallet, the key he hadn't been able to bring himself to hand over on his last day at the cemetery. So far, Ben hadn't asked for it back.

Haley unlocked the door and stepped into the office, which seemed to have just been fled: the radio on the mini-fridge murmuring news, a breeze from an open window rustling papers on the desk. Alongside the dig register was a sweating, open can of Ben's beverage of choice: ginger ale.

Haley had come here on a mission, and now he set off to accomplish it. He made for the left file cabinet, pulled out the bottom drawer, and removed from behind the last file a

159

paper-swaddled package. Inside it was a handmade weed pipe identical to one Haley had seen Pete smoke from a day or so after he met him, an "artisanal" work of blue-glazed ceramic, created by Pete's cousin. ("She's making a killing with these things," Pete explained, "on Etsy.")

Knowing his wife would love the pipe—she had a collection of about twenty, in nearly as many colors—Haley put in an order through Pete and received the pipe during his last week at the cemetery. Not wanting his wife to discover it before her birthday arrived, Haley had stashed the pipe in the office drawer, knowing he could collect it when the time came, which it had: Vicky's birthday was tomorrow.

Haley stuffed the pipe into his back pocket and departed the office. As he locked the door he felt suddenly adrift, uncertain. *Stay or go?*

Stay, of course.

He hadn't kept any keys to the cemetery gates, but it had never been difficult for him to shove a toe between the fence's iron curlicues and hoist himself up and over the decorative spikes. Now, he climbed the fence adjoining the East Gate, dropped down by the storage shed, and moved forward, past the lights of the parking lot and into a darkness relieved only by a clouded moon. Even in total blackness, even blindfolded, he would have found his way, he was certain. These grounds were that familiar to him, and that familiarity, the realization of just how much he missed it, was the main reason it had taken him so long to return.

These days, Haley reported for work in button-down shirts and khakis, his hands never dirtied by anything more than printer toner, his movements limited mostly to trips between his cubicle and the coffee pot, the restroom, the photocopier, and Carl Jenks's office. Although the pay was better, although he'd received an extra week's vacation, although his abilities at office work had so far been praised, even by Jenks, he couldn't help but feel that he'd made a serious mistake.

As Haley headed toward the main hub of the irrigation system, his best guess as to where Ben and Pete might be, the sound of an acoustic guitar rose up from the distance, to his right. Someone was plucking out the intro to a familiar tune. Then came a male voice—no, two voices—singing in harmony. Within a few bars Haley recognized the song: "Don't Fear the Reaper."

Fucking perfect, he thought. He stood still for a minute or so, just listening, far enough away that the lyrics were indistinct but the vocals discernible: Pete and Ben. No, Pete and Nick Graves.

The closer Haley got to the singing and guitar, the more they seemed to come from all around him, a trick of acoustics, perhaps, the play of sound waves across the rolling hills, against the stands of tombstones. The tune seemed to be rising from the ground, as naturally as night vapors.

Then as quickly as it started, it ended.

⁂

"I thought you wanted to do covers, Pete. Only covers."

Ben shifted on the bench, trying to "make peace with the twinges," as his father used to say. Of all the desires he'd experienced over his many evenings in this cemetery, it didn't seem possible that any of one them could have exceeded the longing he now felt for a butt cushion.

"I didn't think you'd have a problem with original stuff."

"I *don't.* I was just hoping we could keep things simple between us, stick with the familiar."

What Ben didn't want to say, what he hoped Pete understood, was that he didn't want to spend hours working on and rehearsing new tunes for some open-mike gigs in which, frankly, he had little personal interest.

"It's just *one* song, Ben. And I already wrote the lyrics. I roughed out how it might sound, too."

"I'm impressed," Ben said.

He was also uneasy, because he would have to listen to the song and, in all likelihood, register an opinion. What were the chances it wouldn't suck?

"I bet you'll be more impressed when you hear what it's about."

161

"Oh yeah? Tell me."

Now it was Pete who shifted on the bench.

"It's about your spore suit."

"Shit. *Really?*"

"Really."

A few nights back, after their post-work session of phone calls, Pete had discovered one of Ben's spore catalogs on the desk and started asking more questions about his interest in mushrooms. Ben blamed an assortment of circumstances for what happened next: fatigue from a long day's work, the single beer he'd unwisely indulged in, Pete's sincere and oddly moving interest in the spores and their cultivation.

Ben told Pete all about the petri dishes in his cellar, those nurseries for the spores that were variously feeding off of, or rejecting, shavings of himself. He told Pete about possible designs for the shroud/suit, and about how it might be constructed, then laced with the spores.

"Well," Ben said, "I'm honored. But I'm also a little embarrassed."

"Aw, really? I wasn't out to embarrass you."

"I know, but—"

A sound from the left froze Ben.

"What?" Pete asked.

Ben grabbed Pete's arm to shush him, and in the silence heard someone approaching. Seconds later, a figure emerged from the dark: Haley.

"My men," Haley called. "You sounded awesome."

Ben rose to Haley's high-five invitation. So did Pete.

"You going to be able to make it to our gig Wednesday night?" Pete said.

"It's in my calendar. And Vicky's coming, too—a belated birthday gift. Speaking of that—" Haley looked to Pete. "I just picked up that other gift for her, from the office. Thanks for holding on to it for me."

"No sweat, man," Pete said.

As Haley and Pete exchanged more small talk, Ben found himself distracted by the ways in which Haley had changed, ever so slightly. His hands seemed softer, and his complexion had subtly paled. He slouched in a way Ben didn't recall.

"How's that new job treating you?" Ben said. "Or shouldn't I ask?"

Haley shrugged. "It's paying the bills."

"Geez," Ben said. "Is it that bad?"

"No, no, no. It's fine. Some days even good. What about you guys? What brings you out here to make your music?"

Haley seemed eager to change the subject, and Ben was happy to oblige.

"Most times we rehearse in the office. But nice nights like this, it's good to be outdoors."

"Sure is," Haley said, attempting a smile that, to Ben, suggested its opposite.

"Speaking of music," Pete said. "I have a favor to ask you, Haley."

"Oh yeah? What?"

"I've written a song, and I'd like you to listen to it, tell me if you think it's worthy of additional performances. And eventual accompaniment by guitar."

"Sure," Haley said, looking genuinely pleased.

"And you have to be absolutely honest."

"All right."

With this permission, Pete pulled a sheet of what seemed to be lyrics from his back pocket. But all the while he sang, he never once looked at it, making Ben realize that much rehearsing had led up to this moment.

Pete's voice could stand without accompaniment; it was as mournful and clear as an Irish balladeer's. Still, Ben picked up his guitar and came in at the start of the third verse, and they played through the song a second time, together.

Ben D, the man knows it's an honor
To tread
That borderland in between
Living and dead

163

And from all of the graves
That he's toiled in
Ben D and mushrooms,
They've become nearly kin

After years in the dirt
Ben's most certainly
Found
It's not so bad being a part of
The ground
Just ask and he'll tell you
Of all that you'll
Miss
If you only look skyward
For heavenly
Bliss

Once Ben's entered that grave that has
No exit doors
In a suit that's festooned with some
Ben-loving spores

May those spores crank up
Some strong fungal ignition
So Ben will succeed
In his last earthly mission

After years in the dirt
Ben's most certainly
Found
It's not so bad being a part of
The ground
Just ask and he'll tell you
Of all that you'll
Miss
If you only look skyward
For heavenly
Bliss

Ben's working things out in a few petri
Dishes
And it is among his most deeply held
Wishes

To mushroomly enhance
His own grave's vegetation
And spread Ben-ish spores
To the next generation

After years in the dirt
Ben's most certainly
Found
It's not so bad being a part of
The ground
Just ask and he'll tell you
Of all that you'll
Miss
If you only look skyward
For heavenly
Bliss

Haley applauded loudly, and apparently sincerely. "I love it! And you should definitely keep playing it."

"Thanks," Pete said. "I think we will. If you agree, Ben."

Ben didn't answer right away. He was coming down from the disorienting, Tom Sawyer-ish feeling of having made an appearance at his own funeral, of having played himself out.

"Why not?" he said, at last.

"Good," Haley said. "Now tell me about this spore-festooned suit. How much fact and how much science fiction?"

"I'm not quite sure," Ben said. "The lines are kind of blurred."

He told Haley, as briefly as he could, about his experiments in the cellar. "Clearly, I won't be around to see if I've achieved success. But I'm pretty determined to give it a try."

Haley went quiet for a moment, then said, "So is this going to be part of your Green Initiative?"

Ben found it curious that Haley always said *"your* Green Initiative," as if he had no connection to the project, even though he'd helped carry out parts of it while working on the grounds. Ben wondered if serving under Jenks had further tainted Haley's attitude toward the endeavor.

"No," Ben said. "Not for the moment, anyway."

"Well, keep me posted about it. I'll be wishing you luck."

"Hey," Ben said. "Speaking of the Green Initiative, we've been getting more and more calls from people requesting green burials. Do you have a sense of whether that's happening in the central office?"

Haley cast Ben a quizzical look. "You never heard of the call log?"

"The call log?"

"Yeah. Whenever people call in with special requests or complaints, whoever's answering the phone is supposed to record them in this electronic file and make sure they get forwarded to the proper party. It's apparently a requirement for all town offices, a way to make sure we're being held accountable to taxpayers."

It sounded promising to Ben, but who knew how well the log was maintained, if at all? "You think I could get a printout of whatever's in the file?"

"From me, I presume."

"From you."

Haley didn't look pleased. "I'm not sure that would be in keeping with the rules, Ben."

"What do you mean? Aren't I one of the *accountable parties*? At least potentially?"

Haley kept quiet, still not looking pleased.

"You get me the printout, you get a bottle of that bourbon you're always talking about. The stuff you tried at that wedding."

Haley kept silent for some time, apparently mulling over Ben's proposal. Then he said, "All right. When do you need it?"

"As soon as you can get it to me."

"How about Tuesday, after work?"

"Your bourbon will be waiting."

Chapter 24

In the interest of sparing unnecessary effort and expense regarding the planned exhumation at Lot 3 of the cemetery (the grave of the Unknown Vagrant) I ordered a forensic analysis of soil samples extracted from the site. My conclusion is that an exhumation, for any purpose, would be unproductive.

Soils with a pH of 5.3 or less are inhospitable to the integrity of bone and muscle tissues; in fact, such conditions can lead to rapid bone degradation. Given that the samples extracted from Lot 3 were found to have an average pH of 4.7 pH, I believe it highly unlikely that an exhumation would uncover skeletal remains, much less allow for extraction of viable DNA. Furthermore, the soil probing revealed no burial-relevant subsurface features (e.g., casket remnants) other than a coffin nail.

—From a memo to the Board of Directors of the Bolster Hill Cemetery and the Bolster Hill Historical Society, by Meredith Kurtz, Ph.D.

⁂

Rossmore B. (Ross) Dirjery, 52, died unexpectedly on Wednesday, September 2nd. For more than thirty years, Mr. Dirjery was employed by Bolster Hill Cemetery, since 1978 as grounds manager. Although he was a meticulous and talented landscaper and an exacting performer and supervisor of interments, he may be best remembered for the comfort

167

he provided to countless mourners during his tenure at the cemetery. "He's like a walking therapist," said longtime Bolster resident Mel Lorett, in a 1987 profile of Mr. Dirjery ("Man of the Grounds," *Bolster Register*, 5/23/87). "He's like the best kind of bartender, only without the booze." In that same profile, Mr. Dirjery described the reverence with which he performed the most important of his tasks. "For me," he said, "digging someone's last earthly home is an activity every bit as spiritual as physical."

—From the *Bolster Register*, September 6, 1992

Lot 502
Mid-morning, June 28

By the time he was knee-deep into the dig, Ben's T-shirt was sweat-soaked, his heart pounding in his ears.

He paused and leaned against the shovel, wondering if it was time to end this annual tradition the sensible way, with a backhoe instead of what was feeling more and more likely: an ambulance. He wasn't a teenager anymore, wasn't even in shouting distance of thirty. Then again, he rarely worked this quickly, fueled by so much frustration, and anger.

Use some common sense, he thought. *Pace yourself.*

Once he'd settled himself down, he grabbed the shovel handle and started back in, got into an easier groove.

"Ben?"

Meredith's voice. He chucked the shovel into the ground and turned to face her.

Seeing him her smile dimmed, as if she sensed his mood. "You got the good news, I presume."

"Yes," he said. Early that morning, Jenks phoned him with word that the exhumation had been called off. "And I'm really thankful for everything you did. Those soil tests made all the difference."

"You deserve as much thanks as I do. That's what I told the guy who gave me the word. Carl Something."

"Carl Jenks." Ben flexed his hands, feeling blisters rising, even with the gloves.

"Yeah. He called me just a little bit ago, while I was stopping to get some gas. And since I was just down the road from you, I thought I'd drop by."

"I'm glad you did," Ben said, trying to smile. His grudge against Jenks, just refreshed and feeling especially raw, was nothing she should have to suffer from.

That morning, when Jenks called him with the news, Ben wasted no time reminding him that he, Ben, was *owed something*—Jenks's words—if the soil testing worked out.

Jenks's response: "You'll be getting a handsome bonus this year. You have my word."

"How about I take a pass on a bonus, if we can give Dolores Fielding what she wants? In time for it to matter."

In the pause that followed, Ben imagined Jenks's face purpling.

"Let's not keep having the same old argument, Ben. It's not the least bit productive."

Before Ben could get another word in, Jenks signed off, pleading an incoming call.

In truth, what troubled Ben the most now was beyond his or Jenks's powers. Dolores had grown too weak to leave her home, much less make her usual rounds at the cemetery. Because of Dolores's frail state, Ben now kept in touch with her through her daughter, Jenny, occasionally sending pictures of mushrooms he'd discovered on the grounds.

He hoped Dolores could hang in there at least until the July twenty-sixth board meeting, his last shot at making a green burial happen for her at Bolster Hill Cemetery.

Meredith stepped closer to Ben and cast a puzzled look over the grave-in-progress. "Is there any reason you're digging this by hand?"

The question, one Ben was rarely asked, made him just slightly uncomfortable. Then again, if he could pick one person who might understand the reasons for the hand digging, it would be Meredith.

"It's something I do every once in a while, just to remind myself of what this job is. That it shouldn't just be some impersonal business."

He also mentioned that it was a tradition of his father's, one that Ben had carried forward.

"I always try to dig the grave on or about his birthday."

"That's lovely."

Meredith looked over the grave again, as if some other question were lingering in her mind. Then she said, "You don't look as happy as I'd imagined you'd be, given the news. Is something wrong?"

He didn't want to go into the business with Jenks, for his own sake as much as hers. But Meredith's words brought to the surface the other thing that had been troubling him. They felt like permission to speak of it.

"I just want to apologize for my behavior the other night."

Meredith looked puzzled, as if she didn't know what he was talking about. Then, the memory seemed to dawn on her.

"There's no need to, really."

After collecting the soil samples they'd gone to a hole-in-the wall bar, The Tin Whistle, and nearly closed the place down, not by steady drinking—Meredith had had a glass of wine and some soda water, Ben a couple of beers—but by talking.

She told him more about her past fieldwork and her upcoming research in Arizona.

She told him of her recent trip to India, of pyres burning by the Ganges and tended by Ben's sooty brethren.

She told him of her time at a former military base in Guatemala, the site of one of her clearest memories: the exhumation of a girl wearing hand-embroidered slippers, a girl who was never identified. The picture of those blue slippers stayed with Ben. So did the memory of Meredith telling the story, in their dark corner of the near-empty bar, candlelight flickering in her eyes.

When he reached for her hand during that story, she took it and didn't let go.

Ben told her a bit more about his work, and about Cole.

And then, perhaps because Meredith was holding his hand and listening, perhaps because he didn't know her well, he told her of the music he'd started writing—something he hadn't mentioned to Pete, much less to Cole. This felt strangely like a confession, if not of a sin, then of something just as linked to darkness and desire, at least when songwriting was going well for Ben.

His talk of the music and the kind way she'd listened, with so many thoughtful questions. The way she'd kept hold of his hand and looked into his eyes. All these things and simple longing, they'd given him a courage that, in retrospect, looked far more like beer-fueled foolishness. In The Tin Whistle's rain-misted parking lot, as they readied to part ways, Ben drew close—perhaps too suddenly—and moved to kiss her. She turned her face away.

"Sorry, not tonight," she'd whispered.

Sorry, not ever, was what he saw in her expression, then in her haste to climb into her car. At that moment, he'd cursed himself for not reading the signs that should have been plain to him all along: her terse mention, midway through their time at the bar, of a recent breakup; her eagerness to start her new life in Arizona.

Now, Meredith unshouldered her ever-present backpack, took a paper-bagged item from the side pocket.

"Elodie's was on my way, so I wondered if you'd be up for a snack break." She lifted the bag and smiled. "Two prosciutto and cheddar scones."

"My favorite," Ben said. "Should we sit and eat or walk and eat?"

"Up to you. You're the one who's been digging a grave."

"Let's walk."

He climbed out of the grave, ditched his gloves, and accepted one of the scones. Its buttery, breakfasty smell got his mouth watering, and he took a big bite of it.

"Good?" Meredith asked.

His mouth full, Ben could only nod.

Meredith slung her backpack over her shoulder, and as they made their way forward, she started in on her own scone.

Ben didn't care where they roamed. It just felt good to enjoy this break, and Meredith's company.

"Hey," she said, stopping. "Your dad's buried here, right?"

"Yep." He downed the last of the scone and whisked the crumbs from his hands.

"Wanna pay him a birthday visit?"

"Sure."

The word *visit* conjured an image of Meredith meeting the living Ross, who would have been as interested in the stories of her forensic digs as Ben was. Ben could see the look on Ross's face as she talked, enchanted equally by her words and her beauty, and eager to test his charms. But as little as he knew of Meredith, Ben sensed that she was minimally tolerant of bullshit, even the charming kind. Ross wouldn't have gotten very far.

As Ben led the way toward Section C, he and Meredith kept quiet for some time. Then she said, "We talked so much about my work the other night. When I got home, all these questions came to my mind, about what you do."

"Like what?"

She finished her scone and tucked the empty bag into her pack.

"When I was in Varanasi, watching those men stoking the pyres, it seemed like it was second nature to them, almost like any other job. But I couldn't help but wonder if it took a toll on them, over time. So I guess I'm just wondering if digging graves, being in graves, is ever hard on you."

Ben had to think this over. "Every so often, yes. How much detail do you want me to go into?"

"As much as you can give me."

He pictured the grave to which they were heading. That got him started.

"When my father died, other people offered to bury him: the junior man here and the main groundskeeper from a cemetery in the next town. But I felt like that wouldn't be right, because I was his son, and he'd taught me everything about this job there was to know. I felt like I owed him that much.

"The usual thing, as you know, would be to dig the grave with a backhoe, and maybe use a shovel for touchup. With a simple plot and a backhoe, you can get the job done inside of twenty minutes. But because there was a good amount of unfinished business between my father and me, I decided to use a shovel for the whole grave."

Ben led the way toward Gentian Path. From there, they'd climb the hill to Ross's plot.

"I'd say I got one foot deep in fifteen minutes, on pure anger. I was pissed that he'd died unexpectedly, not because that was tragic or sad, which it was, but because I felt cheated."

Ben spotted a stray floral ribbon and stooped to pick it up. "I felt cheated because I'd been living under the assumption that my dad would live long enough to see me exceed him. Exactly how I'd exceed him, I didn't know. But I was determined I'd be something more than a charmer with a work ethic. At a bare minimum I'd be a better husband than him, someone who wasn't running around with at least one other woman at any given time."

The ribbon, absent of its flowers, reminded Ben of the mystery these women had been to him. He stuffed it into his pocket.

"But of course he never got to see any of this. His heart gave out on him while he was in bed with his mistress *du jour*."

"Jesus," Meredith said. "How'd you find that out?"

"Well, a couple nights after this happened, she worked up the nerve to call me. She told me that death had dropped over him like a net: quick and merciful, and for that I should be thankful. And call me an asshole, but I wasn't thankful in the least, other than for the courage it took for her to pick up the phone and dial my number. I was resentful. Because he'd died just the way he would have wanted to: in the middle of something that pleased him, without a shadow of regret, fear, or doubt."

Meredith was shaking her head, her face slack with what Ben took as disbelief. "What a thing to take in all at once. From a stranger, I presume?"

"Yeah, she was a stranger. And I never heard from her again."

But Ben always wondered if she was one of the three or four unfamiliar women who, just days after this phone call, lurked in the shadows of Ross's memorial service.

"Go on," Meredith said.

Ben's mind returned to Ross's grave. "When I got about two feet down, fatigue set in, and I started feeling lost. Because as hard as I'd been digging against my anger, against my father, I came around to seeing that I was absolutely alone: whatever I was going to do with my life, it was all on me. There was no blaming him for what I would or wouldn't make of myself."

As they climbed the hill to Ross's plot, Ben told Meredith about his time with the Vagrants. He told her how he dreamed of touring with them before Leah got pregnant with their first child, and how the dream resurfaced after they lost the baby.

"As horrible as it sounds I felt a thrill just then, the thrill of re-opening a door I'd locked, presumably for good. I had a second chance with my music, with going on the road with the band. And while I loved my wife and had no thought of leaving her, I found myself imagining scraps of a future that didn't include her."

Ben interrupted his story to steer Meredith rightward, to the foot of Ross's grave.

"Here he is." Then he gestured to the right. "And there's my mom."

He wondered if Meredith sensed that the space between his parents' stones was more than physical, just as he always had. Now, she focused on Ross's stone only, giving it the same *You shit heel* stare his mother once turned on the man himself.

He wasn't all bad, Ben wanted to say. *Sometimes, he could even be great.* But now wasn't the time.

"So you were thinking of going on the road," Meredith said. "With the Vagrants."

Ben nodded. "It might not be fair, but I felt like the urge to follow that temptation came directly from this guy." Ben waved toward Ross's stone. "And the truth is, I wish like hell I'd asked him what he would have done, in my shoes. I'd have taken his opinion as I'm sure he would have wanted me to take it: not as instructions but as food for thought. But he died when I was in the middle of thinking through all this, and that brought me back to feeling lost."

Ben stepped closer to Ross's stone.

"That last foot of the dig, I felt like I was only going through the motions, but I got the job done. If it had been another grave, I would have climbed out at that point. But instead I eased myself down onto my back and put my head right about here." Ben drew closer and patted the ground right in front of Ross's stone. "Where his would be. The cool earth felt good on that hot day, and it was nice to lie in the darkness and look up at the sky.

"If you'd asked me then why I was doing this, I don't think I would have been able to tell you. But looking back, I think some part of me realized this was the closest I'd ever be to my father again."

Meredith's expression softened, just slightly.

"And as I was lying in that hole, staring at the sky, a strange kind of feeling came over me. Like I was lying in two graves, both this one and the one I'd dug for my son. Or, rather, one grave was the same as the other. When I closed my eyes I once again saw my son."

Now as then, Ben pictured the black-haired baby, with the chin that might have been his own and the mouth that was most certainly Leah's.

"If I hadn't seen him before the burial, he might have remained an abstraction, something easier to move on from. But because I *had* seen him, all those specifics, all the possibilities he represented, continued to haunt me, and these stood apart from my feelings about my dad, my music, even my marriage. That little person by the grave, he was unfinished business. And by the time I re-opened my eyes I'd confirmed a decision I'd already made subconsciously: that I *needed* to be a father again, and a good one—or at least the best one I could be. Even if that meant putting music on hold. That decision might have been one of the few smart ones I ever made."

Ben stood up from the grave and returned to Meredith's side.

"So coming back to your question, I guess digging graves can be an existential kind of hard for me, at times. Especially when I'm down in a hole by myself, instead of working with someone else, or with a backhoe."

He tried to explain how down in a grave, with nothing to distract him, it could be hard to escape his most troubling thoughts, though not as hard as it once had been.

"But a couple of months ago another strange feeling came over me. While I was squaring the walls of a grave. I was struck by how weathered, how old my hands had become—how much they now resembled my father's."

Ben held his hands out before him, took in his reddened, line-etched palms, his callused fingers.

"And it occurred to me how I'd become so much more like him than not, for good and ill. Maybe because of that, I can't really be that angry at him anymore."

He lowered his hands and looked to Meredith. "Does that answer your question?"

"Yes. Beautifully." She studied his face for some time, as if gathering her thoughts. "And you know what? I bet you were a good son, or tried to be, and I bet you're a good father, or trying to be. And your work here maybe helps you figure out some of the sad and hard stuff, rather than creating it."

Ben thought that when it came to his fitness as a son and father, *tried* and *trying* had a solid lead on the *good*.

"You know what else I think?"

"What?"

"It's really great that you're working on your music again. It sounds like that was really important to you."

It was, he thought. *Maybe still is.*

Ben remembered how he'd taken her hand at The Tin Whistle, during a moment very much like this one: a weighted pause.

This time, he let the moment pass.

"You'd make a damned good psychiatrist, Meredith Kurtz."

"Hah! That would have made my mother *so* much happier, believe me."

"Really?"

176

"Really. But that's a whole other story. Speaking of which, would you have time for a celebratory dinner? Maybe tonight? Or tomorrow?"

"Sure," Ben said. "Only if it's on me. I think tonight would probably be better, but let me just check with Cole."

"You know how to reach me. Meantime, I've got to return a call from a reporter, about the soil analysis. It came into my voicemail when I was on the phone with Mr. Jenks."

"Wow. Word spreads fast."

Ben wondered if some other curious parties had called her since then. Her phone had buzzed a few times while they headed to Ross's grave.

"Seems so," she said. "When I pulled into the cemetery, some folks were already having a little celebration on the Vagrant's grave. Nothing too outrageous, mind you."

Ben hadn't yet seen any signs of merrymaking. Then again, he'd gotten into the habit of steering clear of the North Gate area, unless he had work to do there. Maybe things were finally going to change for the better at that spot, once this latest excitement died down.

As Ben walked Meredith to the exit, he tried to tell himself that by a *celebratory dinner,* she'd meant just that: an opportunity to toast a good deed accomplished, to continue their conversation over a respectable but not overly elegant meal and a minimal amount of alcohol, and finally to part, warmly but chastely, at a decent hour.

If she had anything else in mind, it was going to be her call.

Chapter 25

Saturday, July 21 – Mercy's Lounge
Stone Monkeys with
Keith's Hell and
The Vagrants
2 SHOWS! – 7 p.m.: All ages – 9 p.m.: 21 and over
Tickets $3 only!

—Show flier, summer 1990

Home

After dark, June 28

"If we want the name of the band to really pop, we need to focus on contrast first, color second," Miranda said. "At least according to my mom."

Cole was already heading to the basement, phone to her ear. "I'm sure I've got everything covered: contrast, color . . . sparkles."

Miranda laughed. "Sparkles would be *awesome.*"

"All right. I'll let you know what I find."

On the other end of the line, Cole heard the fury of fries descending into hot oil. It was one of Miranda's nights at the Snack Shack.

"Cole? I'm really glad we're still doing this show."

"Me too."

The band was getting tighter with every practice, and Cole

was proud of how the songs were coming together, proud of what she was bringing to them.

"Okay. Talk to you soon."

Cole pocketed her phone and flicked on the light switch by the basement door. As she descended the stairs she considered, once again, how much had happened since she got out of bed this morning. As soon as she reported for work at the cemetery, her dad told her about the exhumation being called off. Though Cole knew that was for the best, and what she herself would have wanted at any other time in her life, she couldn't help but feel disappointed: it seemed there was no longer any reason for a protest concert, for which they had a firm date (August fifth) and a venue (Randolph Park).

But in the eyes of Meg Tirella, the cause had never been lost. Because her mother worked at the *Bolster Register*, Meg had gotten the news about the exhumation early, and by lunchtime she'd contacted Miranda and Grif with an alternate plan: to make the concert a celebration instead of a protest. By the time Cole left work, everyone involved with the concert was onboard with Meg's new plan.

Cole had expected her father to be indifferent to this development, at best, but when she told him about it, he seemed genuinely pleased—perhaps only because of his own news: he was going out for dinner that evening with the woman he helped do the soil testing: Meredith.

(*"Is this a date, Dad?"*

"I don't think so."

"That sounds like a maybe, at least.")

Cole's current mission was to locate material left over from a fiber-arts class her mother had taken years ago, as an undergraduate. According to her mom, there were at least two boxes of the stuff, "some of it bland, some of it pretty wild," somewhere in the basement storage room. If Cole could find any decent swatches, she'd pass them on to Miranda, whose own mother, an accomplished seamstress, was making a stage banner for the band.

To Cole, the basement had always looked haunted and sad,

but never more so than since her parents' divorce. Upstairs, life had moved on: most of her mother's art supplies and paintings had departed with her to Boston, along with other random items—blown-glass vases, a set of shelves with her favorite books, some inherited odds and ends—that Cole's father had no special claim on. The beat-up couch and chairs in the living room, the center of so much of the family's pre-divorce life, were hauled away the day after her mom's move, and replaced with brand-new furniture, free of memories.

The basement, though, remained entangled in the past. Aside from her father's mushroom experimentation station, little had changed over the years, and whether this was at all intentional or purely the result of neglect, Cole didn't know and didn't want to. All three of their bikes, as well as her old tricycle, still hung from the ceiling of the darkest, most distant corner. And Cole knew that if she took a close look at the shelves along the left wall, a temptation she now avoided, she would find not only gardening tools, bags of grass seed, and other household miscellany but also the rolled-up, mildewed camping tent they'd last used, together, four summers ago; a trio of scuffed-up ice skates, battered from regular winter outings to Bolster Pond; and highest up and farthest down, a dusty stack of board games, including a one-time favorite of Cole and her mom: "You're It!" If there were such a thing as a graveyard for their family, the family they'd once been, this basement would be it.

Cole headed for the storage room, across from the shelves, and within it encountered a concentration of the smell outside its door: must and general staleness, like the breath of someone who'd slept a long time with their mouth closed.

In the dimness she found the pull-chain for the light and turned it on, revealing shelves of boxes on either side of the door: most of them generic cardboard moving boxes, most of them labeled with her mother's handwriting: *X-mas Decorations; Halloween Decorations; Cole's Drawings— Kindergarten; Cole's Schoolwork—Bolster Elementary; Linens; Fiber Arts Materials* . . .

Cole pulled down this last box, and another one behind

it with the same label. Turning back to the gap she'd opened in the shelves, she noticed a smallish box crammed up against the wall, behind a larger carton. The handwriting on its side, block letters in black marker, wasn't her mother's, but Cole couldn't be sure it was her father's either. *BAND*, it said.

She yanked the box out of its nook and opened it, finding first a stack of crumpled photocopies:

Saturday, July 21 – Mercy's Lounge – Stone Monkeys with Keith's Hell and The Vagrants

Friday, Aug. 3 – Weeker Auditorium – Clubbed Med and The Vagrants

Thursday, Sept. 6 – The Vagrants at Willow Tavern – Southridge

It was odd that either one of her parents would have held on to show fliers, even if they'd once been Vagrants fans. The fact that this stuff had been kept so long, in hiding, suggested something more significant. Perhaps her mom had dated one of the Vagrants—Vince Resklar, the purported lady-bait of the band? If this were true, it might explain why her dad seemed so distant whenever the subject of the Vagrants, and Vince Resklar in particular, came up.

As Cole dug deeper into the box, uncovering more fliers, Vagrants pins and stickers, and handwritten set lists, her theory started feeling more plausible, and also unsettling. This collection seemed strangely obsessive, nothing Cole would ever have associated with her mom, even as a possibly love-struck young woman.

Deeper in the box were two plastic-cased cassettes labeled "Demo Tape." Deeper still was a manila folder labeled "Press Kit." Opening it, Cole found more stickers, an envelope, and a press release, dated July 10, 1990:

Blending garage punk and the melody-rooted guitar sounds of the sixties, the New England-based foursome the

Vagrants will be launching a four-state tour on July 15 (dates and venues enclosed). Two of the band's songs, "Leave Me in Peace" and "Getting Out," are gaining more and more airplay at college stations, as well as early praise from such publications as Tuned, *which calls the Vagrants "an up-and-coming group to pay attention to." (These songs are included in the enclosed demo.)* . . .

Skimming ahead in the press release, Cole found the list of band members:

> *Vince Resklar – Vocals, guitar*
> *Nick Graves – Vocals, guitar*
> *Tuke Masters – Bass*
> *Dave Pecora – Drums*

Vince's name was familiar to Cole, Tuke Masters's name more vaguely so. But she had no clear recollection of a Dave Pecora or a Nick Graves. The only Vagrants guitarist she remembered from her online reading, other than Vince, was Tommy Something.

Cole set aside the press release and withdrew a black-and-white photo from the envelope. It showed the four Vagrants standing in a cemetery (Bolster Hill Cemetery; Cole recognized it from the Crane Mausoleum, in the background), Vince out in front of the others, the point of a *V.* None of them looked much older than Cole, and all of them wore the usual rocker stony face. The caption: *Left to right: Dave Pecora, Tuke Masters, Vince Resklar, Nick Graves.*

Nick Graves, the only one in sunglasses. Even without seeing his eyes, Cole recognized the long, sharp nose and oval face, the slightly clefted chin and broad forehead that, to Cole's maternal grandmother, inspired comparisons to Richard Burton.

Nick Graves was Ben Dirjery. Nick Graves was her dad.

Cole rummaged more quickly through the rest of the box, finding some news clippings—reviews, profiles from college newspapers—and more pictures of the band: some of them from gigs, one of them a close-up of her dad playing the Rickenbacker, his eyes closed as if he was lost in a song. She understood, now, why the singing she'd overheard in his office, the growl-humming, had sounded so familiar. It must have been part of some of the older MP3s she'd picked up from the Vagrants' online music trove.

Cole had become restless, too distracted to take anything else in. She barged out of the storage room, leaving the band mementoes, the fabric, and everything else behind her. She wanted to be out of this house, in the fresh air. She wanted to ask her dad what he'd been thinking, what he'd been hiding, and why.

Cole bolted up the basement stairs then out onto the front porch, where she paced back and forth in the humid darkness. At some point, she pulled out her phone, thinking she'd just call him. Then she remembered his date. What about her mother? What did she know? Cole scrolled for her name in the directory, then returned her phone to her pocket. This explanation was going to have to come from her father, from him alone.

Chapter 26

For some yarn taggers, the biggest challenge is coming to peace with the temporary nature of their works. If this is one of your concerns, my advice is that you try to seek the greatest pleasure from the process of creation, and from the understanding that your works will provide others with a meaningful and possibly memorable visual experience, even if only briefly.

—From *The Yarn Tagger's Handbook*

Memory Garden
Early morning, June 29th

By Peg's count, the yarn sunset lasted at least two days. It had been standing when she came by the day after she installed it, and also when she returned the following evening, feeling like one of those malefactors who are driven to revisit the scenes of their crimes. How long it had lasted into yesterday, its third day, Peg had no idea. She'd been too busy with appointments and errands to stop by the cemetery.

Now, all that remained of her work was one of the outer poles, apparently forgotten by the maintenance crew. In the morning mist it looked orphaned and lost.

Peg's first impulse was to grab the pole and take it home, but for what purpose? She wasn't going to re-create a yarn sunset here or anywhere else. And she was pretty sure this first yarn bombing was also going to be her last. As unsophisticated as this might sound to Martha and to all the other Needlers who'd gushed about this form of *public art*, the investment hardly seemed worth the payoff to Peg. With time, she'd grown more and more biased toward things that lasted, more and more tired of change, and loss.

As for Martha's decoration of the Unknown Vagrant's grave, it hadn't made it to the end of its first day, not because it was any less worthy of preservation, to Peg's mind. Being so visible, and in such a controversial spot, its doom had felt sealed from the start.

Scanning the Memory Garden's foliage for stray bits of yarn or other leavings, Peg found nothing. But as she looked toward one of the stone benches, some purplish writing caught her eye: graffiti, in lipstick, written across the seat. She stepped closer to read it.

WHY did you tear the sunburst down?

Underneath this another message had been scrawled in a different color of lipstick—sparkly pink—and in larger, more rounded handwriting:

Bring back the sunburst, you <u>*HEATHENS!!!*</u>

On another day, "Heathens" might have made Peg laugh, but now her throat tightened, and she felt close to tears.

She pictured two young women, wondering if they were anything like she herself had been in her own sparkly lipstick days: constantly verging on goofiness, at times mean and judgmental, at times "overly emotional" (never her own description), and almost always underestimated. If her yarn work, if its absence, had given these girls even a fleeting opportunity to express passion and anger over the fact that life was too often unjust, that was fine with Peg. Maybe even enough.

Had she brought her camera, Peg would have photographed the lipsticked complaints, just as she'd photographed the yarn sunset a few nights before. But the truth was, she rarely looked back on pictures she'd taken. When a moment was gone it was gone.

Chapter 27

I'll show my thanks by disappearing, taking with me all you lost.

—From "Taillights," a song on the Vagrants' final album (1993)

Home

Labor Day evening, 1993

A wedge of light widened in the dark, and a woman's form stepped into it. Leah. She pushed the door open a little more and softly walked toward him.

"I'm awake," he said.

"Just thought I'd check on you. Feeling any better?"

"A little, I think."

The truth was, it seemed there was less of him to feel anything. Like he was part mass, part vapor.

"Can I bring you anything?"

"No, I'm good. I'm fine."

She stayed where she was, watching him, as if she didn't quite believe his words.

"I'm sorry, doll," he said.

"What are you sorry about? You're the one with the hurt back." He'd strained it at work a few days before.

"I'm sorry because this is your big party. I should be downstairs, mixing it up. Acting like a real host."

She sat down on the edge of the bed, laid a hand across his arm.

"You ordered that beautiful cake and all that food. You got me the perfect graduation gift. That's more than enough."

Despite his back, despite the pills that had drowsed him and dulled his pain, Ben wanted to pull her down beside him, fold her into the blue hum of himself.

Laughter rippled through the downstairs, interfering, reminding him of the drinkers, talkers, and smokers who crowded the living room and kitchen and spilled onto the porch and lawn, of whoever was moving to the music thumping up from the basement, its rhythm ready at any time to slip back into his subconscious. He found it surprisingly conducive to sleep.

"What time is it?" he asked.

Leah angled her wristwatch into the light from the hall. "Almost ten thirty."

"Shit. Really?"

The last he remembered, it was just past nine.

"I could start shutting things down," she said. "I don't think anyone will feel cheated at this point. Certainly not me."

If it were up to Ben, everything but Leah, himself, and their bed would drop into oblivion, immediately and until some undetermined point in the future. But this night was not about him.

"Doll," he said, "it's your party, and you should let it roll on as long as you'd like. As long as you don't mind me keeping a low profile."

"Of course I don't."

Leah reached for the plastic cup on the nightstand. "Let me get you some fresh water."

She paused and sniffed the cup, made a face. "Honey, beer's not a good mix with muscle relaxants."

"I just wanted a taste of it, a sip."

It was true that he missed beer: the taste of it and more. Since the finals for her master's program, Leah hadn't had a single drink—part of their try at another baby. In an act of solidarity, Ben had stopped bringing any kind of alcohol into the house, even for himself. The booze for the party was a single exception.

It wasn't true that, tonight, he'd had just a sip of alcohol. What Leah was carrying away from him now, back toward the hall, was the start of a second—or was it a third?—beer.

"Well, sorry," she said. "But I'm going to replace this one with water."

Soon after Leah left the room, Ben heard a car door slam out front, then the sounds of cheerful commotion: hoots and *heys*.

By the time she returned, the shouting was loud enough to draw her attention to the front window.

"What's going on out there?" Ben asked her. "Can you tell?"

Leah set the water on the nightstand and stepped over to the window, pushed aside the sheers. She craned her neck this way and that, then lowered her head for a better look, peering beneath the open sash. After a moment, she glanced back to Ben.

"Unless my eyes are deceiving me, Vince Resklar has arrived."

"No shit," Ben said.

Vince was the last person Ben had expected, and they hadn't seen each other since that early morning in the cemetery, more than a year before. Lately, the only Vagrant he'd kept in touch with was Dave, and when Dave mentioned he'd be in town over Labor Day weekend, Ben had invited him to the party. "Let Vince know, too," Ben told him. "If you think of it, and if he'll be around." These days, he wasn't sure how to reach Vince himself.

It turned out that Dave couldn't make it. As for Tuke, he'd already come and gone. And he was a Vagrant no more. Tommy Nemec, the new co-lead/rhythm guitarist and co-singer/songwriter—Lord Tom, according to Dave—had replaced Tuke with his own bass player. *His own*—as if bass players were mere possessions, objects.

Another wave of drowsiness rolled through Ben, the blue hum buzzing in his head.

"Leah? Would you mind telling him I'll be down soon? I just need a few minutes."

"Why don't I send him up here?"

"No, I want to get up. It'll be good to stretch my legs."

Ben kept his true feelings private: A bedside visit from Vince would be an invitation for pity.

"Okay. I'll see you downstairs, whenever you're up for it."

Leah stepped from the room and all but closed the door. Despite the chatter downstairs and in the yard, despite the music thumping from the cellar—or maybe because of it—Ben drifted back into sleep.

When he woke the house was silent, or nearly so. He got up and hobbled to the dresser, pulled away the T-shirt he'd thrown over the alarm clock's glow: it was twenty of twelve.

"Shit."

His lower back throbbed like a beacon, pulsing pain down his legs.

Pills. His next dose was long overdue.

He scanned the dresser and the top of the nightstand. The bottle was nowhere in sight. He looked through drawers and under his bed, even lifted his pillow. Nothing. Then he remembered: he'd taken the last one downstairs, washed it down with a beer.

As he lurched along the hallway then down the stairs, signs of life floated up to him: from the living room, low-volume banjo and fiddle, one of his dad's old bluegrass records; from the kitchen, a murmur of voices, and the stale haze of smokers present and departed.

In the downstairs bathroom, a toilet flushed, and when the door opened Ben was grateful to see a stranger—a young woman in a floor-length black dress, her eyes made up like a raccoon's. Most likely, one of Leah's art-school friends. No one he felt obligated to talk to.

Once she was gone he checked the medicine chest and the cabinet under the sink. No pills.

Leah. Maybe she'd seen them.

He exited the bathroom and crept along the hall, peering first into the living room and next into the kitchen, finding more strangers and then a cousin of Leah's whom he escaped with a wave. He moved ahead to the dining room, and it was here where he finally found her.

Cleared of its table and chairs, the space had been made into an impromptu gallery of what Leah considered her best paintings, the best of those that hadn't yet sold. The most visible space, the wall across from the entrance where Ben now stood, had been devoted to one of her newest and largest works. Composed mostly of thick-stroked blues and greens, the painting called to mind an underwater commotion. Flung to the edges were dissipated, vaguely human shapes that on this particular evening reminded Ben very much of his semi-drugged self.

Leah stood in front of the painting, speaking in a low voice to the tall, slightly stoop-shouldered man beside her.

Vince.

His closely cropped hair, his sharkskin-ish blue-gray jacket had briefly thrown Ben off.

Vince followed Leah's gaze and pointing finger to various parts of the painting, listening intently to whatever she was saying, now and then murmuring responses, questions.

How do the colors . . .

Yes, I was trying to get across a feeling of displacement . . .

And this part here, what is . . .

Ben heard words and phrases but failed to connect them. What he could not fail to see was a shift in Vince's attention. At some moment, as Leah pointed, explained, and described, Vince turned his gaze to her and kept it there, his expression rapt and private, just as when he was pulled into music.

Leah didn't notice, or pretended not to, until she turned about to face him, as if he'd taken her by the shoulders. They stared at each other—Leah entranced and uneasy, Vince unchanged, the painting as good as invisible.

Ben waited, heart pounding, his curiosity equal to his fear.

Then a glass shattered in the kitchen.

Vince looked to the doorway, seeing Ben. Just as Leah turned, Ben fled, hearing her question—"What?"—but not Vince's answer.

He limped back toward the stairs, jealous, panicked, and confused. Part of him was certain he'd interrupted a seduction;

part of him was almost as certain that the benzodiazepines had granted him fresh admission to the theater of paranoia, which he'd quit pot to avoid. Either way, Ben considered it best to distance himself from all human society, including Vince's—especially Vince's—at least until this party was over.

Climbing the stairs brought fresh jolts of pain, and he reflexively patted his chest.

His shirt pocket. That's where he'd stashed the pills. And if he was remembering correctly, he'd stripped down to his T-shirt before climbing into bed, thrown his over shirt onto a chair.

He hauled himself up the stairs, not before grabbing a half-full bottle of beer that had been abandoned on the hall table. Back in the bedroom, he closed the door and found the pills just where he'd guessed they'd be: in his shirt pocket. He washed one down with some beer then sat there, quickly coming to the conclusion that he could get away with another. Right now, his back hurt like hell.

A knock sounded on the door, not Leah's.

"Yeah?" Ben hoped his irritation was clear.

"It's me. Vince."

"Come in."

Vince did. In the shadows, he seemed even less familiar to Ben. It wasn't just the shorter hair and shiny jacket; he looked hollowed-out thin, hungry.

"Don't get up," Vince said.

Ben felt no inclination to. He was glad that, at the very least, he wasn't on his back.

Vince grabbed the chair by the bed and gave Ben a *May I?* look. When Ben nodded yes, Vince took a seat.

"I thought you were going to stick around down there," he said. "I'd been waiting for you to make an appearance."

"Had to flee, sorry. The pain was really getting to me."

"I'm sorry about your back."

Ben swallowed more of the beer and set the bottle on the nightstand. "That's what I get for lifting a bag of cement all by myself."

Vince had no reply to this. For some time, they sat in silence, the kind of silence that fell between near strangers. Music, music they played or listened to or talked about, had always been a constant of their times together, the main thing that connected them. Without it, they were merely sharing space.

"That new album of yours," Ben said. "When's it coming out?"

"November first, if all goes as planned."

"I heard a couple preview songs on the radio. They're really good."

"Thanks."

Ben's compliment was sincere. If the two songs were any indication of the album as a whole, the Vagrants were on to a different sound, something both rougher and more melodic—Tommy Nemec's influence, no doubt. Ben was grateful for the change, and grateful that he heard nothing of himself in the new songs. There was nothing, as well, of the riffs Vince had given him on that cassette.

After a while, Vince said, "I still think of your dad, from time to time."

Ross died less than a month after Vince asked Ben to rejoin the Vagrants. By the time Ben dug his father's grave, by the time he made the decision not to return to the band, Vince was already on his way out of the country, ready to resume touring. He hadn't made it to the funeral.

Vince went on: "He was a good man."

Ben let this compliment float between them, unanswered.

Vince waited a bit, shifting in his chair. Then he said, "I don't think I ever told you this, but you remind me of him. In a lot of ways."

An olive branch? If Vince had been on the way to seducing Leah, this was as close as he'd ever get to an apology, Ben was sure.

"I'm not sure I should take that as a compliment, considering he was a cheating shit."

Vince flashed a look Ben recognized from old arguments, old disputes about the directions of songs. It said, *Don't push it.*

Ben's back pain was beginning to recede, the throbbing now like a distant signal. He slouched against the bed pillows, settling himself.

"Listen, Vince. Don't think I'm anything but grateful to my dad. I mean, look what I've inherited from him: I'm now king of the cemetery grounds, at almost double the pay. And the benefits at management level—well, they pretty much put the rock-n-roll lifestyle to shame."

Vince stared at Ben, no longer angry. Now, in the look on his face, in the tone of his voice, he seemed to be aiming for a cautious neutrality. As if Ben were not an old friend but a mentally unstable stranger, which he might, in fact, have become.

"Leah told me they're covering your tuition for—what is it you've been studying? Environmental management?"

Ben didn't answer, at least not the question Vince had asked. Part of him wanted to say, *Do yourself a favor and leave. Right now.* But that part didn't win.

He said, "Let's bring this back to you, Vince. I feel like congratulations are in order."

Ben took Vince's silence as permission to proceed.

"I couldn't help but notice that your shakes are gone, and you look really good. Nice and mellow and steady."

"Shakes?"

"From back when you visited me at the cemetery. When you were about to give Boskin the hammer."

Below them, someone called goodnight through the downstairs hall. Seconds later, a car door slammed, an engine started.

"I never thought I'd say this, Vince. But I guess some good can come of trading uppers for heroin."

The *Don't push it* look returned to Vince. He slid to the edge of his chair, poised for a move.

"Where did you hear that?"

"Come on. The story's everywhere."

Ben first heard it the year before, and in confidence, from Dave. Earlier tonight, Tuke—newly bitter and considerably drunk—repeated it, loud enough to be picked up by anyone in earshot.

"And you believe it?"

"I believe what I see."

Vince stood up, his eyes still fixed on Ben.

He said, "What a bitter, self-pitying ass you've become. I never imagined this for you, Ben."

Ben leaned back against the pillows, let them take his full weight. "Well, I'm always happy to exceed expectations. As for your little habit, I'm in no position to judge."

He reached for the bottle of pills.

"Thank God for drugs, I say. Thank God for every single thing that kills our pain."

Ben shook out a benzo and washed it down with beer. Then he set the pill bottle back on the nightstand, took one last glance at Vince.

"Help yourself," he said. "Everything that's mine is, and always has been, yours."

The blue hum rose up, quicker than before. He rolled over and into it, let it swallow him whole.

Chapter 28

"That would be a good thing for them to cut on my tombstone: Wherever she went, including here, it was against her better judgment."

—Dorothy Parker

General Grounds and Lot 421
Mid-evening, June 29 (present day)

Miranda was the last of them to climb the fence and land on the cemetery side.

"There's no place like home," she said, looking around as if to reacquaint herself.

"Indeed," Alex replied.

Since her father and Pete had started keeping longer hours at the cemetery, Cole had steered her bandmates away from it. After practice, they'd linger an hour or so longer in Miranda's basement, listening to other people's songs, old and new, and eating the cheapest food that could be delivered. Or they'd just pack it in for the night.

The week before, they'd driven out to the planned site of their concert, Randolph Park, a grassy expanse as soulless as a golf course. They'd brought their blanket and cooler to the park but didn't set them down right away. When they did decide to stay, it wasn't for long. They sipped their drinks but never sang, and when they spoke they whispered. What was the problem, Cole wondered, with big, featureless spaces at night? For her, it seemed to be this: she felt both like easy prey and diluted matter, insignificant. She missed the sense of protection and privacy offered by the cemetery's gravestones and rolling hills.

Tonight, though, as Cole led the way across the cemetery grounds, back to Vince Resklar's plot, she took little comfort from her surroundings. She'd been distracted all evening, even during practice, causing her to fuck up three times and eventually get the eye from Grif: a first, for her.

Sorry, man. I'm having Daddy Issues.

Though that was the truth, it was nothing she would ever say out loud, to Grif or anyone else in the band. She and her dad were going to have to work this thing out between themselves.

The problem was, she hadn't yet been able to speak to him. By the time he got home last night, or early this morning, Cole had fallen into a deep enough sleep that she hadn't heard his arrival. When she woke up, he was already gone, having left a note on the kitchen table: *Away at an off-site meeting today. See you after your band practice. (Help yourself to lasagna in freezer.)*

Cole could have called him during the day, but she didn't want to have this conversation over the phone. She was determined, though, that it was going to happen this evening, as soon as she got home. Even if she had to get him out of bed.

Now as before, Miranda unfurled their blanket over Vince Resklar's grave, and Alex started passing out their usual drinks of choice. Before he could hand Cole a limeade, she said, "I'll take a beer this time."

She hoped it might relax her, take the edge off things.

Alex smiled and tossed her a can of Narragansett.

Cole cracked it open and forced down as big a gulp as she could stand. It was just as bitter as she remembered.

Once he'd settled in with his own drink, Grif said it again, grimly, as if pronouncing a sentence.

"Five."

He said it to all of them. He said it to no one. He stared toward some spot beyond his outstretched legs, as if that evil number had nestled there.

Alex made a *Not this again* face and took a sip of his beer.

Five was the number of original songs worthy of a concert performance. Damned good ones, Cole thought. Though they were working on a few other numbers, it was uncertain these would be ready in time.

"Six, actually," Miranda said. "If we count the Vagrants cover. Are we counting the Vagrants cover?"

"Okay, *six,*" Grif said.

"Guys," Alex said, laying a hand to his chest. "Allow me to be the voice of reason. We have four songs in the three-minute range and two that are about four minutes. Add in some stage patter, and that'll give us at least twenty minutes of material, which I think is pretty respectable. Considering we're not the only act." Seeing the blank look on Miranda's face, he said, "Or am I mistaken?"

"No," Miranda said, "you're not mistaken. Meg Tirella scored that neo-funk band, and she's fishing around for other acts."

Cole forced down another sip of beer. "What's up with that magician dude? That friend of your brother's."

Miranda wrinkled her nose, as if her own drink had gone bitter. "I just saw some of his videos, and let me spare you from doing the same."

"That bad, huh?"

"That bad. But remember that stand-up comic I told you about? The one from Lincoln Falls? I saw some of her stuff online, and it's really good. I'll send you guys the links."

Cole thought of Pete, knowing he'd gladly come to their rescue with his covers. Then she remembered that her father was his guitarist. The black-and-white photos of him and his Rickenbacker flashed through her mind.

Pete Kovak and Nick Graves.

Wanting to clear her head, she breathed deeply, taking in the peppery sweetness of the Nicotiana flowers that she and her father had planted around the grounds in late spring. When he told her their fragrance was strongest at night, Cole wanted to ask him, *Who's the smell for—the dead?* Now, she was grateful for the fragrance, and for the mild buzz of the beer, which was just starting to set in. Together they were unknotting the tension in her shoulders, down her spine.

Miranda set aside her drink and looked to Grif.

"Speaking of the Vagrants cover. Could we maybe sing through it one more time? I feel like we could figure the problem out better without the instruments."

Miranda and Grif insisted the "problem" was with the harmony, but nothing sounded wrong to Cole. To her, their two voices were ideal collaborators, aligning when they needed to, working against each other when the words or music called for it. When, in the chorus of the Vagrants' song, Miranda's and Grif's voices circled each other uncertainly, that uncertainty felt necessary, nothing that needed to be fixed.

It was just the same when they started in again.

Numbers, here's my numbers, four and twelve, and twelve and eight
There's a question in them—Answer me, it's getting late.

Midway into the second verse, Cole saw a figure rushing forward from the distance. Despite the darkness she recognized the stride, steady yet hitched from some old injury. It was her father.

Because she alone faced him, the others were oblivious to his approach. Cole thought of stopping them, warning them, but he was already well on his way. Alex had pitched his own empty back into the cooler, reasonably out of sight, but her own beer was still at her side. She loosened the work shirt she'd tied around her waist and draped it over the can, already understanding that the effort was futile.

Her father was moving with ever greater speed, from the Section B fountain to the graves just past it, and then emerging into the lamplight on the nearest path. Here, he paused, as if deciding what to do, or maybe just observing the musician's courtesy of never interrupting another's song, of letting it play out to the end.

Cole doubted he could see her, or any of them—not clearly, anyway, because he was in the light and they were in the dark. So as he listened to the singing, she never took her eyes from his face, which she'd last seen in the photographs from the basement. It looked as intent and unreadable as in the press-kit picture.

Though Miranda and Grif hadn't changed a word of the old Vagrants' song, they had made it their own—to Cole, something stranger and more haunting. Whatever her father heard in their version, and whether it pleased or repulsed him, she had no idea.

After the song wound down, as Miranda and Grif began talking through the harmony problem, pinning it to notes in the bridge, Ben moved forward again, with determination, a determination that made Cole certain she'd been spotted, and that she was in trouble.

By the time Alex, then Grif and Miranda, looked to where Cole was staring, her father was just a few yards away. In seconds, he was looming over Vince Resklar's headstone.

"Dad," Cole said, getting to her feet, "these are my bandmates."

And, guys, this is my father, Ben Dirjery, a.k.a., Nick Graves. One of the original Vagrants. By bringing this up, she might steer things down another track, but possibly a worse one. So she held her tongue.

Grif was the second of them to get up. He reached over the headstone to shake Ben's hand, introduce himself. Miranda and Alex followed.

Ben's return of their greetings was cheerless, an afterthought. All the while his eyes roved over the ground, taking in the cooler, the open cans of limeade. Like a hound on a scent trail, he stepped around the headstone and headed right for Cole's work shirt, pulled it aside. He examined the can quietly, as if not quite believing his eyes. Then he turned to Cole.

"Is this yours?"

Yes. And I'm really sorry.

Fuck yes, it's mine, and it was long overdue.

"I asked you a question, Cole." His voice was level and cold.

"Yes. It's mine."

He glanced toward the cooler and the other scattered cans, then looked back at Cole.

"So what you told me about keeping things clean, that wasn't the truth."

For a moment words escaped her. How could she make him understand how tame this all was, really? It wasn't like they had heroin, or even pot. This made her more grateful than ever that her joint-smoking days were behind her.

"This is the first beer I ever drank here, Dad. I swear."

Alex glanced nervously from Cole to Ben. "She's right. I'm usually the only drinker."

Grif stepped in. "That's true. And I'm his ride home."

It was as if Ben hadn't heard them. He walked to the cooler and lifted the lid, sending a cold shock of embarrassment through Cole.

He looked over the contents and closed the lid. Then he turned to Alex.

"So the only drinkers need twelve beers. And a six pack of soda's good enough for the rest of you."

Cole stepped forward. "Come on, Dad!"

Alex glanced to Grif, as if for help. "With all due respect sir, we . . . I mean, I—" He stopped for a moment, his usual eloquence escaping him. "I wasn't planning on drinking them all at once."

"Great," Ben said. "I'll sleep a whole lot better tonight."

Cole wanted nothing more than to vanish into the earth, away from her father, away from these kids she'd started to think of as friends.

She glanced from Alex to Miranda to Grif and hoped they saw that she was sorry. She said, "You guys should go. Please. I'll see you on Sunday." This mention of their next practice was a hope, and a question.

Before any of them could answer it, Ben said, "We'll see about that."

Then he was back to the cooler. He lifted the lid and pulled out the two cardboard carriers of beer. He set these aside and replaced the lid, and nodded toward the beers.

"Those are going into the dumpster. And you can take these"—he knocked on the top of the cooler, still holding the limeades—"home."

Alex shouldered his backpack, and he and Grif grabbed the handles on either side of the cooler, lifted it from the ground.

"And one last thing," Ben said. "If I catch any of you with beer again, or with anything else you shouldn't be drinking, or smoking, you won't get off so easy. Understand?"

They agreed to his terms, with a word or a nod. But Grif and Alex seemed, in spirit, to have already fled. Now, only Miranda seemed wholly present. She kept her eyes on Cole, as if reluctant to leave her to whatever was next.

"Go ahead," Cole told her. "I'll be okay."

Miranda balled up the blanket, tucked it under her arm, and started following Grif and Alex toward the East Gate. Then she turned and said to Cole, "I'll call you."

Only three words, and perhaps an empty promise. But Miranda had said them boldly, almost in defiance. And this brought Cole to tears.

Ben acted as if he didn't notice. He looked over the grave as if to make sure nothing else was out of line, then he picked up the beer carriers. "Okay," he said. "Let's go."

As he started out ahead of Cole, she felt as if everything was moving too quickly, away from her and out of her control.

"Dad?"

He couldn't hear her or was outright ignoring her; she couldn't tell. He just kept moving, making her pick up her pace.

"Hey Dad! *Wait!*"

When that failed she stopped and shouted as loud as she could: "*Nick Graves!*"

This brought him to a stop, froze him still, and he stood there silently even as she drew closer. Cole wondered if he was thinking the same thing she was, that it was her turn for some answers.

When he turned to face her, he looked like he'd been pulled over by a cop.

"Who told you about Nick Graves?" He said the name as if it had nothing to do with him.

"No one *told* me. I found your band mementoes in the basement. The fliers and stuff. And it made me wonder why you never told me you were in the band. Why you said you didn't really know Vince Resklar."

He kept silent, as if considering what he would and wouldn't tell her.

"The more I think about it—and I've thought about it a lot—the more I'm convinced the stuff in the basement is a clue to a mystery. The mystery of this weird thing with you and music."

He set down the beers, no longer so intent to leave. "What do you mean by *this weird thing* with me and music?"

Cole took another breath of the night air and the Nicotiana, whose scent seemed to have intensified.

"When I was a little girl, I heard you playing the guitar once, and it sounded so beautiful, like you were really enjoying yourself. But I never heard you play again."

He lowered his head, but Cole could tell from the brightness of his eyes that he was taking in every word.

"When you told me you *grew out* of wanting to play music, I believed you, but I also sensed a kind of sadness in you. And when I started playing the drums, seriously, you acted like you were happy for me, but I saw that same kind of sadness in you, and I didn't know what that was all about."

Slowly, he lowered himself onto the ground, and Cole sat down beside him.

"Since I found that stuff in the basement, I've been feeling more and more like the sadness goes back to you and the Vagrants, like your time in the band is connected to something pretty bad."

He cast her a level look, absent of anger or denial.

"You're a good detective, Cole. But the problem wasn't with the Vagrants; it was with me."

"I don't understand."

He looked away from her, into the distance. In the long silence that fell between them, Cole wondered if he'd already reached the limit of what he was willing to tell her. Then he spoke.

"A long time ago I did something I don't feel very good about. Something concerning Vince Resklar. I never told anyone about it, not even your mother. But I think it might explain a few things."

He told her about the night of her mother's graduation party, which was also the last night of Vince Resklar's life. He told her about his suspicion that Vince was flirting with her mom, about his tense conversation with Vince, about the pills. The whole time, Cole didn't move or speak. It hardly felt like she even breathed as she tried to keep up with the flood of information about Vince and her dad, someone she thought she knew so well.

Recalling the date on Vince's stone—September 6, 1993—Cole now understood that it didn't just mark his death. It marked a change in her father equally worthy of being etched into granite.

"I can't really trust many memories of that night," he said. "But one thing is certain: when I looked for the pills the next day, they were nowhere to be found. And when I learned how Vince had died, I could come to just one conclusion."

From her internet searching, Cole knew that Vince had crashed his car into a tree, that drugs and alcohol had been found in his system. There were stories, too, about Vince and heroin. After his death, these seemed to break out everywhere.

"So what if he took your pills, Dad? Whether he did or didn't, every choice he made that night was his. I don't see how any of it could be your fault."

Though he was staring off, Cole could tell he was taking in her words. "And what about him just letting you pass out in your bed? You could have died, too."

He looked her way and faintly smiled, as if to reassure her. "I doubt it, Cole. I didn't overdo the pills, really. And I couldn't have had more than a few beers. Bottom line is, I saw the next day, and he didn't."

From the distance came the cry of a train's horn, the rumbling of tracks—two of Cole's favorite sounds. She and Ben paused for a moment to listen.

When the train was gone Ben said, "Here's the hard truth, Cole. I *wanted* him to take those pills. And on that particular evening, a part of me wanted him dead. So the ins and outs of *how* he died, they all feel like technicalities to me."

"I understand, Daddy, but you didn't—"

"No *buts*, Cole!"

He looked both angry and bewildered, as if she were his accuser, not himself.

"Sorry," he said in a softer tone. "It's a point you'll never win. Not with me."

Cole believed that, one day, she might. But now wasn't the time to make her case.

"All right, Daddy. I just wish you would give yourself a break."

He laid a hand over hers. "You know what would give me a real break? If you would let me promise you something."

He tightened his hold on her hand.

"I let this guilt about Vince poison music for me, and I don't want whatever's wrong with me to poison it for you. Do you understand?"

Cole wanted to tell him it was time to stop punishing himself over Vince's death. Twenty-some years of that had been more than enough. But she was too close to tears to speak, so she just nodded.

"I want to do whatever I can to support you—in music, in everything."

She squeezed his hand and hoped he got her message: that his words meant more than she could say.

"And that's part of the reason I don't like to see you out here drinking, even if it's only one beer. I don't want any harm to come to you, Cole. Not if I can possibly help it."

"I know, Daddy."

She wanted to bring things back to music, back to him and music. She wanted to tell him that she'd heard him playing guitar and singing in the cemetery office, and that he hadn't sounded poisoned, far from it. Yet that time seemed so private she was wary of mentioning it.

There was one thing she couldn't put aside.

"Remember that song you heard Miranda and Grif singing?"

"'Four or Eight'?"

"Yeah."

"We want to perform it. At the concert."

"Okay."

That was all. It was as if she'd asked him for the time.

"You're sure."

"I'd be honored. The two of them did way better with the vocals than Vince and I ever did."

Though she'd never let on to him, Cole agreed.

"Can I tell them you were Nick Graves?"

He smiled. "Sure. But I doubt they'll know he was in the band."

Slowly, he got to his knees, then to his feet, Cole checking her urge to lend him a hand.

That cement-bag lift from long ago was just one of the ghosts that haunted his back, his knees, his neck, his physical whole. There had been tractor rolls, ditch dives, surely countless other accidents unknown to Cole. Perhaps more taxing than anything was the daily wear and tear. She wondered how many more years of it he'd be able to stand.

When both of them were up, he grabbed the beer carriers. "Let's haul these things to the dumpster. Then I need to get Pete's keys from the office, drop them by his girlfriend's."

"He forgot them?"

"Yep."

As they headed toward the parking lot, Cole remembered something: they were close to where that lady had pointed out the glowing mushrooms.

"Dad, can I show you something?"

"Sure."

Even as she posed her question, she realized the glow might have faded out for good. But it hadn't. The moment they passed the Memory Garden, a faint green light illuminated the grass ahead, beneath the old birch.

"My God!" he cried, shaking her by both shoulders. She

wasn't sure she'd ever seen him this ecstatic. "Dolores Fielding's holy grail."

Dolores Fielding, the mushroom lady. Cole had met her once or twice and knew she was very sick.

She waited as her father stepped forward and snapped pictures with his phone.

"Hold on," he said, typing out a text. "I just want to get these to her daughter."

When this was done he led the way to the parking lot, quickly, as if energized by the mushroom sighting. When they arrived, he paused at the door of his truck.

He said, "A week or so ago, didn't you mention you'd recorded some of your songs?"

"Yeah. But the recordings are pretty shitty."

"Are they somewhere we could listen to them? Tonight?"

"Sure. They're on the computer."

"Let's do it."

Just then, his phone pinged with a message. "Dolores Fielding's daughter," he announced, then read the message aloud: "My mom says, 'Our beauties discovered, at last!'"

Chapter 29

"I write purely with one dramatic structure and that is the rite of passage. . . . Rock and roll itself can be described as music to accompany the rite of passage."

–Pete Townshend

General Grounds and Oak Corner
Some October afternoon, 1989

"Ce-me-te-ry cliché, ce-me-*tahr-y* cliché! Ce-me-te-ry cliché, ce-me-*tahr*-y cliché!"

Ben sang in time to the tape as he roamed ahead, with words his surroundings had nudged to the surface of his mind: gold and orange leaves flickering down from the maples and oaks, onto graves, gardens, and statues, onto the lake that mirrored the blue of the sky. Bright and chiming, the guitar chords seemed part of the colors all around him.

"Ce-me-te-ry cliché, ce-me-*tahr-y* cliché! Ce-me-te-ry cliché, ce-me-*tahr*-y cliché!"

At the bridge of his song-in-progress, the chords turned darker, lower—like the smells he kicked up from the fallen leaves, the bittersweet of something going, going, almost gone—until they returned to bright and loud, flowing through him like blood. Like life.

"Ce-me-te-ry cliché, ce-me-*tahr-y* cliché! Ce-me-te-ry cliché, ce-me-*tahr*-y cliché!"

An incomplete song, but a damned good one. Maybe the best he'd written so far.

"Ce-me-te-ry cliché, ce-me-*tahr-y* cliché! Ce-me-te-ry cliché, ce-me-*tahr*-y cliché!"

Vince is going to like this one.

Leah is going to love it.

Nearing Oak Corner, Ben spotted the mushrooms he'd first seen the previous weekend: bright orange ruffles crowding the base of the dead oak and climbing partway up its side.

This time, a hatted figure stood alongside them, giving him a ship-deck wave. Dolores.

She must have heard him singing, but he wasn't embarrassed. He was just glad to see her. He shut off the tape deck, dropped his headphones to his neck, and hurried toward her.

"Bunch of show-offs, huh?" Ben said, waving toward the mushrooms.

Dolores laughed. "They're that, indeed."

"What are they, though, really?"

"Chicken of the woods. Good to eat if you catch them at the right time, which I hope I have."

Ben spied her usual basket at her feet, partly filled with orange ruffles. "I'm glad you got to them before it was too late. My dad tells me this tree has a date with a chainsaw."

Dolores followed his gaze to one of the lowest limbs, the only one populated by leaves, the same bright orange as those on the nearby oaks—last hurrahs. The higher branches had been bare for several seasons.

"I figured that time was near." Dolores dropped her harvesting knife into the basket and whisked her hands clean. "Let's talk about something with a future: you. What was that I heard you singing—*cemetery chalet? Croquet?*"

"Cliché. Cemetery cliché. Just some nonsense lyrics for a song I'm working on."

Ben decided not to go into the whole story behind the phrase: his mom's label for postcard-worthy scenes in the cemetery, which were never more abundant than in the fall, when the combination of colorful trees and gravestones suggested that death could have a bright side, or at least a pretty one, tinged with melancholy and/or Halloweenish thrills.

"It's music first, lyrics second," Ben said. "At least for me. And maybe I'll leave the words part to my bandmates."

"You're in a band?"

"Yeah."

"Wonderful!"

"We're playing a hole-in-the-wall gig here this weekend. Which is why I'm back in town."

"That's great," Dolores said. "And it's nice to see you listening to your *own* music here, and enjoying it. So it seems."

Ben smiled. "I *am* enjoying it. Does that make me some kind of self-involved ass?"

"No. It makes you lucky, in my book."

If anyone could understand why he was drawn to the cemetery for a walk-and-listen, even though he wasn't working here now, it would be Dolores. Now and then back at school, scenes from this place flashed through his mind while he worked on songs, as if his old habit of roaming the grounds with his Walkman had forged some lasting connection between this cemetery and music. For some reason, this place seemed to spark something in him.

Dolores pushed back her hat, looked him in the eye. "Would it be overstepping to ask for a listen?"

Ben hesitated, not because he thought she was overstepping but because he respected her opinions. If she thought his guitar work sucked, it probably did. And he was sure this judgment would show in her eyes, silently overruling whatever kind thing she might say.

"Not at all," he said.

As he rewound the cassette, Dolores tossed her hat aside. He passed her the tape deck and headphones. "Just press *play*." She put on the headphones and did as he said.

For an uncomfortably long stretch, her expression was unreadable, especially because she kept her eyes closed. Then, she started nodding along to what she was hearing, a faint smile playing across her lips.

From moment to moment, he wondered what part of the song she was on—one of the bright stretches, or one of the turns to the dark, which back when these chords first came to him felt unexpected yet right, like a gift from someone else. Someone who understood how music worked.

Eventually, she pressed *stop* and opened her eyes, which he couldn't quite read. They shone like she was close to tears. She stayed silent for a bit, then pulled the headphones away, handed them back to Ben, along with the tape deck.

"That took me away from myself, in all the best ways. And I heard not a single cliché." Here, she smiled.

"So you think it's a keeper?"

"Oh, yes. I want to hear the final version, whenever you have it."

"You will. I promise."

Ben tucked the tape deck and headphones into his jacket and checked his watch on the sly. Almost time to meet up with Leah.

Glancing up, he caught Dolores studying him. She didn't look away.

"You've never looked happier to me, Ben. It's really nice to see."

He didn't know what to say to this—*Thanks?* No. He simply nodded and smiled, and a moment later, he and Dolores said their goodbyes.

Now and then in the years that followed, Ben returned to this scene in his mind. In his darkest times, he believed it quite possibly marked the height of all his promise, before his own limitations and failings caught up with him.

Chapter 30

Meeting Agenda, Bolster Hill Cemetery Board of Directors

1. Overview of financials – Carl Jenks, President
2. Recommendations for irrigation and drainage upgrades – Igor Volnakov, Sacred Grounds Consulting
3. Review of equipment and service requests – Pepper Lloyd, Board Member
4. Sculptural improvements to Memory Garden – Leah Dirjery, Consulting Artist
5. Miscellaneous matters – Benjamin Dirjery, Grounds Manager

Events Tent, Section E
After 7 p.m., July 26 (present day)

"I understand why the yarn art had to be removed. That's cemetery policy. But I don't think anyone would dispute how much people liked it. Especially the work in the Memory Garden."

Pacing before the board in her white linen suit, Leah looked more like a prosecuting attorney than an artist. And like a good attorney, she'd done her homework.

She walked to the end of the function table and turned to Marcy Walsh, the board's most junior member, and overlord of the cemetery's website.

"What about all those favorable comments on the website, Marcy?"

Marcy glanced toward her colleagues, as if to ask permission. Then she said, quietly, "We got quite a few of them. Especially after those photos appeared in the *Register*."

Leah nodded then made her way toward the center of the table, toward the more senior board members, including Jenks. She stopped and looked to Ted Santos.

"And, Ted, what about all those complaints that came in once the yarn art was taken down?"

He spoke boldly, right into the mike: "We were surprised about how many came in. They overloaded our voice mail. And our email account."

Satisfied, Leah headed back to her easeled drawings, collectively labeled "Perpetual Sunset."

"I would argue, then, that this sculpture would be public art in the most basic and respectful sense. I think it would greatly enhance the Memory Garden and the cemetery as a whole."

After an interval of silence, she said, "Any questions?"

Dependably, Al Crider rose to the aisle mike, just to the left of Ben and Pete. Al made a point of sitting by the mike at every board meeting. And at most every meeting Ben could remember, he used it.

"I don't think of yarn as a lasting material," Al said. "You're going to be using something else, I assume."

"That's correct. The sculptor will be working with nylon, steel, and steel wire—all durable and weather resistant. Anything else?"

"What's the cost?"

Davis Wooten's question—now, previously, and forever more.

The most senior board member, Wooten nixed every expenditure without fail, even outlays for shovels and grass seed. More than once, Ross had said that if it were in Wooten's power, the cemetery corporation would be dissolved immediately, and the land sold to a developer of anything more profitable than a cemetery. This was only partly a joke.

Leah seemed to have remembered Ross's words. She was prepared and unfazed.

She said, "According to the budget for the current fiscal

year, five hundred and twenty-six dollars remain for non-land-scaped grounds enhancements. I've priced out the materials, and the costs will come in at no more than five hundred dollars, for which I will gladly provide receipts. As for labor costs, the sculptor and I will be donating our time."

Silence.

Santos looked up and down the table then leaned toward his mike. "Okay, comrades. Can we come to a decision on this?"

The others agreed, and the board voted: eight *yeses* and one *no*: Wooten's.

In the applause that followed, Ben caught Leah's eye and gave her a thumbs-up. He was proud of her and grateful, and he thought once again of the thank-you dinner she'd insisted wasn't necessary. He was now determined to make it happen. Or, barring that, he was going to buy her a very expensive bottle of champagne. Soon, but not tonight. Tonight, she'd told Ben, she and Adam would be driving to Northeast Vermont for a long weekend. It was possible that Adam was already in the parking lot, waiting.

In spite of this, she took back the mike and looked to the board.

"May I say something else? Quickly?"

From the table, nods and mumbles of approval.

Leah turned to the audience.

"A painting of mine was said to be the inspiration for the yarn art in the Memory Garden. But I can't really take credit for the plans I just presented to you. The sense of place and space that the yarn artist brought to this work is theirs alone and truly something to be recognized and commended. I have been reaching out, trying to find this person, so far without success. So if any of you have any leads, grab one of my cards, and please let me know. Thanks very much, all of you."

Leah pulled a stack of cards from her pocket, waved them over her head, and left them on the display table. Then she grabbed her bag and headed for the exit, casting one last look at Ben.

"Good luck," she mouthed. Then she was gone.

It seemed she took with her a share of Ben's courage and determination. He'd spoken at countless board meetings, and up until this moment the experience had never been more stressful than singing in the shower. Now, an electrical current seemed to be flowing through him.

As if sensing Ben's nervousness, Haley, who was sitting to his left, slapped his back. Pete, on Ben's right, grabbed his arm and whispered, "You're going to kick some ass up there, man."

"Maybe my own."

"No chance."

Ben patted Pete's shoulder, then willed himself to his feet and down the aisle, toward the presenter's mike. Straight ahead, Jenks glared at him from his spot at the table, reminding Ben of their encounter just before the meeting was brought to order. Jenks had cornered him, shaking a copy of the agenda in his face.

"What the hell," he'd hissed, "are *miscellaneous matters*?" Ben's response: "You're about to find out."

Surely, and rightly, Jenks suspected skullduggery. Yet it was skullduggery of the most banal sort. Ben had simply waited until last week, the start of Jenks's vacation, to add his agenda item, and the final document came back from the copier just a few hours before the meeting.

Now, Ben was glad to turn away from Jenks and toward the crowd. He was grateful for the near silence all around him, the only sound being the pulse of crickets.

The audience was the largest Ben could recall for a board meeting. In addition to the regulars, like Al Crider, it seemed that every person he and Pete were counting on had made it. This restored a measure of his courage, as did the presence of Cole in the second row, next to her bandmates. She smiled at him, and he smiled back.

Ben's only disappointment: Meredith was nowhere in sight. Then again, this was perhaps for the best, considering how things might very well go.

He took a deep breath and spoke into the mike.

"Ben Dirjery here. I want to thank all of you for coming tonight.

"Looking out at the crowd, I'm guessing that about twenty-five percent of you know exactly why I'm here and what I'm going to talk about.

"I want to say, first, that you're right about my topic, mostly. And, second, I hope you'll listen nonetheless. Because I'm going to try something a little different tonight. Something I hope will make good sense to every single person in this tent.

"For the last few years, I've been in charge of the cemetery's Green Initiative, which means that at meetings like these, I stand in front of charts and tables and talk about the percentages by which the cemetery has reduced water or pesticide usage, or increased its appeal to so-called green consumers. The board asks me for numbers and data, and I do my best to oblige. And if I can show that doing some good improves the balance sheet, so much the better.

"Of course, there's nothing wrong with doing well by doing good. In fact, there's a whole lot right with it. But, as I've discovered, working from numbers alone has some real limitations, which I'll get to in just a minute.

"First, though, let me give a little background to anyone who hasn't had the fortune of hearing about what, to me, has become the most important goal of the Green Initiative. And it goes to the heart of our central mission at Bolster Hill Cemetery: burying the dead in a way that respects their wishes and those of their loved ones. For more and more people, that means respecting the earth as well—going into it as directly as possible, without embalming chemicals or the quote-unquote *protection* of a heavy casket, or a concrete liner or vault.

"As many of you know, I've made the point that we at the cemetery should be listening to these folks. And I've suggested devoting half of the plots in our new wing, Section E, to green burials. Of course, the cemetery management wanted to know what this would mean in terms of numbers. Most importantly, what kind of revenue might come in and what, if anything, might be lost?

"So I did a lot of research and ran a bunch of numbers. And I put together lots of tables and bar charts and projections that, in my opinion, show why my proposal makes good financial sense. By now everyone sitting behind me, and every single person in management, has a copy of my report. And if anyone else wants to see it, there's a bunch of copies on that table over there. Please help yourself."

Glancing toward the table, Ben saw that Meredith had arrived. She was cruising along the rows of chairs, looking for a seat.

"But as some of you may know, few things do a better job of making nothing happen than a report. This one hit the in-boxes like an anchor, just like every other report I've ever done. And when I started pushing for action, for decisions, I discovered that the best numbers in the world wouldn't be enough to get things rolling. Especially when they come up against old, entrenched systems and fear of change.

"So, tonight, I want to talk about something that transcends numbers—or that should for a cemetery. That is the needs and wishes of the people we're supposed to be serving. People in our community, like Dolores Fielding, who would be here tonight if she could.

"As many of you know, Dolores has been a fixture of the cemetery for years. She's led the mushroom walks every fall, and she stood up for the flora here long before anyone else did. She kept after cemetery managers to cut back on pesticides years before we finally did, and she was the first person to encourage us to protect, even reintroduce, native plants. In short, she was the real start of the Green Initiative, and a big motivator, for me, in keeping it going. So tonight, I would very much like to return the favor."

Ben looked to Jenny Fielding, in the front row. Saw that she was waiting, ready. So were the others he and Pete had been in touch with.

"Right now, Dolores is very sick. But when she was still able to walk these grounds, she took me aside and asked if she could have a green burial in the cemetery. I would have said *yes* on the spot if it were up to me alone. Especially since both of Dolores's parents are buried here. But of course it isn't up to just me. So I'm asking the board to say *yes* to her, and to my proposition for Section E. Tonight. Because Dolores is running out of time, and because it's just the right thing to do—not just for her, but for all the other people who want just what she does. And there are a lot of them."

He glanced toward Haley, who looked as on edge as Ben felt. "According to my review of call logs, the central office received thirty-one inquiries about green burials between January first of this year and the end of June. That's almost double the inquiries received the entire year before.

"But enough of my talking." Ben turned toward the board. "Do any of you have questions for me?"

Jenks, now lowered to a simmer, was the first to speak: "I don't have any questions so much as a comment: You say good-bye to the vaults, you say hello to the sinkage. If your proposition goes forward, Section E will look like a field of ski moguls."

"No, it won't," Ben said. "Not with the right type of filling. As I've said many times before. And as I describe—in great detail—in the report."

Ben noticed that other board members, not Jenks, had started flipping through the copies of the report Pete had left at their places. Guessing the nature of their next questions, and hoping to save some time and embarrassment, Ben said, "I'm sure that many of you were impressed by the financial projections for my proposal. They're on pages twelve and thirteen, in case you'd like to take another look."

Giving them time to absorb the numbers, Ben turned away and searched the crowd for Meredith, found her seated in the last row. Catching her eye, he smiled, and she flashed him a thumbs-up.

"Ben?"

He turned to see Davis Wooten staring over the top of his reading glasses.

"This certification we need for green burials. What's the cost?"

"Not even a half a percent of the annual budget. Check out page seventeen."

Wooten flipped ahead and searched the page. "Okay, I see it."

After some more page shuffling and murmuring among members of the board, Ted Santos said, "Okay, folks. Are we ready to vote on this?"

A cold, fresh rush of anxiety flowed through Ben. It was almost time. There was just one more thing that needed to be done.

He said, "Hold on a sec, Ted. Can I make a final point?"

"You can."

"Actually, I'm going to ask for some help with this one." Ben turned back to the crowd. "Jenny?"

She rose from her seat and took the mike, bringing some of her mother with her—in the set of her shoulders, in the direct, level tone of her voice.

"I'm Jenny Fielding, Dolores's daughter. It goes without saying that my mother is ready and willing to pay the one thousand five-hundred-dollar fee proposed for a green-burial plot in Section E. But I also want to make a personal pledge: that if the board votes *yes* on Ben's proposition, I will pay that fee, in advance, for my own plot. And I am not alone. Several people here tonight have made the very same pledge, and I'd like them to stand as I read their names:

"Ellie Whitlin. Gus Vance. Adam and Joseph Chisholm-Davies. Lucas and Abigail Everly. Tina and Mitch Gomes. Ryan Hughes. Penelope Mayhew . . . "

Name by name Ben watched them rise, some with the speed and ease of youth, others with the help of a cane or friendly arm. A few he knew by more than name: longtime members of the cemetery association, and Dolores's fellow mushroom hunters—like her, regulars on the grounds. Others had, until now, been only names—prospects for his and Pete's cold calls, gathered in every way Ben could think of.

Through the weeks of calls and calculations, Ben didn't dare imagine the scene before him, of friends, acquaintances, and strangers rising to this purpose. Nor did he expect the effect on him, this thickness in his throat.

" . . . Karen and Tom Tirella. Shirlene Washington. Jane Amato. Christina Baird. And, finally, Ben Dirjery.

"That is twenty-six people, right here in this tent." Jenny lifted her voice: "And another seven people who weren't able to be here have also made the pledge. So that's thirty-three pledgers altogether. And a total of forty-nine thousand, five hundred dollars."

Applause rippled through the crowd, gathering momentum, bringing on cheers and whistles. Waiting this out, Ben glanced toward Pete and Haley and found them looking equally pleased and stunned. Just like himself.

When the applause died down, Ben took back the mike. "Thank you, Jenny. And thank you to all the pledgers, and to my colleague, Pete Kovak, who helped make this happen."

Then he turned to the board. "We've given you both the people and the numbers. Now we just need your vote."

Ben wandered to the shadowy region of trash bins and detritus, as far as he could get from the crowd and the board and still be in the tent. During the wait, he didn't want to speak with anyone, or hear possibly jinxing *Good lucks.*

Once again, he studied Jenks, who was no longer at a simmer. Right now, he was all about twisting and untwisting the candy wrapper in front of him, looking tired and, yes, defeated. Ben had never meant this to be a battle between the two of them, or merely that. He hoped Jenks understood as much, or that he might one day.

"All right, ladies and gents," Ted Santos said. "We have before us a measure to allow green burials in two hundred and ten of the four hundred and twenty plots in Section E, set to officially open on September twelfth. Tell us, each of you, *yea* or *nay*."

One by one they called their votes:

"Yea."

"Yea."

"Yea."

"Nay." (Wooten)

"Yea." (Jenks!)

"Yea."

"Yea."

"Yea."

"Yea."

Ted took a moment to consult his scratch pad. "I count eight *yeas* and a single *nay*, meaning the *yeas* have it!"

Another round of applause and cheers. As Ted called an end to the meeting, Ben headed for Jenks and held out his hand. Jenks took it.

"Thank you, Carl," he said. "This means a lot to me."

"You made a good case, Ben. No one can deny that."

Ben felt a hand on his back. Turning, he saw Jenny and gave her a hug, led her out of earshot of Jenks.

He said, "You tell me when the time comes, all right? Even if it's before September twelfth. We're going to take care of your mother, just like I promised."

"I know you will. Thanks, Ben."

Ben let himself be carried along by congratulations, well wishes, and occasional questions, feeling like a groom at an impromptu wedding. It took him close to an hour to approach the exit, by which time the tent had almost emptied out. Pete and Haley had taken off shortly after the vote, asking for a rain check on beers. Cole and her bandmates followed Pete and Haley, after being assured—not just by Ben—that Section F would be a fine place for a late-summer concert. Now that the exhumation had been called off, the political charge had been sapped from every part of the cemetery grounds.

All the while, Ben was aware of Meredith, of where she sat or stood, of whom she was talking to.

She was wearing a bright red sundress, with matching sandals and lipstick, the most dressed up Ben had ever seen her. She looked exceptionally pretty.

He was hoping she would wait for him, and she did. At nine o'clock it was down to her, Ben, and the two members of the tear-down crew.

"Nice work up there," she said, when they were finally face to face.

"Thanks. And thanks for coming tonight."

"Of course."

When it was clear the tear-down crew wanted to dissemble the tent, Ben and Meredith stepped outside of it, onto the grass and into the moonlight. This evening, it was unusually bright.

"Hey," Meredith said. "Would you have any interest in going to my place? My mom's playing poker at a girlfriend's, then staying overnight."

"She's getting around better, apparently."

"Yep. She's off her crutches and raising hell."

"Glad to hear it," Ben said, though he knew this was one more step in Meredith's exit from town. "And to answer your question, yes."

Chapter 31

A concert originally planned to protest the exhumation of the Unknown Vagrant in Bolster Hill Cemetery has been transformed into a celebratory fundraiser.

"When the exhumation was called off, we didn't want to waste the great momentum we'd built in our protest," says Bolster High senior Meg Tirella, one of the concert organizers. "We decided to channel it to some other good causes."

Originally scheduled for August fifth in Randolph Park, the concert will now be held from noon until 3 p.m. on Labor Day in the newly cleared but unbroken grounds of Section F in the cemetery. The headlining act will be the Genteel Hooligans, a rock band made up of students from Bolster High and Bolster Academy.

The purpose of the concert is now twofold, according to Tirella and other organizers: (1) to celebrate the opening of Section E of the cemetery, half of which will be devoted to green burials, and (2) to help fund, through admissions, a monument honoring the Unknown Vagrant. This monument, whose design has been overseen by the Bolster Hill Historical Society, is set to be erected in Section C. According to cemetery president Carl Jenks, the marker currently in place at the Unknown Vagrant's roadside grave will be removed to reduce visitation there and, thus, risks of traffic injuries and fatalities. However, the grave itself will not be disturbed.

Commenting on the decision to offer green burials, Jenks said, "I've always been a fan of getting out ahead of what the public wants and needs. It's nice to see that strategy paying off."

At the time this article went to press, forty-three green burial plots had been sold in advance, according to Jenks.

While pleased with this development, Ben Dirjery, grounds manager and head of the cemetery's Green Initiative, said, "We could always be doing more, and I'm hoping we'll keep moving in the right direction."

The week after the concert, Dirjery will be attending a green burial conference in Michigan. There, he will take part in a panel discussion on building community support for such burials.

—From "Protest Turns to Celebration," the *Bolster Register*

General Grounds
Early afternoon, Labor Day

As they moved through the crowd by the main gate, Martha checked her watch. "You said two, right? Not two thirty?"

"Two is what we decided on," Peg said.

By *we*, Peg meant herself and Leah Dirjery. Thus far, they'd communicated only by email, after being connected by a mutual acquaintance, Catherine—like Leah, a painter.

Because Catherine had supplied Peg with the postcard of Leah's painting, the inspiration for the yarn bombing in the Memory Garden, she'd felt obligated to do her part.

Peg discovered that her yarn work had in turn inspired Leah to install a permanent sculpture in the garden, where she, Peg, and Martha would be meeting today.

"You deserve this way more than I do," Peg said to Martha after receiving the news about the sculpture. "You're the artist, the *real* artist."

"And who says *you're* not?" Martha had replied. "Some great deity of culture? If such a being exists, I want out."

Martha appeared not the least bit jealous of Peg, or resentful of the fact that her own yarn bombing—far more inventive and thought-provoking, in Peg's opinion—had been removed from the cemetery without fanfare. In fact, Martha seemed genuinely happy for Peg. And she'd readily accepted Peg's offer to join her today, to see the sculpture. According to Leah, it had just been finished.

Of all the day's events, the thing Peg least looked forward to was the rock music, more particularly the volume of it. Having determined in advance that the concert stage wouldn't be far from the Memory Garden, Peg had come prepared. Before leaving home, she'd stuffed a set of earplugs into the pocket of her shorts.

Right now, the music was a harmless and distant thump mingled with wordless singing. It contributed to the strange carnival atmosphere all around, life amid death. As far as Peg could see, kids barely taller than the gravestones were zipping among them, and the smells of popcorn and cotton candy wafted through the air.

As Peg and Martha made their way along Acanthus Lane, the main drag through the cemetery, they saw that food and drink stands, carts of balloons and various other amusements, and the requisite face-painting station had been set up on the left, evidently the pleasure side of the lane.

The business side, on the right, was the land of civic-minded literature, arrayed on folding tables with the occasional donation can. Peg and Martha passed artist's renderings of the Unknown Vagrant memorial, brochures promoting assorted volunteer organizations, and literature on green landscaping and green burial. At the last table, it was objects, not literature, that drew Peg's eye.

To the table's left, lined up along the lane, were three caskets: one of plain pine, one of wicker, one of cardboard. Peg looked back to the table's front banner, which read "Eco Exit: Helping You Go Out Lightly."

"Can I answer any questions for you?"

A young woman was smiling at Peg from her station behind the table.

"No, thank you. These things pretty much speak for themselves."

The woman's smile dimmed by a lumen or two.

"Hey, Peg! Come see this."

Martha, holding one of the brochures from the table, looked as if she'd scored a point in a treasure hunt.

"Custom-made shrouds," she said.

So? Peg thought. But she kept her mouth shut and looked through one of the brochures herself.

Apparently, Eco Exit also made biodegradable burial shrouds of cotton and linen, "tailored to the customer's aesthetic preferences and/or religious faith." Some of the shrouds pictured in the brochure were rather plain. Others were elaborately embroidered, or rendered in colorful fabrics.

Looking between Peg and the brochure, Martha said, "Just think of what we could do."

Peg didn't get it; then she did. "By knitting shrouds?"

"Yes."

The idea seemed absurd, at first. Then Peg's mind got going. She pictured shrouds that were cabled, netted, or multi-patterned. She pictured decorative crocheted flowers and vines. Then there were all the possible colors.

"We don't have to decide anything here, Peg. Let's just hold on to the thought for now, let it percolate some. All right?"

"All right."

They tucked the brochures into their pockets and headed up the hill, toward the Memory Garden. At this distance, the music was more audible, its sound nothing Peg had expected. The harmonizing voices, male and female, called to mind bluegrass singing, but with a raw, more plaintive edge.

Miranda knows
He's turning away and going away and gone

Miranda knows
He'll be in her town and then in her room by dawn

Miranda knows
She'd rather not see

And rather not feel

. . .

And rather not know

Peg continued to listen to the song, not feeling the need to put in her earplugs, not just yet.

Nearing the garden, she looked out for someone matching the description Leah had given her: a woman in a bright yellow dress, with dark hair pulled back in a ponytail. Peg soon found her, waiting expectantly in front of the southern entrance to the garden. Beside her stood a tall man in shorts and a stylish blue shirt, his head topped with a straw fedora.

"Leah?"

"Peg?"

"That's me."

Peg stepped forward uncertainly, began to extend her hand. But Leah got ahead of her and gave her a quick but firm hug.

"I'm so glad to finally meet you."

"Likewise," Peg said. "And this is my friend Martha, a fellow yarn bomber who is far more talented than me."

"I don't know about that," Martha said, as she took Leah's hand.

"And this is Adam," Leah said, nodding to her left. "My boyfriend."

"Pleased to meet you," he said, tipping his hat. "Both of you. Leah has really been looking forward to this day."

He seemed a gentleman, Peg thought, and a catch.

She glanced toward the center of the garden, where something the size of a large shed was covered in blue tarps.

"Is that it?" she asked.

"Yes," Leah said, looking a little nervous. "There's a lot I could say right now, but it might be best for me just to show it to you. If you're ready."

"I'm ready," Peg said, though she was nervous herself.

Leah took Peg by the arm and guided her back a ways. "You'll get the whole picture best if you start from a distance."

Leah turned to Adam and said, "Okay, let's go."

The two of them walked to opposite sides of the sculpture and pulled away the tarps.

The colors and structure were as Peg remembered them: multiple lines of yellow, gold, red, and orange radiating from the top of a central pole to poles of various heights all around the garden. The lines weren't coiled or chained as Peg's crocheted ones had been; they were free of complications or distractions, and the longer Peg studied them the more they seemed pure rays of color without substance, shifting in perspective as Peg circled the work then walked into it.

Sensing that Leah was waiting for a response, Peg said, "I'm quite impressed."

That much was true. But did she *like* what she saw? She didn't know. She never knew what it was to like art anyway. It either interested her or it didn't. She decided this thing did.

Martha, too, seemed intrigued. Like Peg, she was walking around and through the work, studying the lines and angles.

Looking a little less tense, Leah said, "Obviously, we had to use something more durable than yarn. I was worried that would be kind of limiting. But I'm hoping things came out okay."

Martha smiled at her and said, "It's more than okay. The materials really suit the work, and this space."

Thank God for Martha, Peg thought, for her words had done the trick. Leah looked relieved, and pleased.

Martha stepped back to a sign staked into the ground, just beyond the north side of the sculpture. She read it aloud: "'Perpetual Sunset,' inspired by Margaret (Peg) Beckwith's original yarn sculpture at this site."

Peg found the phrase *yarn sculpture* amusing. She'd never thought of what she'd done here as a sculpture.

"We'd like to make that sign a permanent fixture," Leah said to Peg. "In other words, switch out the cardboard for bronze."

"I'd be honored," Peg said. "Really I would. But shouldn't your name be on it, too?"

Leah looked more contemplative than flattered. "I appreciate that. But it's enough for me to just make this happen.

Whatever inspiration you took from me, this work is really yours."

Peg wanted to say something more. She wanted to tell Leah how much her painting had meant to her, how it had taken her back to those evenings in the kitchen with Roger, the memories of which were shadowed by his absence. Yet what Peg had made of Leah's painting, what stood all around her now, echoed the living, present Roger and his strange and lovely optimism. She supposed, and hoped, it would remain to outlast her.

In the end, Peg said nothing to Leah. She didn't want to bore her, or intrude upon whatever memories, dreams, or thoughts had inspired her painting. That was private property and none of Peg's business, unless at some point Leah decided otherwise.

Instead, Peg took another spin around and through the sculpture, listening as the band launched into an upbeat number about singing and driving. The brightness of the song resounded in the colored lines above her, as if they'd been strummed. She guessed that Roger, another genuine artist, would approve of both.

When the song ended, the amplifiers let loose an ear-curdling squeal. It seemed that someone had turned up the volume, for the voice that followed the squeal, a young woman's, carried clearly across the cemetery and over the applause:

"Thanks again for coming, everyone. It's been really fun getting our songs out to you."

Peg stepped out of the garden and looked toward the stage, which was obscured by a stand of trees. Glancing back to the sculpture, she found Leah listening, transfixed, as if she were awaiting crucial news. Noticing Peg's curiosity, Adam stepped over and explained, "It's Leah's daughter up there. She's the drummer."

"Oh no," Peg said. "I've kept Leah away all this time?"

"It's all right, really. She's heard most of the songs many times. Just not this next one."

"I see."

"I hope you'll excuse us," he said.

"Of course."

Adam tipped his fedora and collected Leah, and the two of them moved closer to the stage. Peg stayed behind, still tuned in to the amplified voice:

"In a few minutes you'll be hearing from a great musician who happens to be my father, Ben Dirjery, also known as Nick Graves. And I'm going to tell you something he probably won't. The song we're about to perform is one he wrote many years ago for a little local band, the Unknown Vagrants."

Another, louder, wave of applause rolled through the crowd, accompanied by hoots and whistles. When the noise died down, the young woman continued:

"A lot of people don't know, or don't remember, that my dad was one of the original Vagrants. But when he was he gave it his all. So this one's going out to him. And my mom."

⁂

Ben was the sole occupant of the "green room," a section of the stage hidden from the audience by plywood framing draped with moving blankets. He sat on a wobble-legged chair, his guitar strapped prematurely over his shoulder and warming itself against his middle.

He watched Cole climb back behind her kit and count out the start of the song, listened as she and her bandmates launched into it.

By now, he'd heard most of the Hooligans' numbers multiple times—live at one practice, recorded on other occasions. This song was the only one Cole had been afraid to let him hear.

"I'm not going to judge you," he said the last time she expressed her reservations. But his words had no effect. The truth was, he understood her. If the bands he and Pete covered ever showed up at open-mike night, he'd surely be on edge.

What he hoped she knew, what he'd tried to say at different times, was that she and her bandmates were on to something. Most likely, the Hooligans would break up upon graduation, maybe before. But they'd made some great songs—fresh, off-beat, and occasionally moving. As Ben recognized from his own experience with music, they'd pushed themselves into new territory from which there was no going back, together or apart. Watching Cole driving the beat, working the fills, he thought again about what a great drummer she was becoming. This talent had nothing to do with him; it was between her and the music, which as she drummed, swallowed her up and away from him and everything else in this world. At such times the only connection he could claim to her was that he understood the feeling.

I just need to know
Will you let me know?
Four or eight by twelve, which one?
Four or eight by twelve, which one?

As the band wound down the first pass through the chorus, a cold tension rose up and through Ben. Although it had been years since he'd had a case of stage nerves—open-mike nights never gave him trouble—the sensation was as familiar to him as razor burn. Automatically, he resorted to an old trick for soothing himself: he held his guitar closer and murmured, "We'll be fine, We'll be fine, We'll be fine. . . . " This time, the words brought him back to their earliest days.

He was seventeen, and the twelve-string Rickenbacker 360 in the window of Carlo's Instruments was $1,720: "a deal," according to Carlo Jr. And it probably was to a guitar enthusiast whose earnings were reasonably north of the minimum wage. Ben's weren't. It was summer into fall of 1987, and he was earning between thirty and one hundred and seventy dollars a week doing odd jobs for his dad at the cemetery. His newly opened savings account contained approximately four hundred dollars.

Fortunately, Carlo's Instruments offered an installment plan. Ben put two hundred dollars down and committed to paying at least one hundred and fifty dollars a month until the deal was done. "As soon as you make that last payment," Carlo Jr. told him, "you walk that baby out of here."

Until then, as often as he could, Ben dropped by the store

and had Carlo Jr. or whoever else was on duty take down the Rickenbacker and hand it over, and he'd make his way to one of four sound-proofed practice rooms, plug the guitar into an amp, and start in, sometimes just messing around, other times dumbing his way through tabs he'd copied or ripped from music books—for "She Said She Said," "Pretty Persuasion," or various tunes by the Byrds—alternating between states of frustration and semi-hypnosis, and experiencing rare moments of joy when he nailed a few bars created by another or came up with something interesting on his own.

It got to the point where Carlo Jr. took down the guitar the moment Ben walked through the door. Then he'd check Ben's balance and call out encouragement: "Congratulations. You dropped to the triple digits, man." "It's below eight hundred now, my friend." "I see you hit five hundred. At this rate, it'll be just another month or two."

Early that fall, Ben's junky Cavalier broke down. For a couple of evenings, while the car was in the shop, Ross dropped him off at the store, on his way to unspecified destinations.

On the first night, Ross didn't ask any questions. On the second night, he put the truck into park outside of the shop and said, "Did you get a second job, son?"

"No. I just go in there and play a guitar."

"Any guitar?"

"One I really like."

"How long have you been doing this?"

"I don't know. Since the end of July?"

Ross let out a low whistle. "Can't you just buy the thing and bring it home?"

"It's really expensive. I'm on a payment plan."

Ross leaned closer and studied Ben's face, as if trying to identify just exactly what had gone wrong with him. Then he smiled.

"I know that look, son. You're in love."

No, I'm not, he wanted to say. But his dad wasn't wrong.

"How much more do you owe on it?"

"Four hundred and forty-five dollars."

Ross looked out toward the road, as if running calculations in his mind. Then he said, "Sit tight. I'll be back in a minute."

A few minutes later, Ross stepped out of the shop with a guitar case, looking pleased with himself.

He knocked on Ben's window and signaled for him to roll it down.

"Okay for me to put this on the back seat? Or would you rather hold it in your lap?"

Ben took this as a joke, but Ross was waiting for an answer.

"The back seat would be fine. And thanks so much, Dad."

"You're more than welcome, son. We don't often get what we most want in this life. You deserve at least one good turn."

Holding on to the guitar now, Ben was once again grateful for it. He was grateful to Cole for bringing him back to it, and for turning out as she had, so much like her mother.

Ben was grateful even to his father. It seemed to him, now, that he'd inherited from Ross more good things than bad, including this work on these grounds—work he'd grown to love, in spite of himself. If Ben was in fact a later-model Ross, he supposed there were worse things to be, as long as he could keep learning from his mistakes instead of denying them.

As Cole and her bandmates wrapped up their number, Pete appeared. He climbed the impromptu stairs to the green room and nodded a greeting to Ben.

"Better late than never," Ben said.

"I've been pacing the mausoleums. I'm nervous as hell."

He looked it. Sweat shone on his face and had soaked a circle into the chest of his T-shirt.

"Why the mausoleums?"

"I don't know. I guess maybe because they look kind of cold and indifferent. I find that comforting."

"Comforting?"

"Yeah. Like if they were the audience and I fucked up bad, they wouldn't care."

"You're not going to fuck up."

"Promise?"

Ben didn't like to make promises about things he couldn't control. Still, he said, "Sure."

"From Nick Graves' mouth to God's ear," Pete said, looking satisfied.

As Ben learned only recently, Pete had found out that Ben was Nick Graves, and a former member of the Vagrants, by his second week on the job, well before he'd approached Ben about the open-mike night. The snitch: Haley, of course.

Still, Ben couldn't bring himself to hold a grudge against Haley, or to call off his mission to rescue him from his office job. There was a lot of work to be done in Section F, and elsewhere on the grounds, and if Haley wanted to help with it, the job would be his for the taking.

Now, Ben and Pete listened to the applause and cheers for the Hooligans, who remained on the stage. Once again, Cole took the mike:

"I'm happy to introduce Ben Dirjery and Pete Kovak, also known as the Grounds Men. Since my bandmates will be sitting in with them, we'll have the continued pleasure of your company. Here they are, ladies and gentlemen, *the Grounds Men!* . . ."

Ben jogged onto the stage, making his way to Cole. He hugged her and murmured into her ear, over the noise of the crowd.

"You guys sounded great. Better than we ever did."

"I'm not so sure. But we tried."

"*I'm* sure."

She kissed his cheek and ran back to her kit. As Ben took one of the main mikes, Pete stepped up to the other one, ready to go.

Of all the years he'd been in the cemetery, Ben had never seen it in quite this way: from the height of a stage, at the northernmost and newly cleared part of the grounds. From here, the greatest extent of the cemetery was visible, rolling downward and southward, as far as the Old Post Road. Section F, still ungraved and the home of the stage, was crowded with people of all ages, reclined on blankets or beach towels, or milling about—some tossing Frisbees or pushing strollers. Farther out, stragglers had set up camp in Sections E and D.

This mingling of the familiar and unfamiliar settled Ben's

nerves. He cleared his throat and spoke. "Thank you, Cole, and thank you, Hooligans. It's an honor to follow such an impressive performance.

"Now, I'd like to introduce you to the gentleman standing behind me, Pete Kovak, the lead singer of the Grounds Men." Ben motioned toward Pete, who took a bow and waved. When the applause had run its course, Ben turned back to the mike.

"Before we start in, I want to bring things back to the Vagrants, and to one Vagrant in particular, one who's buried about three hundred yards south of this stage. Vince Resklar."

Looking toward Oak Corner, Ben spotted Meredith, who must have finally escaped the barbecue at her mother's. She was edging her way through the crowd and toward the stage. He went on:

"About a year before he died, Vince gave me a cassette tape, bits and starts of new songs he'd recorded on his guitar. He was on the road with the Vagrants then, and I was out of the band, back at home. The idea was, I'd listen to the tape and work with Vince on some new songs. Then life kind of got in the way for me, and it wasn't long before Vince was gone. The cassette went into a drawer and stayed there.

"But not long ago I returned to it, thanks to inspiration from Pete, and thanks mostly to my dear daughter, Cole. Pete and I have been able to work out some new numbers based on the tape, and we're going to perform them for you, with the help and talent of the Hooligans."

Ben saw that Meredith had made it to the front right of the stage, surely unaware that Leah and Adam stood two rows behind her—Adam, whom Ben had finally met and decided he might even like, in time. Farther back were Tuke and Dave, who'd flown in on a lark the day before, and Jenny Fielding.

Not quite a week ago, after dark, Ben had helped Jenny and one of her cousins lower Dolores's shrouded body into the first grave of Section E, a grave he'd dug himself, by hand. Neither Jenny nor Dolores had asked for hand shoveling, and it wasn't a requirement of green burial. Yet the mechanical swiftness and noise of a backhoe seemed contrary to Dolores's manner and to her long, quiet presence on the grounds.

As he helped lower her body, as he filled her grave, he thought of what Dolores had said to him years before, about the kinds of things, even seemingly insignificant things, that add up to a well-lived life. She'd been right all along, and she'd been more significant to him than he could ever express.

Ben caught Meredith's eye and waved, and she waved back. Even at this distance he felt a familiar thrill, desire mingled with fear.

Whatever the future held for the two of them, together, only the next week of it was less than foggy. Sometime after the concert, they'd load their bags into Ben's truck and make their way west, over-nighting somewhere in Upstate New York, and pushing ahead to Ann Arbor, and the green burial conference, the following morning. There, they'd spend their longest uninterrupted time together since they'd met: five days.

Now, Ben said his final words to the crowd:

"I'd like to dedicate every song we're about to play to Vince, because he was the start of them all. But this first one also goes out to everyone here, the living and the dead. It's called 'In This Ground.'"

Cole counted out the start and Ben dived in, all of them did. From that instant on he was no longer nervous, freed by habit and practice and by the music itself. He played first in the foreground and next in the background. He ran through a call-and-response with Pete's voice and Miranda's guitar. They conjured Vince incompletely but enough, Ben hoped, to do him justice.

In the end, even Vince vanished from Ben's mind. The music pulled him up and out of himself, nearly out of the world. Still, he felt Cole's drumming within himself, like a second beat to his heart.

Acknowledgments

I am incredibly thankful that, once again, I have had the good fortune of working with Laurel Dile King, publisher and editor of Garland Press. As with my novel *Marion Hatley,* Laurel suggested many smart revisions, and I'm grateful for all of the care and attention she has given *In This Ground.* Laurel also provided valuable insights from Garland Press's advisory board: Robin Cuneo, Anne Pound, and Sam Paradise. Their comments helped me shape a book I can be proud of.

I am also greatly indebted to Bobby Burke, who digs graves (among many other things) at Fairview Cemetery in Hyde Park, Massachusetts. Bobby gave generously of his time to explain the logistics of grave making and burial. He also described the moving, strange, comical, and occasionally law-breaking goings-on that make for interesting days—and nights—at a cemetery.

Several other people provided valuable support as I researched, wrote, and revised *In This Ground:*

Daniel J. Wescott, director of the Forensic Anthropology Center at Texas State University, helped me figure out how it might be possible, from a forensic standpoint, to leave the Unknown Vagrant in peace.

Editor William Boggess helped me get the book worthy of submitting to publishers, turning a careful eye to the novel at both the sentence and big-picture level. The book benefited greatly from his thoughtful and insightful suggestions.

My writing-group companions (and other dear friends) responded to earlier drafts of this novel in great detail: Beth Gylys, Karen Henry, Chris Juzwiak, Audrey Schulman, Grace Talusan, Gilmore Tamny, and Patty Wise. Earlier group members, Bill Routhier and David Rowell, were also crucial to my development as a writer.

Once again, Garland Press and I were fortunate to work with the talented cover designer William Boardman, who created an inviting and intriguing cover for the novel. We are also grateful to Diane Vanaskie Mulligan for her lovely interior design, and to Tara Masih for her careful proofreading,

My husband, John, has been an unfailing champion of my writing, never questioning the many hours, days, and years I've devoted to it. He smartly critiqued many aspects of this novel, from the perspective of both a book editor and a former rock guitarist. I will never forget his kindness and support.

Finally, I will be forever grateful to my parents, Barbara and Nelson. Barbara always kept plenty of books within my reach and never let bedtime or a sunny, play-outdoors-worthy day interfere with a good read. Nelson introduced me to the power and joys of music—inseparable, to both of us, from a life worth living.

Discussion Guide

Note: If you would like Beth Castrodale to join a discussion of *In This Ground* in person or via phone or Skype, she would love to hear from you. She can be reached at bcastrodale@gmail.com.

1. Two graves at Bolster Hill Cemetery, the Unknown Vagrant's and Vince Resklar's, have become public attractions. Why are people drawn to these sites?

2. Early in the novel, Cole reflects on her father's (Ben's) distaste for the Vagrants' hit "Leave Me in Peace" and on the fact that he doesn't play guitar anymore. Why are the Vagrants—and the lasting popularity of Vince Resklar, in particular—such a sore spot for Ben? Why is "I grew out of it" an unsatisfactory explanation for why he decided to put music behind him?

3. Why, aside from attraction to another woman, might Ben have made the decision to cheat on his wife, Leah? What does this decision say about his attitude toward their marriage at the time of the infidelity?

4. What might explain Ben's relatively new interest in mushroom cultivation, and in creating a mushroom-spore burial suit? Do you think this interest is healthy? troubling? something else?

5. While in India, Meredith experiences an "easy intermingling of death and life," which she finds "essentially and reassuringly human." In what ways might that observation also apply to Bolster Hill Cemetery?

6. Consider Meredith's experience at Manikarnika Ghat in India. What personal challenges does she seem to be facing based on the advice she gets from Wes and Sanjeet?

7. Peg, one of the yarn bombers at the cemetery, doesn't seem to regard herself as a "real artist." How do others' reactions to her creation in the Memory Garden counter this view?

8. When Ben is a young man, Dolores Fielding tells him that "the enjoyment you get from playing the guitar, even the frustration of learning it, is not insignificant. It's the kind of experience that adds up to a well-lived life." Ben seems to dismiss this advice in his youth. How does his attitude toward it change?

9. What lessons does Ben seem to have learned from the ways, good and bad, in which his father conducted himself—as a cemetery manager, husband, and father? Do you think Ben's attitude toward his father changes at all over the course of the novel? If so, how?

10. Although Vince Resklar is a pivotal character in the novel, none of the story is told from his point of view. Why might the author have made this choice?

11. Do you think that Cole is right when she tells Ben that he shouldn't hold himself responsible for Vince's death? Does Ben overcome his guilt over Vince's death to any degree? What thoughts or behaviors of his lead you to this conclusion?

12. How do you feel about the ending of the novel? Would you describe it as happy? bittersweet? something else? Did you find it satisfying?

13. Did this novel change the way you view cemeteries? If so, in what ways?